MURDER AT CLARIDGE'S

JIM ELDRIDGE

Allison & Busby Limited
11 Wardour Mews
London W1F 8AN
allisonandbusby.com

First published in Great Britain by Allison & Busby in 2022.

A CIP catalogue record for this book is available from
the British Library.

First Edition

ISBN 978-0-7490-2806-0

Typeset in 11/16 pt Sabon LT Pro by
Allison & Busby Ltd.

FSC
www.fsc.org
MIX
Paper from
responsible sources
FSC® C171272

Printed and bound by
CPI Group (UK) Ltd, Croydon, CR0 4YY

This one, again, for Lynne

CHAPTER ONE

Tuesday 15th October 1940, London

Henry Kenneth Morton – known as Hooky to his associates – sat at his private table in the saloon bar of his pub, the Dark Horse, in King's Cross, perusing the heavy ledger open in front of him and comparing some of the figures with a pile of tickets from his tankers. They didn't add up. According to the tickets, certain amounts of petrol or diesel had been delivered as verified by the vehicles' meters and the drivers' dipsticks, but the sums showing in the ledger as payments received from some of them were short.

Someone had been ripping him off and now he knew who that someone was.

He shut the ledger, a grim look on his face. He ought to feel satisfied, the war had been good to him: rationing had meant there was scope for a black market. And his contacts with the tanker drivers of the legit outfits, especially those who were happy to learn how to alter the bypass on their vehicle so that air instead of fuel passed through the meter and get well paid for the extra gallons on their tanker at the end of their rounds, should be putting a smile on his face. But two things were blotting things for him.

One was the fact that he'd just discovered he was being short-changed on the black-market fuel being sold on. And the other was the fact that three times now his boys had gone out on a job, only to find a rival mob had just been there.

Coincidence? No! He was being shafted, and it had to be by someone in his own crew.

Hooky had fingers in many pies. Rationing had offered him a great business opportunity: as well as the black-market fuel there was meat. In the same way that the fuel he sold was stolen, so was the meat, taken wholesale from different butchers. The same was also true of eggs and butter. Whatever was in short supply, and Hooky knew that soon everything was going to be in short supply, Hooky knew a place where it could be got hold of. A sledgehammer breaking open a locked door of a warehouse in the middle of the night, with an empty truck outside waiting to be filled. And there were plenty of isolated farms on the edges of London with fields full of sheep and lambs, and chickens, ready to be shepherded into a truck and be sold to an eager public. And if the farmer came looking to see what all the noise was about, a blast from a shotgun or a pistol usually sent them scurrying back indoors.

But three times in the last month his boys had gone out on a raid, only to find another rival gang had already been there and taken everything. And the raids had taken place just hours before his own men were supposed to be there.

He was being set up. And what was worse, he was being laughed at by the other outfits.

Someone was taking him for a ride.

'Boss?'

Hooky, jerked out of his reverie, looked up. His lieutenant, Dobbin Edwards, a tall, stringy man, was looking down at him, and Hooky could tell by the awkward look on his face that he had some bad news to tell him. The thing was, he trusted Dobbin. Whatever Dobbin told him would be straight and true, no beating about the bush. Dobbin was worth his weight in gold to Hooky.

Both men were about the same age, Hooky was forty-two, Dobbin forty, and both had grown up in the same part of London, round the back of King's Cross Station. It had definitely been the school of hard knocks, and Hooky had been just that little bit harder than most others. His adage had been: if you think the other bloke's going to do something to you, do it to him first. He called it 'getting your revenge in beforehand'. As a result, he had become feared in the King's Cross area. One day some local thugs had banded together to bring Hooky down a peg, and it had been Dobbin Edwards who'd turned up and joined in on Hooky's behalf, wielding a bicycle chain.

That cemented the relationship between them. From that moment on, Dobbin was the one person Hooky really trusted. If there was something he wanted done, or nosed about, it was Dobbin he called on.

Hooky looked enquiringly at Dobbin, who pulled a chair to the table and sat down. He leant forward so he could keep his voice low.

'You know you asked me to keep an eye open on who might be leaking to the opposition when we've got a job on?'

Hooky nodded.

'Well, Nutty saw Patch Peters coming out of Roly Fitt's joint in Curzon Street.'

Roly Fitt ran a rival organisation to Hooky around the Mayfair area.

'What was Nutty doing around Roly Fitt's place?' asked Hooky.

'I asked him to keep an eye on it, see if any of our blokes went in, after I got word that some of Roly's blokes had been involved in the raids on the places we'd had targeted.'

Hooky nodded thoughtfully.

'Patch was on all three raids that went pear-shaped, wasn't he?' he said.

Dobbin nodded. 'He was.'

'So it looks like Patch has been earning himself a few bob by leaking what we're about to do, and when it's going to happen, to Roly Fitt,' mused Hooky grimly.

'That's what it looks like,' said Dobbin.

Hooky nodded to himself, his face grim and also very, very determined.

He couldn't have this. Being shafted like this without retribution made him look weak. And weak men didn't survive long in this business, there were too many sharks swimming in the same pond. It was time to show people that he wasn't to be made a fool of.

So, there were two people to be made an example of. Patch Peters, and that scum at Claridge's. And he'd deal with both of them personally. That was the only way to keep proper order.

CHAPTER TWO

Wednesday 16th October 1940

It was 5.15 a.m. Janos Mila wheeled the trolley laden with boxes of potatoes, tomatoes, mushrooms and other vegetables, along with sides of bacon and different sorts of sausages through the kitchen at Claridge's Hotel and left them on the thick wooden tables where the chefs were busy preparing the hundreds of breakfasts. As he did so, he scanned the tables for a spare knife that someone had left unwatched, unguarded. The knives were of different sizes and blades, thin ones for paring apples and pears, thicker ones with well-honed edges for slicing the bacon into thin rashers. He saw one that was perfect for the task ahead of him: a razor-sharp blade that would slice through the carotid artery in the neck, along with a sharp point that would slide easily between muscles and ribs into the heart. At the moment, this particular station where the knife lay was unmanned, the chef being absent. How long would he be absent for, Janos wondered? Chefs were very protective about their knives. If this station was still unmanned in four minutes and the knife still here, he would snaffle it. Hide it in the inside pocket of his kitchen porter's whites. Everyone here in the kitchens wore whites, from the chef of chefs down through all the levels to the porters.

He put a side of bacon down on the table on top of the knife, obscuring it from view, making sure that no one else would take it before he returned, if the chef didn't come back soon.

He was moving on to the next table when Alexandru Hagi stopped him. Alexandru was one of two other Romanians who worked in this kitchen. The other was Josef Malic. Janos did not like Malic. He was an immoral man. A man with no honour.

'There is a man outside in the street who says he needs to talk to you?' said Alexandru.

Janos frowned. 'I do not know anyone,' he said, puzzled. It was true. Janos had come to England just two months before, and all he'd done since his arrival was work here in the kitchen, waiting for instructions. Was the man who was outside calling with a change to those instructions? If so, why?

'Did he ask for me by name?' he asked.

'He did,' said Alexandru. 'Please tell Janos Mila I must talk to him.'

Janos shot a concerned glance towards the burly figure of Marcel Devaux, the overall chef in charge who was bellowing in French at some unfortunate minor chef.

'I will not be long,' Janos murmured, and he made for the back door that led to the street.

Kill one of the kings currently in residence at the hotel, that was his mission. Do it at 6 a.m., the time when they will be least expecting it. Kill the bodyguard first, then gain entry to the royal suite and cut the throat of the sleeping monarch. He will be alone in his bedroom, Janos had been assured.

12

Janos pulled open the door and went out into the street. A man was standing there in the shadows of a doorway. Janos approached him and heard the man whisper: 'Janos Mila?'

'Yes,' said Janos.

The next second he felt a movement behind him, then something was dropped over his head and down to his neck. He started to turn, but there was a sudden pain as something sharp bit into the skin of his neck, and as it bit deeper he found himself unable to breathe. He struck out, but it was no good, and he felt himself falling.

Detective Inspector Arnold Lomax of the Metropolitan Police force struggled out of bed as the ringing of the telephone penetrated his sleepy state.

He looked at his wife, Muriel, in bed next to him, who was just starting to stir.

'What's that noise?' she asked.

'It's the telephone,' he said. 'I'm getting it.'

He pulled on his dressing gown and hurried downstairs. Muriel still hadn't got used to the telephone. Very few people had their own private phone. He only had one because his superintendent, Jeremy Moffatt, had insisted. 'Serious crime happens at any time of night or day, Inspector,' he'd said. And so the telephone had gone in. Muriel still looked at it suspiciously, reluctant to pick it up when it rang. She hadn't got used to the idea of a disembodied voice at the other end of the line.

He lifted the phone from its cradle and said '"Arnold Lomax".'

'Sorry to trouble you at this early hour, sir,' came the voice of his detective sergeant, Joe Potteridge. 'Only there's been a murder at Claridge's Hotel.'

'One of the guests?' asked Lomax hopefully. He'd wanted a high-profile murder to investigate for a long time, one with which he could push himself further up the promotion ladder.

'No, sir. One of the kitchen staff. It looks like he was strangled.'

'In the kitchen?'

'No, sir. His body was found in the street by the rear entrance. But he was wearing his kitchen uniform.'

'All right, Sergeant. Come and pick me up. I'll get dressed and we'll get along there.'

He went back upstairs.

'Who was it?' Muriel asked.

'Sergeant Potteridge. There's been a murder at Claridge's, the big hotel. I've got to go.'

'Anyone important?'

'No,' he sighed. 'Just someone who worked in the kitchens.'

Lomax and Potteridge arrived at Claridge's accompanied by a uniformed sergeant and a constable and made their way down the two flights of stairs to the kitchen. Lomax recoiled as he pushed open the double doors and they entered what seemed to be a blistering inferno filled with shouting in foreign languages and the rattling of wooden shoes.

'They've all got clogs on,' said Potteridge, surprised.

Lomax stopped a man who was hurrying past with a box of vegetables and demanded: 'Who's in charge here?'

A tall, burly man dressed in chef's whites, complete with

14

a tall chef's hat joined them.

'I am!' he boomed. 'Marcel Devaux.'

'Inspector Lomax from Mayfair police station,' Lomax informed him. 'Where's this dead body?'

'We have left him in one of the cold rooms.'

'Is that where he was killed? I was told he was murdered out in the street.'

'That is where his body was found, but we could not let it lay there for all to see.'

'Why not?' thundered Lomax angrily. 'If that was the murder scene, we need to have examined it.'

'You can still examine it, but the body had to be brought in,' said Devaux firmly. 'Follow me and I will show you.'

As the policemen followed the chef, Lomax muttered angrily: 'Bloody French. They've got no idea of the proper way to do things.'

Devaux opened a door to a room not much bigger than a cupboard. Blocks of ice were on the shelves, along with salad vegetables. On the floor lay the body of a man in kitchen whites. A ring of freshly dried blood ran around his neck.

'What's his name?' asked Lomax.

'Janos Mila.'

Lomax gestured to the uniformed officers. 'Drag him out so we can get a look at him.'

The officers pulled the dead man out of the room and into the kitchen. Lomax knelt down beside him.

'It looks like he was strangled with a piece of wire,' he said to Potteridge. 'Thin wire. A garrotte. You don't see much of that in this country.' He looked at Devaux. 'What nationality was he?'

'Romanian,' said Devaux.

'Who found the body?'

'Another of the kitchen workers. Alexandru Hagi.'

'Nationality?'

'Romanian.'

'Does he speak English?'

'Yes. He has been in this country for many years,' said Devaux angrily. There was no mistaking his dislike of Lomax.

'Get him for me,' ordered Lomax. He wiped his sleeve across his sweating brow. 'I can't work in this heat. It's like being in an oven. Send this Hagi to me outside in the corridor.' He looked at the uniformed officers. 'You two arrange to have the body removed. Take it to Middlesex Hospital. And put it back in that cold room until the ambulance arrives, otherwise it'll go off in this heat.'

'Yes, sir,' said the sergeant. He turned to the constable and said: 'Put it back in there. I'll arrange an ambulance to pick it up.'

He left to go up to reception to use the phone to call for transport while Lomax and Potteridge walked through the double doors into the corridor.

'Thank God for that,' said Lomax. 'All that noise and that infernal heat. A man can't think properly.'

The doors opened and a man in a white jacket peered out nervously at them.

'Police?' he asked.

'Detective Inspector Lomax and Detective Sergeant Potteridge,' nodded Lomax. 'You are Alexandru Hagi?'

'Yes.'

'You were the one who found the body of this Janos Mila?'

'Yes.'

'How?'

'I told Janos that a man was out in the street asking for him, and Janos went out. When Janos didn't come back, I went out to see where he was. He was on the ground, not moving. He looked dead.'

'How did you talk to this man who asked for Janos? Were you out in the street already?'

Hagi shook his head.

'No. I was near the door and it opened and I heard someone call. I went to the door and looked out, and there was a man there. He said he wanted to speak to Janos Mila.'

'What did he look like?'

'I did not see his face. It was dark. And he had a hat pulled down and his coat collar was up. He also had a scarf pulled up over his face.'

'Didn't that strike you as suspicious?'

'No. It is cold outside at that time of the morning.'

'And when you went out again to look for this Janos, was this man still around?'

'No. Just Janos lying on the ground.'

'What did you do?'

'I told Pierre, and he told M'sieur Devaux.'

'Who's Pierre?'

'He is my boss for my section.'

'Right,' said Lomax. 'Show us exactly where you found the body.'

Lomax and Potteridge followed Hagi through the kitchen and out the door to the street at the back.

'There,' said Hagi, pointing.

17

'Right,' said Lomax. 'That's all we need for the moment. We'll talk to you later if we need to.'

'I can go?'

Lomax nodded. Hagi went back into the kitchen.

'We need to walk along this street and see if anyone was around who saw anything,' Lomax told Potteridge. 'You start that while I go and get this Mila's address and details about him. I'll join you in a minute.' He shook his head in disbelief. 'Garrotted? Who garrottes people these days?'

CHAPTER THREE

'Thousands of you in this country have had to leave your homes and be separated from your fathers and mothers. My sister, Margaret Rose, and I feel so much for you as we know from experience what it means to be away from those we love most of all.'

Detective Chief Inspector Edgar Saxe-Coburg came from the bathroom, wiping the excess of shaving cream from his face, and looked at his wife, Rosa, as she sat in their kitchen, listening intently to the voice of the young girl coming from the wireless set.

'Who's that?' he asked, curious.

'Princess Elizabeth,' said Rosa. Adding, with her finger to her lips: 'Ssssh.'

'The Princess Elizabeth?' asked Coburg.

He sat down and joined her in listening as the young princess continued: 'All of us children who are still at home think continually of our friends and relations who have gone overseas – who have travelled thousands of miles to find a wartime home and a kindly welcome in Canada, Australia, New Zealand, South Africa and the United States of America. My sister and I feel we know quite a lot about these countries. Our father and mother have often talked to us of their visits to different parts of the world. So it is not difficult for us to picture the sort of life you are all leading, and to think of all the new sights you must be seeing, and the adventures you must be having.

'But I am sure that you, too, are often thinking of the Old Country. I know you won't forget us. It is just because we are not forgetting you that I want, on behalf of all the children at home, to send our love and best wishes – to you and your kind hosts as well.

'Before I finish, I can truthfully say to you all that we children at home are full of cheerfulness and courage. We are trying to do all we can to help our gallant sailors, soldiers and airmen, and we are trying, too, to bear our own share of the danger and sadness of war. We know, every one of us, that in the end all will be well; for God will care for us and give us victory and peace. And when peace comes, remember it will be for us, the children of today, to make the world of tomorrow a better and happier place.

'My sister is by my side and we are both going to say goodnight to you. Come on, Margaret.'

Then another girl's voice was heard, this one much younger, saying: 'Goodnight, children,' followed by Princess Elizabeth's: 'Goodnight, and good luck to you all.'

There was a brief pause, then an announcer said in formal tones: 'That was a repeat of last Sunday's broadcast on *Children's Hour* by their majesties, the Princesses Elizabeth and Margaret, to the children of the world.'

When he finished there came an orchestral version of 'God Save the King'.

'My God, that was a very professional performance for

one so young,' said Coburg, impressed. 'How old is she? Fifteen?'

'Fourteen,' said Rosa. 'And her sister's just ten. They recorded it at Windsor Castle. It's aimed at all those children from Britain who've been sent abroad for their own safety.'

'But the Princesses haven't been evacuated.'

'No,' said Rosa. 'The Queen Mother says her family will stay in Britain and share in what the people are having to put up with. However, as they've already been bombed twice at Buckingham Palace, I think she considers the girls are safer at Windsor.'

'Until Windsor gets bombed,' said Coburg with a rueful sigh.

The ringing of the telephone had him crossing the room and lifting the receiver.

'Coburg,' he said.

'Superintendent Allison here,' said the clipped voice at the other end. 'Just checking you're coming in this morning.'

'Yes, sir. I'm just about to leave to collect Sergeant Lampson.'

'Report to me when you arrive,' said the superintendent. 'An issue has arisen.'

Rosa looked inquisitively at Coburg as he hung up.

'That was the boss,' said Coburg. 'An issue has arisen.'

'What sort of issue?'

'Who knows?' said Coburg. 'Perhaps there'll be something on the news that'll alert me.'

He turned his attention back to the wireless as the national anthem finished, and the announcer said: 'This is the BBC Home Service. Here is the news read by Alvar Lidell for Wednesday 16th October.'

They listened to the news headlines, which included a report of a battle between the Royal Navy and Italian ships off the coast of Malta, resulting in a victory for the British. Coburg reflected that the battle would have been a few days ago, because the propaganda ministry was very careful to vet reports to make sure that the morale of the public was kept high, and if the battle had gone the other way and the Italians had been victorious, he doubted if it would have made it to the airwaves.

'What time are you due at Paddington?' he asked.

Rosa, as well as being a well-known jazz singer and pianist, also volunteered as an ambulance driver, based at the St John Ambulance depot close to Paddington station.

'I told them I'd be there at ten,' she said.

Most of the emergency action didn't happen until the evening, when the bombing raids were in full swing, but the morning always bought reports of injuries sustained overnight where the casualties had only just been discovered.

'I'll drop you off, if you don't mind being early,' Coburg offered.

'No, that'd be great,' said Rosa. 'I'll be on hand if anything comes in, and if not, I can always grab a coffee with the crew.'

'So long as you stay safe,' said Coburg.

Rosa went to him and held him and kissed him, then whispered: 'And you stay safe, too.'

After Coburg had delivered Rosa to the St John Ambulance station at Paddington, he headed for Somers Town in north London, where his detective sergeant, Ted Lampson, was waiting for him outside his small terraced house. Coburg shifted over to the passenger seat so that Lampson could slide behind the steering wheel. It was a routine they'd adopted. Even though the vehicle was a police car and not Coburg's prized Bentley, which had been locked away in a garage as part of the restrictions on the use of private cars to conserve petrol for the war effort, Coburg was glad of this sharing routine. For his part, Lampson loved driving, but with no car of his own he rarely got the chance to engage. From Coburg's perspective, although he enjoyed motoring on the open road in the countryside, the traffic in London, even with petrol rationing reducing it, was a pain in the neck, and Lampson's driving them to Scotland Yard in the mornings, and occasionally driving them to a crime scene, meant that Coburg was able to think without worrying about crashing into something or someone because his mind was preoccupied. Right now, he was wondering what sort of 'issue' he would be faced with when he met the superintendent.

Lampson looked at the radio telephone that had only recently been installed in their car. Coburg had lowered the volume so there was a general background hum from it, with occasional calls from Control to different vehicles. Coburg's vehicle had been allocated the call sign Echo Seven.

'We're getting very modern,' grinned Lampson. 'You wouldn't have been able to have this in your old Bentley.'

'True,' conceded Coburg. 'At least we'll be saved from racing all over London on wild goose chases.'

'Did you hear the Princesses on the wireless this morning?' asked Lampson.

'I did,' said Coburg. 'I thought they did an excellent job. Or, rather, Princess Elizabeth did a good job, because she was the one doing the talking.'

Lampson chuckled. 'My old man stood to attention the whole way through it,' he laughed. 'He's such a patriot! I think if he actually met the Royal Family he'd die of fright. It was good, though. With all that's going on it needed something like that talk to lift people's spirits. I know the RAF are doing their best, but this constant bombing is wearing me down. And everyone else I know. You never know when it's gonna be your name on it. Did you hear about the air raid up at the Angel, Islington last night?'

'No.'

'A hundred dead, men, women and children all in the basement shelter at a school there. They reckon it was a direct hit. Bastards. And did you see that bus in Balham?'

Coburg nodded. Every newspaper had had the same picture: two days previously a German bomb had exploded on the road by Balham station, creating an enormous crater. That night, during the blackout, a bus had driven into the deep hole, killing sixty-six people.

'How are you and Terry coping with the air raids?' asked Coburg.

'We go to the underground, along with my mum and dad. It's better now they've opened the stations.' Changing the subject, he asked: 'Is it Mrs Nicholson today?'

'Yes,' said Coburg. 'I'm sure this will wrap it up. I get the impression she wants to talk.'

Joanne Nicholson, forty-five years old, who'd been battered by her louse of a husband, Eric, for most of the twenty years of their marriage, had been picked up by police on Waterloo Bridge as she stood staring down into the murky waters of the Thames. She'd refused to say who she was or what she was doing there, but a sympathetic

24

police constable had persuaded her to let him look through her handbag, where he found a ration book with her name and address on. Concerned about her mental state, a police car had taken her home to her address in Lambeth, where they discovered the body of Eric Nicholson in the scullery, his head smashed in and a hammer lying beside his body in a pool of blood.

At first, Joanne Nicholson had insisted she'd come home and found his body, and that it must have been an intruder who'd done it. But questions asked of her neighbours had revealed the noise of frequent rows and beatings administered to Joanne by Eric, and on this last occasion Joanne's screams and yells of pain had been mingled with shouts of alarm from Eric. A medical examination of Joanne had revealed bruises to her body, some very old, some very recent. When the hammer had been examined for fingerprints, those of both Eric and Joanne had been found on the handle. Joanne insisted she'd only used the hammer to break coal for the fire.

'You talk to her this morning while I go and see the super,' said Coburg. 'He says he's got something he wants to see me about.'

'Right,' said Lampson. 'She did it. And, to be honest, if half the stories we heard about her husband are true, I don't blame her.'

'Be sympathetic when you talk to her,' said Coburg. 'Don't pressurise her. Have a WPC sitting with you at the table. If Joanne feels intimidated, she'll only retreat into silence.'

'She won't want to hang. That'll keep her from admitting she did it.'

'I'll see if we can't arrange for her to have a good lawyer

and barrister. Tell her that we'll do everything we can to look after her. Tell her we believe it was self-defence, that her husband was attacking her with the hammer and she tried to stop him. You know the drill.'

'People from Lambeth don't trust us. The police, that is.'

'She'll trust you. And if it looks like she doesn't, I'll have a word with her after I've seen the super.'

'You've no idea what he wants?'

'No. An issue, he said.'

'Could be anything.'

'It could, but I bet it's not going to be compliments thrown at us.'

CHAPTER FOUR

Superintendent Edward Allison was a short, thin, wiry man in his fifties. Like Coburg, he'd served in the First War, in his case at Gallipoli, while Coburg had fought, and been seriously wounded, in the trenches in France. The superintendent still maintained his military air: stiff-backed, head held high, a penetrating look in his gimlet eyes. He looked up from his desk as Coburg knocked at his office door and then entered at the call of 'Come!'

Allison gestured for Coburg to take a seat by his desk and asked. 'How's the Nicholson case?'

'Sergeant Lampson's just tying everything up at this moment,' said Coburg.

'She did it?'

'She did,' nodded Coburg. 'I'm fairly sure she'll make a full confession.' He looked inquisitively at the superintendent. 'On the telephone you mentioned an issue, sir.'

'Yes, there's been a murder at Claridge's. One of their kitchen staff has been found dead, apparently strangled. They've requested you take charge.'

'When you say "they" . . . ?' asked Coburg.

'Specifically, the owner of Claridge's, Rupert D'Oyly

Carte,' said Allison. 'I'm sorry about this, Edgar, but D'Oyly Carte has the ear of important figures in the government.'

'One of the kitchen staff, you say.'

'Yes, and ordinarily it would be a job for a local inspector and his team. But these are not ordinary times. With the war on, most of the exiled kings and queens of Europe have taken up residence at Claridge's.' He ticked them off on his fingers. 'King Haakon of Norway, Queen Wilhelmina of the Netherlands and her son-in-law Prince Bernhard, as well as King Peter II and Queen Alexandra of Yugoslavia. And King George of Greece is registered there as a "Mr Brown". Tact and diplomacy is called for when dealing with these crowned heads, and that's why Mr D'Oyly Carte requested you. Whether you like it or not, these people are less likely to complain about police interference in their daily lives and those of their staff if the officer in charge is the Honourable Edgar Walter Septimus Saxe-Coburg. These people still remember when their British cousins, the King and Queen, were called Saxe-Coburg before they changed their name to Windsor.'

'Saxe-Coburg-Gotha,' Coburg corrected him.

'Yes, all right, one hyphen less,' sighed Allison. 'But you take my point? Or, rather, the point that Rupert D'Oyly Carte was keen to make.'

'I am not a member of the Royal Family,' said Coburg. 'I do not attend grand dinners and functions at Buckingham Palace or Windsor.'

'But your brother, the Earl of Dawlish, does. And I understand he is also very close to the prime minister.'

'Is that another factor in why I've been chosen for this investigation?'

28

'Whether you like it or not, Chief Inspector, this is a time for politics and who knows whom, and who is to be trusted by those in charge. The Germans are massing on the French coast and prepared to launch an invasion of these shores at any moment. The RAF are valiantly resisting the constant attacks by Germany's bombers, but there is no guarantee they'll be able to keep holding off the Luftwaffe. This island is the last place in Europe not under Nazi control and our military are unable to mount effective attacks on the enemy. Not to mention the fact that fifth columnists and German spies seem to be everywhere here undermining our war effort.'

'And with all that, the strangulation of a kitchen worker at Claridge's is to be given prominence of investigation,' said Coburg pointedly.

'We hope there will come a time when we will need Norway, Greece, the Netherlands and Yugoslavia and the rest of Europe to rebuild stable and democratic societies after the Nazis have been defeated. And it will help if their rulers and heads of governments say: Ah yes, the British were the very personification of tact and diplomacy when a certain incident occurred in London during the war. We can work with them.'

Rosa had barely finished her early morning coffee at the Paddington St John Ambulance station when Chesney Warren, the district supervisor, came in to the crew quarters with a piece of paper, which he handed to her.

'Two kids playing near a bomb crater fell in. One of them's got what sounds like a broken leg. Here's the address.'

Rosa looked at it. 'Where is it?' she asked.

'I'll go with you,' offered Derek Peers. 'I know every street in this area.' He looked at Warren. 'Unless you've got something else for me.'

'No, that'd be great, Derek.'

Rosa and Peers headed out towards their ambulance. Rosa had been on a couple of shouts with Derek and liked him. He was in his early fifties, very reliable, and had been with St John Ambulance for at least ten years, from what she could gather. He was handicapped by only having one arm, his left arm ending in a stump just above his elbow, but he didn't let it stop him doing as much as he could. Although he couldn't drive, a leather strap with a loop at the end dangled from his shoulder. Tied around his stump, it enabled him to carry a stretcher using his one good hand and the strap. He was also amazingly adept at dealing with bad injuries with just one hand.

He climbed into the passenger seat, while Rosa took her place behind the steering wheel.

'It's not far,' said Peers, looking at the address Warren had given them. 'Honestly, you'd think parents would know better than to let their kids wander around near bomb craters. There could well be an unexploded bomb in it.'

They set off, with Peers navigating Rosa out of the station and heading in the right direction.

'If it's a bad break we might have to put the splint on together,' he said, and gave a rueful sigh. 'It's at times like this I really miss having my left hand.'

'How did you lose your arm?' asked Rosa.

'During the last war. In France.'

'You were in the trenches?' asked Rosa. 'My husband

was in the trenches in that one. He lost a lung.'

'No,' said Derek. 'I was doing ambulance work. And before you ask, yes, I was a conscientious objector. I'm a Quaker, you see.' His tone became slightly bitter as he added: 'Although there were other words used to describe us: coward, softie, traitor, Hun-lover.'

'That was then,' said Rosa. 'Times are different now.'

'Sadly, they're not,' said Derek ruefully. 'Quaker friends of mine are still being called names and beaten up once people find out they're a conchie. The war brings out the worst as well as the best in people.' He patted the stump of his left arm. 'I was collecting an injured soldier from one of the trenches when a bomb went off right beside us. Blew my mate, another conchie, to bits and took half my arm off. The only one who was untouched by it was the injured soldier in the trench waiting for us to pick him up. The good thing about it was it made me realise what I wanted to do. So after the war I joined St John Ambulance as a volunteer. I knew I wouldn't be able to drive, but I could learn first aid, even with one arm. And over the years I've learnt a lot more. I can do almost everything now to save a life. I've often thought I'd like to train as a doctor, but I'm too old for that. And they wouldn't let me, having only one arm. But this is just as good for me. Going out, saving lives.' He grinned. 'Especially with a driver like you. You'd be surprised how bloody awful some of the drivers are. Downright dangerous. Trouble is, drivers are in short supply, what with the war.'

In the interview room in the basement of Scotland Yard, Lampson sat at a bare wooden table. Joanne Nicholson

31

sat on the other side, facing him. Next to her sat a woman police constable, WPC Wendy Merton, in her mid-twenties. In front of Lampson lay a writing pad and a fountain pen.

'Mrs Nicholson – first: may I call you Joanne?' asked Lampson gently.

Nicholson hesitated, then nodded.

'Joanne, I know you're worried about being here, but I want to reassure you that this is all just procedure. It's what happens when someone dies unexpectedly, and in this case the evidence found at your home raises questions. But it doesn't mean we think you murdered your husband. In fact, the opposite. From the evidence, the picture we've got is that your husband, Eric, attacked you with a hammer in your scullery. Is that what happened?'

Nicholson didn't answer, just looked at him, then dropped her eyes to the table.

'Our guess is that he accidentally dropped the hammer on the floor, and he bent down to pick it up to continue his assault on you. It's possible he picked it up, but somehow you managed to defend yourself from his attack and you found the hammer in your hand. You were in a state of panic and fear, you were afraid of what he'd do to you with it, so you struck out with it to try to scare him off, and he was knocked to the ground.

'Because you knew the sort of man your husband was, violent and dangerous, you were terrified that, if he got up, he'd batter you to death. So you struck him once more in an attempt to stop that happening.' He paused, then asked gently: 'Was that what happened?'

Again, she didn't answer, just looked at him, then looked away.

'Again, you panicked,' Lampson continued, 'so you struck him again to stop him getting up, and then once more. That wasn't murder, Joanne. Murder is premeditated, planned in advance. This was self-defence. The prosecution may claim it was manslaughter, but manslaughter isn't murder. People don't get hanged for manslaughter. And a death caused as a result of self-defence, when you were in fear of your life . . .' Lampson left the sentence unfinished.

'That's the evidence we shall give, if called for,' Lampson continued. 'And Chief Inspector Coburg has told me to tell you we'll arrange for the very best defence for you: a top barrister. If everything goes as we hope, there shouldn't be any time in prison, except the time you spend on remand waiting for a trial. If there is one. It may not even come to that. But the court, if there is a trial, will need to hear your side of the story. About how Eric used to attack you. What you suffered for all those years. And how the hammer came to be in the scullery.' He tapped the writing pad in front of him. 'We need to put it down, Joanne. We need what you have to say.'

She looked directly at him, and her lips moved but no sound came from them.

'I need to hear what you have to say,' said Lampson gently.

'The Angel of Death is upon me,' she said softly.

And then she stopped speaking, her eyes still fixed on him.

CHAPTER FIVE

Inspector Lomax stared at Superintendent Moffatt, his boss at Mayfair police station, shocked.

'DCI Coburg has taken it off me!' he burst out, outraged. 'Again!'

'He hasn't taken it off you, Inspector,' said Moffatt. 'The Top Brass have decided, due to the delicate nature of the clientele who are staying at Claridge's who may well need to be questioned—'

'This happened before!' raged Lomax. 'When there was that titled bloke killed at the Savoy. I caught the initial shout, and they took it off me and gave it to Coburg. Just because of who he is!'

'It's politics,' said Moffatt, trying to smooth the situation. 'The commissioner feels—'

'The commissioner feels that because I'm just an ordinary bloke who didn't go to Eton and doesn't hobnob with royalty . . .' chuntered Lomax angrily.

'It's not that at all,' said Moffatt.

'What is it, then, sir?'

'It's about diplomacy with all these foreign kings and queens staying at Claridge's.'

'Because he's one of them,' scowled Lomax.

'I'm sorry, Inspector, but that's the way it is,' said Moffatt stiffly. 'As I said, it's politics. It's not a reflection on you.'

Oh, yes it is, thought Lomax angrily as he returned to his office where Sergeant Potteridge was waiting for him.

'What's up, boss?' asked Potteridge, recognising the anger on Lomax's face.

'We've been taken off the Claridge's job. The murder of that kitchen bloke.'

'Taken off? Why?'

'Because it's been given to DCI Saxe-bloody-Coburg! His toffee-nosed friends in high places want him there.'

'Rather him than us in that place,' said Potteridge sagely. 'All that heat. All that noise. All shouting at one another in French.'

'That's not the point!' exclaimed Lomax. 'I'm a detective inspector, not just some tinpot constable. I should have been a DCI by now. I've had the same amount of experience in the police as Coburg. My arrest record shows I'm as good as him. But as soon as there's a job in a plum location, a palace or a top hotel or a top West End jewellers, who gets it? Not me! Even though I was first on the scene and by right and protocol it should be mine. No, it gets handed on a plate to High and Mighty snob-face Saxe-bloody-Coburg. That's what being born with a silver spoon in your mouth is all about, Sergeant. Getting the plum jobs. The ones that get in the papers and get their name bandied about so that when there are honours and promotions being thrown about, people like Coburg get them.' He slammed his fist down on his desk in fury. 'Well one day I'm gonna get him, Sergeant. Mess him up. Show him up for the clown he is.

Then we'll see how many of his so-called social class still think he's so good.'

Coburg was happy for Lampson to drive them to Claridge's, but he could tell from the grim expression on his sergeant's face that the interview with Joanne Nicholson hadn't gone well.

'She didn't speak,' said Lampson, frustrated. 'Except to say: "The Angel of Death is upon me."'

'Religious?' asked Coburg.

'I don't know,' said Lampson. 'I don't think so. I gave her every opportunity. I let her know we were on her side and that we weren't looking at her for murder; that it was self-defence. But she wouldn't speak up. How did you get on with the superintendent? What did he want?'

Coburg let out a groan, then said: 'I'm thinking of changing my name to Smith.'

'Why?'

'Then I wouldn't keep being roped in for these cases involving foreign royalty. They hear the name Saxe-Coburg and jump to the wrong conclusion.'

'It means they talk to you, which they wouldn't if you were just Chief Inspector Smith. Face it, guv, the name opens doors that would otherwise remain firmly shut to us.'

They arrived at Claridge's and were greeted at reception by the tall, imposing figure of Georges LeGrosse, Claridge's hall porter, resplendent in his uniform of a royal blue tailcoat adorned with gold braid.

'Mr Coburg!' he greeted them with obvious relief. 'Thank heavens! Mr D'Oyly Carte said you would be coming. This is a dreadful situation.'

'One of your kitchen staff has been strangled, I believe,' said Coburg.

'Janos Mila, one of the kitchen porters. His body was found outside in the street by the back door of the kitchens.'

'Where is the body now? Is it still in the kitchen or has it been moved?'

'It's been taken away,' said LeGrosse. 'The first inspector on the scene arranged it.'

Coburg and Lampson exchanged concerned glances. Superintendent Allison hadn't said anything about the case being allocated to anyone else.

'Who was the first inspector who arrived?' he asked.

'An Inspector Lomax from Mayfair police station.'

'Mayfair? Not the Strand?'

'No, although he did say that he used to be based at the Strand, and had been involved with an investigation at our sister hotel, the Savoy.'

Coburg's heart sank. Not Lomax again! For some reason, Lomax viewed Coburg as his sworn enemy, convinced that he'd only been denied promotion to chief inspector because Coburg had been given all the best cases, and that preferment was the result of what Lomax termed Coburg's 'posh friends in high places'.

'Do you know which hospital the body was sent to?'

'I'm not sure. I'm sorry. I don't think the inspector actually said.'

No, he wouldn't, thought Coburg angrily. He'd wait for Coburg to ask him where he'd sent the body, and then he'd take the opportunity to air his view that a case at a prestigious hotel had been taken away from him unfairly because of Coburg's privileged place in society: son of an earl, Eton-educated, the usual bitterness.

Coburg thanked LeGrosse and, after being given the dead man's home address, he and Lampson returned to their car, where Coburg radioed through to Control.

'Echo Seven to Control. Over.'

'Reading you, Echo Seven. Over.'

'DCI Coburg calling. Can you contact Mayfair police station and find out where Inspector Lomax ordered the body found at Claridge's to be taken. Over.'

'Will do, Echo Seven. Stand by. Over.'

Lampson looked at the radio telephone. 'That's brilliant,' he said approvingly. 'Without that, we could have been going from hospital to hospital. The Middlesex, UCH, Paddington.'

'Even worse, we'd have been forced to go to Mayfair and ask Lomax. Which would have given him the opportunity to have a go at us because we've been given the shout.'

It was just a few minutes later that their radio crackled into life with: 'Control to Echo Seven. Do you read? Over.'

'Echo Seven to Control, reading you. Over.'

'The body was taken to the Middlesex Hospital. Over.'

'Thank you, Control. Echo Seven over and out.'

Rosa and Peers delivered the nine-year-old boy with the broken leg, along with his worried mother, to Paddington Hospital, and then headed back to base.

'By the way, I meant to tell you,' said Peers, 'I told my missus I was working with you and she got so excited. "Rosa Weeks!" she said. "The singer?" She couldn't believe it. She's got one of your records at home, and the idea that someone she listens to on the wireless and on record is driving an ambulance here in Paddington . . . well, she was knocked out. Are you going to be appearing anywhere soon?'

'I do still do some,' said Rosa. 'Not as many as I used to because the Blitz and the blackout means most jazz clubs and nightclubs are shut. Mainly I'm playing the big hotels because they've got reinforced building structures, which helps when the bombs fall. I did the Ritz and Savoy recently, and this Sunday evening I'll be at Claridge's. But right now, I'm concentrating on the ambulance work. That's more important than playing the piano.'

'Not to people who like to hear good music and singing,' said Peers.

They pulled into the yard at the ambulance station and were making for the main building, when the figure of Chesney Warren came hurrying out, waving a piece of paper.

'Good timing,' said Warren. 'We've got a suspected heart attack. Woman in her sixties over at St John's Wood.'

'There's a hospital at St John's Wood,' Peers pointed out. 'Wouldn't it be quicker for one of their ambulances to deal with it?'

'It would, if they had one spare. A bomb last night hit their yard and destroyed two of their ambulances. The one they've got left is already out on a call.' He handed them the sheet of paper with the address. 'Here you are.'

'It would help us if we could have a radio in the ambulance,' said Peers, taking it. 'We could have gone straight there instead of coming back here. If it's a heart attack, every second counts.'

'At the moment we're short of vehicles,' said Warren. 'I've asked for radios for all our ambulances, but you're lucky you've actually got an ambulance. Some of our crews are having to use ordinary cars and vans. We had to paint over the words "animal food" on one last week – that wouldn't have gone down well when it arrived at a scene.'

Peers nodded in resignation.

'Point taken,' he said. He turned to Rosa. 'St John's Wood, here we come.'

Coburg and Lampson stood in the mortuary in the basement of the Middlesex Hospital looking down at the naked body of Janos Mila laid out on a metal tray. The mortuary smelt of disinfectant to counteract the smell of rotting flesh from other corpses, along with formaldehyde. To Coburg, the smell was of death.

'He's not just been strangled, he's been garrotted,' said Coburg, pointing to the telltale deep marks left all the way round the dead man's neck from a length of thin wire.

'Whoever did it must have gone equipped,' said Lampson. 'No one just finds a piece of wire lying conveniently around in the middle of an argument.' He peered closer at the indentation. 'It was very thin wire. Thin, but strong. Not a piece of electrical wiring, for example. A professional hitman.'

'Or a soldier,' mused Coburg. 'Commandos are trained to kill silently, and the garrotte is a favourite. Stops the victim shouting out, and so long as the killer hangs on tightly, there's nothing the victim can do.' Like Lampson, he bent closer to examine the mark of the wire deep in the skin. 'With wire this thin, I've known someone to have their head taken off when it was pulled tight.'

'During the war?'

'No, a man called Guy Morris. He killed his wife's lover this way. Sliced right through the neck and just got snagged on the victim's spine.'

'Think we ought to check in with Arsehole Lomax?' asked Lampson as they left the mortuary room. 'See what he picked up. He caught the shout, after all.'

Coburg shook his head. 'Not just yet. I'll only get a mouthful of abuse from him. Let's go to Claridge's and see what we can get from the people Janos worked with. If we draw a blank with them, we'll go and see Lomax.'

CHAPTER SIX

Inspector Arnold Lomax sat at his desk in his office at Mayfair police station and fumed silently. The realisation went like a drill through his mind: once again that bastard DCI Coburg had stolen a high-profile case from under his nose, just because of who he was. And who his friends in high places were.

The murder of a kitchen hand wasn't in itself going to catch the public's eyes, but it was where it had taken place: Claridge's Hotel. One of the top hotels in London, which right now was housing half of the royal families of Europe. That was what would catch the attention of the newspapers and bring celebrity to the detective who solved the crime. The old school network, he thought vengefully. Bloody Eton and Coburg's elder brother, the Earl of Dawlish. The elite looking after one another.

There was a tap at his door, which opened to Sergeant Potteridge.

'Sorry to trouble you, boss,' he said. 'But Patch Peters' body's turned up on a bomb site on Charles Street. He's been shot.'

'Patch Peters?' said Lomax, bewildered. 'He's one of

Hooky Morton's King's Cross mob, isn't he? What's he doing in Mayfair? That's Roly Fitt's neck of the woods.'

'Maybe that's why he got shot. Coming into enemy territory.'

'Rubbish!' snapped Lomax. 'A beating, that's all. Not shot.' He stood up and took his coat from the peg. 'Mind, anything's possible. Let's go and have a word with Roly Fitt and see what he's got to say.'

On their arrival back at Claridge's, Coburg checked with Georges LeGrosse if Marcel Devaux was still the maître chef de cuisines, the chef in overall charge of the kitchens, and on being told he was, asked Georges to phone down and let Monsieur Devaux know he was coming to question the kitchen staff.

'You've never been in the Claridge's kitchen, I assume,' said Coburg as they walked down the stairs.

'No,' said Lampson. 'I've never been in Claridge's before. Too rich for me.'

'It's like hell on earth,' said Coburg. 'Noisy, hot, lots of shouting in French. It's run on the brigade system.'

'What's that?'

'The kitchen staff are divided into sections, each section responsible for different food preparations. The lowest level are those who prepare the soups, the highest are the ones who deal with sauces, but even there the real elite are those who create the velouté and béchamel.'

Lampson shook his head. 'It's all a foreign language to me,' he admitted.

'Yes, it is,' agreed Coburg. 'It's French. As I say, it's very hot, the exception being a cool chamber separate from the main body of the kitchen where salads, canapes, terrines and cold hors d'oeuvres are prepared.'

'How come you know so much about it?' asked Lampson.

'My brother, Charles, is – or rather was – a gourmet. I doubt if he's able to enjoy haute cuisine while he's locked up in a German PoW camp. He knew Marcel Devaux well, and once brought me down here to show me how and why Claridge's produced the best food in London, in his opinion.'

They reached the doors to the kitchen and Coburg pushed them open and they went in, and were immediately assailed by blasts of heat and shouts in French coming through a speaking tube fixed to the walls. The other main sound was of wood crashing on the concrete floor.

'They're all wearing clogs,' said Lampson, stunned.

'Sabots, to give them their proper name,' said Coburg. 'As I said, the kitchen is run on traditional French lines.'

'Ah, M'sieur Coburg!' boomed a hearty deep voice, and a tall, elegant man in chef's whites and wearing a tall chef's hat approached them, hands outstretched. He took both of Coburg's hands in his and kissed him on both cheeks. Lampson, a wary look on his face, took a step back.

'Marcel,' beamed Coburg. 'It's good to see you again. It's a pity it has to be under such circumstances.'

'A murder! Here, in my kitchen! *Incroyable!*'

'This is my sergeant, DS Lampson,' introduced Coburg.

Lampson smiled in greeting, but kept his distance and ensured Coburg was between him and the exuberant French chef.

'What can you tell us about Janos Mila?'

Devaux gave a Gallic shrug. 'I do not know the man. He is a porter, he carries things to and from the kitchen.'

'I may be asking the same questions as the first inspector who came this morning—' began Coburg apologetically, but he was interrupted by an outburst of scorn from Devaux. 'That moron! Inspector Lummox!'

'Lomax,' Coburg corrected the chef, though inwardly he reflected that lummox was a more apt description.

'He ask me nothing!' continued Devaux. 'He ask my staff nothing. He looks at the dead body of Janos, then leaves, complaining it is too hot here. Of course it's hot, it's a kitchen, I tell him.'

'Can you show me where Janos was found. And who found him.'

'Pierre!' shouted Devaux, and a small man with a voluminous brown moustache hurried to join them.

'This is Pierre. He is second head in the salad brigade. He went to a cool cupboard to check on the carrot flowers . . .'

'Carrot flowers?' enquired the puzzled Lampson.

'They carve the carrots in the shape of flowers to go in the salad,' explained Coburg.

'Oui,' nodded Pierre. 'I open the door and am about to go in when Alexandru Hagi, one of the kitchen hands, comes to me and tells me that Janos Mila is dead outside in the street, by the door. I go with him and look, and sure enough, there is Janos, dead on the pavement.'

'Is Alexandru here?' asked Coburg.

'He is,' said Pierre.

'Perhaps you'd find him and ask him to be prepared to talk to us after we've talked to you.'

'Of course,' said Pierre, and he bustled off in search of Alexandru.

'Thank you for your assistance, Marcel, and I apologise

for the disturbance to your routine. We'll do our best to cause as little interruption as possible.'

'For you, M'sieur Coburg, anything,' said Devaux. He looked at the chief inspector, concerned. 'I understand M'sieur Charles is a prisoner in France.'

'Yes, he is. He was captured by the Germans at Dunkirk.'

'If there is anything I can do, a food parcel for him, perhaps?'

'Thank you, Marcel, that's very much appreciated. I'll see what he's permitted to receive.'

A short time later Coburg and Lampson had established themselves in a small room away from the heat of the kitchen. Pierre had little more to offer than what he'd already told them. He'd immediately reported the discovery of the body to Marcel Devaux, who had contacted Georges LeGrosse in reception with instructions to telephone the police.

'We had Janos's body brought in and put in a cold room. We could not leave it out on the pavement,' said Pierre. 'I tied a rope across the door of the cold room to stop anyone going in. The police inspector arrived and looked around, then he ordered Janos's body to be taken away, and shortly after, he left. We expected him to return to ask us questions, but he didn't. So we opened the cold room again.'

'What time did Janos report for work this morning?'

'I did not see him arrive, but his shift begins work at five o'clock.'

'And what time was his body found?'

'Alexandru came to me just before six' o clock with the news. The other police inspector came at about a quarter to seven.'

And Superintendent Allison telephoned about half past

seven, thought Coburg. So D'Oyly Carte must have got on to his important contacts within the Establishment to arrange for me to take over the case, even as Inspector Lomax was arriving.

After Pierre, they were joined by Alexandru Hagi, a short, dark-haired man who regarded them suspiciously as he took his seat across the table from them. He told them the same story he'd told Inspector Lomax: 'I was near the door and it opened, and I heard someone call. I went to the door and looked out, and there was a man there. He said he wanted to speak to Janos Mila.'

'What did he look like?'

'I did not see his face. It was dark. And he had a hat pulled down and his coat collar was up. He also had a scarf pulled up over his face. I went to Janos and told him that a man was out in the street asking for him, and Janos went out. When Janos didn't come back, I went out to see where he was. He was on the ground, not moving. He looked dead.'

'Janos was Romanian?'

Hagi nodded.

'As you are, I'm guessing.'

Again, Hagi nodded. 'I was born in Romania but I have been here in England for over twenty years. My parents moved here when I was ten years old.'

'Had Janos been here as long as you?'

'No. He came to England a few months ago.'

'You were friends?' asked Coburg.

Hagi hesitated, then said in formal tones: 'We worked together.'

'Did you see one another outside of work?'

Hagi shook his head. 'No. I have a wife and child and

the little time I have away from work I spend with them.'

'How did you get on with Janos?'

'He was a good worker.'

'Did you and Janos talk much about Romania?'

'No. There is no time to talk. It is all work.'

'What sort of person was Janos?'

'He was a good man. Very high-minded.'

'About what?'

'About everything.'

'Can you be more specific?'

Hagi paused, then said carefully. 'He objected to some of the things that go on here.'

'Such as?'

Hagi hesitated again, then said reluctantly and with the coldest tones of disapproval: 'The whores.'

'There are whores here?'

'Not just here. They are everywhere. But Janos did not approve of them here. He was very high-minded.'

'Yes, so you said.'

'There is a man who comes here who arranges things.'

'Whores?'

'He makes appointments. Then the girls come in and go to a man's room.'

'Don't they have to pass the main reception desk?'

'They come in through the back door of the kitchens that leads to the street. They are always well dressed so they don't arouse suspicion as they go up through the hotel.'

'I assume that someone in the kitchens is involved in bringing the girls in.'

'Yes,' said the man, his face cold with disapproval. 'Two of them.'

'Their names?' asked Coburg.

The man shook his head. 'These men may not be dangerous, in fact they are weak scum, but the people behind them could be very dangerous, if they are the ones who had Janos killed. All I will tell you is that they pay most of the others to keep quiet about the women coming in. But not everyone takes their filthy money. I don't. And neither did Janos.'

'Why do you think these men killed Janos?'

'Because last week he lost his temper with one of the men after two of the whores had come through the kitchen. He told the man he was a disgrace to his mother country and that he would tell the police about what was going on.'

'This man is also Romanian?'

Hagi opened his mouth to reply, then shut it again. Then he said firmly: 'I will not say.'

'Because if we arrest this man then it will spread bad words about Romanians and raise questions about you and others?'

Again, Hagi said firmly: 'I will not say.'

CHAPTER SEVEN

'Heart attack,' groaned Peers as they drove northwards along Edgware Road, past row after row of rubble where houses and flats had once stood, now demolished. 'If it's a bad one we might well be too late. Too often on a heart attack call it's ended up with us taking the body to the mortuary.' He gave a heartfelt sigh. 'Before the war we had doctors with us. But all that's gone now, all the doctors are tied up with hospital work, what with all the injured being brought in for treatment.'

He looked at the scenes of desolation they were passing. 'It's terrible,' he sighed. 'The whole city's being destroyed. Night after night, bombs raining down. Thank heavens they finally opened up the Tube stations as air raid shelters.'

'I don't think they had much choice,' said Rosa. 'People were going underground because they had nowhere else to go. Trying to lock the station gates against them only led to some pretty dreadful scenes.' She looked out at the street sign and said: 'Maida Vale.'

Peers looked again at the address on the piece of paper on his lap and said: 'Take the next on the right, then first left. It'll be along there. At least we're not far from the hospital.'

Rosa followed Peers' directions, and they found

themselves driving along a street that had been heavily bombed on one side, the few houses that were just about standing showing gaping holes where their fronts had been, the area in front of them piled high with bricks and broken roof tiles, which made driving like an obstacle course as Rosa weaved the ambulance between the heaps of rubble.

'This is it,' said Peers, and Rosa pulled to a halt in front of two houses side by side, both of which the front had fallen out, exposing the furniture, the kitchen, and in one the bath and toilet on the first floor were dangling from pipes, poised perilously over the void below.

'This can't be right,' said Rosa. 'No one can be still living here.'

'You'd be surprised,' said Peers. 'Most people have got nowhere else to go, and even a broken house is a roof over their head.'

'The patient's a Mrs Hibbs,' he said. 'I'll go and see how she's doing if you bring the stretcher.'

Rosa nodded and went to the back of the ambulance.

'By the way,' called Peers suddenly, and now he looked slightly embarrassed. 'I know it's a bit of a cheek, but would you mind doing an autograph for my Elsie? She's such a fan of yours, and it would mean a lot to her. I don't like to ask, but . . .'

'Not at all,' said Rosa. 'It will be my pleasure. Once we've got Mrs Hibbs safely to hospital, I'll do it. I might even have a photograph of me in my handbag. Will that be all right?'

'Even better,' beamed Peers. 'It'll tickle Elsie something special.' He turned and headed for the damaged house as Rosa opened the rear doors of the ambulance and pulled out the canvas stretcher rolled over two long poles.

'Be careful as you walk!' called Peers. 'These houses

51

look like they could come down any second.'

Rosa shut the ambulance doors and made sure she had the ignition key in her pocket. She'd heard stories about thieves opportunistically jumping into vehicles where the driver had left the ignition key in and driving them off. Cars, vans, ambulances, fire engines, it didn't matter, anything on wheels seemed an opportunity.

She was just turning to carry the stretcher towards the house, when there was a noise louder than any explosion she'd heard and the shaking of the ground beneath her feet was so violent it threw her down. Dust blinded and choked her. She couldn't hear, the explosion or whatever it was had deafened her.

Was it a bomb? It was daytime and there had been no signs of aircraft in the sky, not German bombers. The smaller British Spitfires and Hurricanes were seen now and then, flying high, circling like tiny metal guardian angels, ready to give protection. There had been no wail of an air raid siren.

She sat up, spitting the dust from her mouth, then took a handkerchief from her pocket and wrapped it round her nose and mouth. As she sat there, on the broken rubble, the dust slowly began to clear and settle. She looked down at herself and saw that she was completely covered in a grey dust that matted her hair, covered her skin and her uniform. The same grey dust had fallen all around her, covering everything. And where the house had been that Derek Peers had been walking to there was just a hole, and the pile of rubble that had been there before was now as high as the first-floor wreckage of the adjoining house. There was no sign of Derek, just a heap of broken bricks and rubble piled high where she'd last seen him.

CHAPTER EIGHT

After Hagi, Coburg and Lampson spoke to everyone else who'd arrived for work with the five o'clock shift. No one remembered seeing Janos, with the exception of Alexandru Hagi. At that time everyone was too busy picking up information from the previous shift about what work was still to be done, carried over from the night shift.

'So what do you reckon, guv?' asked Lampson. 'Think it's connected to the prostitutes? It's obviously a ring operating.'

'It seems a bit extreme,' said Coburg doubtfully. 'Surely the people behind it would have opted for a warning, or a beating to shut him up. Killing him, especially the way it was done, would only bring the police into the picture. But, as we've got nothing else, we'll need to follow it up. While I talk to Marcel, get on the car radio and ask for a detective constable to be sent here.'

'To watch the back door?'

Coburg nodded.

'I'll arrange for him to be given a set of kitchen whites to put on, but his job will be to watch the door to the street. If any women come in, he's to grab them and arrest them on suspicion. He can phone the Control Room and patch a message through to us and we'll come for him. If we're not available, he can arrange a car to get them to the Yard from reception.'

'It could be a long wait,' observed Lampson.

'It's what most police work is about, Ted, as we both know: hanging about, waiting and watching, and too often with no result. But it's the only lead we've got. We'll also have a word with Vice and see if they've got anything about it. But first, we'll pay a visit to Janos's address and see if there's any clues there as to why someone wants to garrotte him.'

Roly Fitt's club was called The Quiet Mole. Lomax had no idea why. Maybe it was called 'Mole' because it was underground in the deep basement beneath an office block; but from what he could gather it was hardly a quiet place, loud music blaring out at all times of the night. Lomax and Potteridge walked down the winding staircase to the club itself, then walked through the bar to Roly Fitt's office at the back. Staff were clearing up from the previous night, washing the surface of the long bar, wiping down tables, restocking the shelves behind the bar. The staff watched the two policemen walk through, then ignored them and got on with their work. They were used to policemen walking through.

Roly Fitt wasn't roly, or round in any way. Instead, he was tall and thin, very fit-looking for a man in his fifties. Roly was short for Roland and in his way he was a hard man like Hooky Morton, with fingers in many dubious pies. But he dressed smartly and was always genial to his clientele, shaking hands and ensuring free drinks to certain valued clients. It was Mayfair, after all.

Fitt waved the inspector and his sergeant towards two chairs, but they remained standing. Lomax had no intention of being thought of in any way as 'a friend' by Fitt.

'I suppose you've heard about Patch Peters,' said Lomax.

Fitt nodded. 'Found dead. Shot, so I hear.'

'On your area.'

Fitt held up his hands in protest. 'I have business interests here, Inspector. That's all.'

'So why does a man who works for someone with similar business interests, but on the other side of town, end up in your neck of the woods with a bullet in him?'

Fitt shook his head.

'It's a mystery, Inspector.'

'There is a suggestion that he was trespassing where he shouldn't have been.'

Fitt shook his head.

'Absolutely not! In fact, Patch was welcome to come here any time.'

'Was he now?' said Lomax suspiciously. 'One of Hooky Morton's lot being made welcome here?'

'Why not? It's a free city.'

'But parcelled up,' growled Lomax.

'I can assure you, Inspector, neither I nor any of my associates had anything to do with Patch Peters getting shot. The fact his body was found just round the corner from my club makes me think that somebody might be sending me a message.'

'A message?'

'You know, like when a player from one football team thinks about moving to another one, and the manager of that team sends a message telling him to back off.'

'Patch Peters was moving to join your gang?'

'I don't have a gang, Inspector. I have businesses.'

'And Patch Peters was considering transferring his allegiance?'

Fitt shrugged. 'Who's to say, Inspector? Not Patch, not now he's dead. Maybe the person you ought to have a word with is Hooky Morton.'

Janos Mila's home had been a small bedsit at the top of a cramped three-storey, multi-occupied house in Paddington. The pervading smell that greeted them as they mounted the stairs was of damp and boiled cabbage. They'd collected the keys to the house and the room from the mortuary at the Middlesex Hospital, along with the rest of the belongings found in Janos's pockets: some money, a wallet and an identity card. Coburg was relieved that Inspector Lomax hadn't bothered to retain these belongings at Mayfair police station but had been content for them to go to the mortuary; it saved him from having a confrontation with the always resentful inspector, but he knew he wouldn't be able to avoid one for much longer.

They were surprised at how bare the room was of personal possessions. There was a small gas ring, and in a cupboard a few tins of corned beef and vegetables in brine. One cup, one knife, one fork and one spoon indicated that Janos did not entertain guests. There were a few clothes hanging in a small wardrobe, and that was all. There were no papers or documents of any sort in the drawers, or on the small table.

'I may be reading more into this than there is, but it

almost looks as if someone's cleared everything out of the drawers.'

'I was just thinking the same,' agreed Lampson. 'You'd expect to find something, even just scraps of paper about getting shopping, or whatever. But there's nothing.' He looked through the empty drawers again. 'Either Janos left nothing here, or someone's done it. And they did it very neatly, it's not just a grab everything and run.'

'Yes,' nodded Coburg thoughtfully.

'You're thinking the security services?' asked Lampson. 'MI5? MI6? Special Branch?'

'I am,' agreed Coburg.

Detective Constable Peter Witz leant against the wall of Claridge's subterranean kitchen, his eyes fixed on the door in the opposite wall that led to the street. Keep your eyes fixed on it and apprehend any women who come in that way. Those had been his instructions from DCI Coburg, and he was going to make sure he kept to them. The people in white jackets rushing about, the sound of their wooden clogs and the shouting in French that filled the kitchen from the speaking tubes could have been a distraction, but DC Witz was determined he would not be diverted from his task.

The women might protest, he'd been told, insist they have legitimate business, or are even guests of the hotel who've chosen to slip in the back way. Whatever they say, be polite to them, but firm. Your instructions are to escort them to reception and then telephone for a car to take them to Scotland Yard. Do not enlarge on that, don't tell them what this is about. If they insist, tell them you don't know. If they say they will call their solicitor and sue you, tell them their solicitor can meet them at Scotland Yard. Coburg had gone on to say: do not question them, do not even ask them their name, all that will be done by Sergeant Lampson and myself at Scotland Yard.

Two hours had gone by since DC Witz had been given the white jacket and pointed at the door he was to watch. Two hours of watching the door and ignoring all the frantic activity going on around him. Beneath the white jacket he could feel the sweat as the heat of the kitchen swirled around him. Some of the kitchen staff looked at him in curiosity, but none approached him to ask him what he was up to.

'Only the chef in charge, Marcel Devaux, knows why we have stationed you here, and he will not tell anyone,' Coburg had told him. 'Believe me, no one will ask M'sieur Devaux why you are there. He has said you are there and are not to be talked to or disturbed. That will be enough.'

The hands of the clock on the wall moved, although the clock's ticking could not be heard. Frankly, nothing could be heard above the cacophony of shouting, the clatter of plates, the rattle of clogs.

Suddenly, Witz saw the door to the street open slightly, then a woman appeared. She was wearing a fur coat. She shut the door and began to move through the kitchen towards the other entrance, which would take her into the hotel proper. Witz moved forward and placed himself so that she would have to pass him, and as she did, he put a hand on her arm.

'I am Police Detective Constable Witz and I must ask you to accompany me to reception, and thence to Scotland Yard,' he intoned.

'Piss off,' she snapped. 'Get your hands off me.'

One of the kitchen staff, a portly moustachioed man, appeared beside them.

'What is going on?' he demanded nervously.

'This bloke says he's police,' said the woman.

'I am,' said Witz. 'And I must ask you to let me get on with my job.'

'But this woman has done nothing!' protested the man.

Suddenly the imposing figure of Marcel Devaux was there, glaring at the kitchen worker.

'Leave!' he barked.

'Yes, m'sieur,' grovelled the man, and he scurried away.

'As for you, you're coming with me,' said Witz to the woman, and he steered her towards the door to the main hotel.

'You're gonna be in trouble for this,' scowled the woman. 'You're gonna get sued.'

'By all means you can contact your solicitor when we get to Scotland Yard,' said Witz.

He kept a firm grip on her arm as they walked up the stairs to the ground floor and main reception. Georges LeGrosse, who'd been apprised of the situation in advance by Coburg, nodded as the pair approached his desk and was already lifting the receiver of the telephone on his desk.

'Scotland Yard?' asked LeGrosse.

'Please,' said Witz. 'Ask for the Radio Control Room.'

'You've got this all wrong,' said the woman. 'I'm here to see a friend. He's got a room on the second floor. I can prove it.'

During this, LeGrosse had dialled the number, and, when it answered, he passed the receiver to Witz, who took it with his free hand.

'Radio Control? DC Witz at Claridge's Hotel. Would

you inform DCI Coburg I have a suspect in custody . . .
Yes, I'll hold.' He listened to the chatter and click from the
other end of the line, then the operator came back to tell
him: 'DCI Coburg is on his way.'

'Thank you,' said Witz.

He handed the receiver back to LeGrosse and was
turning back to the woman, when suddenly she kicked him
hard on the ankle. Witz gave a yell of pain and let go of her
arm, at which point she ran for the main door to the street.
Witz tried to hobble after her, but she was too quick and he
was too slow, hampered by the sharp pain surging through
his lower leg.

'Bugger!' he groaned, as he sank down on the nearest
chair.

CHAPTER NINE

Rosa pushed herself to her feet as the sound of voices came to her. She could hear again, and the sounds she heard were of panic and concern.

'Are you all right, dear?'

She turned and found herself face to face with a plump, middle-aged woman in a flowered apron who'd obviously come straight from her kitchen to judge by the flour that covered her hands.

'I think so,' said Rosa unsteadily. She looked at the huge pile of rubble. 'My partner's under that.'

'Diana!' shouted the woman, and a tall, thin, red-haired girl edged nervously forward. The woman held out some coins to her. 'Go and phone the emergency people. Tell them what's happened.'

Rosa pulled a St John calling card from her uniform pocket and passed it to the woman. 'Can she phone that number as well? Ask for Mr Warren. His name's on the card. Tell him what's happened. Tell him Rosa Weeks asked you to call.'

The woman passed the card to the girl. 'Go on, Diana. Run.' As the girl darted away, she called after her: 'And remember, press button A when they answer!'

'I'm sorry, sir,' said DC Witz.

And he did indeed look completely apologetic as he stood to attention, shamefaced and embarrassed, in Claridge's reception area and told Coburg and Lampson what had happened, how the woman had got away from him and escaped out into the street.

'That's all right, Constable, it could happen to any of us,' said Coburg sympathetically, remembering that the same thing had happened to him when he had been a young constable in training. 'Did anyone try to interfere when you arrested her?'

'Not really, sir. Some bloke in the kitchen came up and made a sort of protest, said she hadn't done anything, but then the big boss, Mister Devaux, told him to get lost.'

'Who was this man who protested?'

'I'm sorry, sir, I don't know. I didn't think it was important. He was just one of the kitchen staff.'

Coburg and Lampson headed down to the kitchen. 'The bird may have flown, but we may still have a chance,' said Coburg.

'The bloke who interfered,' nodded Lampson. 'I bet he's one of the blokes who gets paid.'

When they found Marcel Devaux, Coburg asked: 'When our officer apprehended the woman, one of your staff tried to intervene.'

'He did,' said Devaux. 'I sent him off with a flea in his ear.'

'Which of your staff was it?'

'His name is Kurt Wenders. He is Belgian.'

'May we borrow him?' asked Coburg. 'I need to take him to Scotland Yard to ask him some questions.'

'By all means,' said Devaux.

'Where will I find him?'

'Pierre!' shouted Devaux.

The small figure of Pierre arrived beside them.

'Yes, M'sieur le Chef?' he asked.

'Take Mr Coburg and the sergeant to Kurt Wenders.'

'Yes, m'sieur.'

Coburg and Lampson followed Pierre to a table at the far side of the kitchen where men in kitchen whites were chopping vegetables. Pierre asked something of one of the men in French, who responded with a few words and some pointing and gesticulations. Pierre turned to the two policemen and told them: 'It seems he has left. This man saw him put on his outdoor coat and go.'

'Was he due to leave?'

'No.'

'Can you get his address for us?' asked Coburg. When Pierre hurried off to check the files, Coburg told Lampson: 'You wait here for it. I want to have another word with Alexandru Hagi.'

Coburg found Hagi and gestured for him to join him away from the mass and the noise of the other kitchen workers.

'Kurt Wenders has disappeared,' he told him. 'He tried to stop our officer taking a woman who came in the back door into custody, and apparently he vanished when he learnt he was a policeman. I assume Wenders was one of the two men you mentioned who passed money around.'

Hagi hesitated, then nodded.

'Wenders was Belgian, so I'm guessing the other one involved was Romanian. In case Janos's death was part of this, I need to know where I can get hold of the other man. Who is he?'

'Josef Malic. But he went away, too. I saw Wenders go up to him and say something when the woman was taken away. I saw him leave with his coat on.'

'Thank you.'

'Am I safe?' asked Hagi. 'If they killed Janos, will they kill me next?'

'We don't know that they killed Janos. Janos's death may have been due to something entirely different. And you didn't tell us who they were before. They will know this from the fact that we only came looking for them after we apprehended the woman, so we didn't know who they were before that.'

'So I am safe?'

'As safe as any of us are during a war,' said Coburg. 'Do you know where Josef Malic lived?'

'Yes. In the same house as Janos. He had a room on the ground floor. They did not like one another.'

Coburg and Lampson returned to the house where Janos Mila had lived, and learnt that Josef Malic had left not long before. 'He had a small suitcase with him,' the neighbour who'd seen him go told the policemen.

They got the same story when they arrived at the boarding house where Kurt Wenders lived.

'The birds are flying,' mused Coburg. 'They won't have gone far, but we could waste a lot of time trying to find them.'

'This bloke Malic lived in the same house as Janos, so he could have been the one who cleared out the papers from Janos's room,' suggested Lampson.

'But the door hadn't been forced and Janos's keys were in his pocket when he was killed,' said Coburg.

'Yes, good point, guv. So, do you think the murder's

connected to the prostitution ring?'

'There's something about the way Janos was killed that makes me doubt it. The garrotte. And surely, if it had been connected with the prostitution ring, Wenders and Malic would have made themselves scarce as soon as they knew that Janos's body had been found.' He shrugged. 'But then, I've been wrong before. The prostitution aspect is still a possibility, but so is the fact that perhaps the security services are involved. You know someone in Vice, don't you?'

'DS Vic Fortune,' nodded Lampson. 'He knows most of what goes on.'

'Then I suggest we split this. You go and see DS Vic Fortune while I go along to Wormwood Scrubs and have a word with Inspector Hibbert of MI5.'

Time seemed frozen to Rosa. She sat, numbed, on a block of broken rubble while the friendly neighbours brought her tea, which she sipped. But all she could do was look at the huge pile of rubble that had buried Derek, and the hole where Mrs Hibbs's house had stood but now was just an empty gap in the row of buildings.

'Are you all right, dear?' asked one concerned woman. 'Are you hurt? Do you want us to get you a doctor?'

It was this that forced Rosa to her feet.

'No, thanks,' she said. 'I'm okay. Just a bit shaken.' She nodded towards her ambulance. 'I'd better be getting that back to base, they'll be needing it.'

She walked to the ambulance, fired up the engine, and drove off.

I need Edgar, she thought. I need him to put his arms around me and tell me everything's going to be all right.

CHAPTER TEN

Lampson was relieved to find that DS Vic Fortune of Vice was in his office, because working police officers spent most of their time out on the road, investigating crime scenes and chasing criminals.

'Me and my guv'nor are investigating a suspected vice ring at Claridge's,' he told him.

Fortune gave a wry grin. 'Why just Claridge's?' asked Fortune. 'They're in every hotel in London. Every big department store.'

'At the moment it's just Claridge's we're interested in. We're not planning to tread on your territory – we're investigating a murder that took place there in the early hours of this morning, and there's a suggestion it may be linked to a prostitution ring. Who's running the high-end girls who do the big hotels?'

'It changes,' said Fortune. 'They seem to swap around. We think we've got tabs on 'em, then one of 'em dies or goes away for a stretch and someone else moves in. The two biggest operators seem to be Jimmy Mussels and Erky Dunbar. We know they've been running girls in the Ritz and the Dorchester, but we can't pin anything concrete on them.'

'Friends in high places?'

'Exactly. Their clients are usually very well connected, which fits with the kind of people staying at those sorts of places. We've been close a few times, but then we've been told to back off. In one case the client was a cabinet minister, another was some rich industrialist with powerful connections in parliament, and another was the fourteen-year-old son of some rich foreign king living at the Ritz who'd bought his boy a girl as a birthday present.'

'Huh, all I got when I was fourteen was a pair of roller skates,' grunted Lampson. 'So, Jimmy Mussels and Erky Dunbar.'

'They seem the most likely, but good luck on getting any evidence against them. From our experience, no one seems willing to talk.'

Chesney Warren looked up as the door of his office opened, and when he saw it was Rosa, her hair and uniform still streaked with grey dust, he got to his feet and went to her, pushing a chair forward for her to sit.

'I'm so sorry.' he said, and Rosa could tell from his tone and his body language that he absolutely meant it.

'I've brought the ambulance back,' she told him. 'It's in the yard.'

'Do you want tea? Or something stronger? I've got some brandy, which is always good at a time like this.'

She shook her head.

'No thanks.' She looked at him, her face showing her distress. 'Derek just vanished. One minute he was there, and then this house fell on him. The house where Mrs Hibbs, our heart attack victim, was.' She shook her head.

'It was awful. I've seen people die before, everyone has during this war, but . . .' She subsided into silence, her eyes looking down at her lap.

'You need to go home,' said Warren.

'No,' she said.

'Yes,' he said, his tone firmer. 'You're in no condition to go out on shouts right now. Take the rest of the day off. Recover. If you feel up to it, come in tomorrow.'

Rosa looked down at herself, at the dust that covered her. 'I need to get rid of this stuff,' she said. 'I can't walk through the streets looking like this.'

'I'll get someone to give you a lift home.'

'No, I'd rather walk. Just let me go to the ladies and give my uniform a good shake. I'll have a bath when I get home.'

With most of the dust shaken off but the memory of how she'd got covered in it still fresh in her mind, Rosa walked the short distance from the ambulance station to the nearest telephone box. She knew that if she'd asked him, Chesney Warren would have allowed her to use the phone in his office, but she also knew that using the telephone at St John Ambulance for private calls was frowned upon, and she didn't want to put him in a position where he was bending the rules.

She dialled Whitehall 1212, and when the switchboard operator answered she pressed button A for the coins to fall into the box and asked for DCI Coburg.

'Who's calling?'

'His wife.'

'One moment.'

There was a series of clicks, and then a male voice she

didn't recognise said: 'DCI Coburg's office.'

'Is DCI Coburg there? It's his wife calling.'

'I'm afraid he's out on a case at Claridge's Hotel. Can I take a message?'

'No, that's all right. Thank you.'

Rosa hung up. Should she wait and see him when he got home? The trouble was she felt so troubled, anguished, she just needed to speak to him, preferably for him to hold her in his arms. She doubted if that would be able to happen while he was working, but if she could just see him it would help.

Claridge's, she said to herself.

Coburg drove to Wormwood Scrubs. No longer operating as a prison, the inmates having been transferred to other jails, the old imposing Victorian buildings now served as the home of MI5. Inspector James Hibbert was in his office and gestured Coburg to take a chair. Hibbert was a bulky, middle-aged man whose general demeanour came across as dour and unfriendly, but he was one of the very few people in the Secret Services that Coburg found to be approachable and co-operative. He was also a man who didn't care for social chit-chat and long-winded introductions, so Coburg came straight to the point.

'Have you had any interest in a man called Janos Mila?'

Hibbert shook his head.

'It doesn't ring a bell. Who is he?'

'He worked in the kitchen at Claridge's until someone garrotted him. He's supposed to be Romanian.'

'Supposed to be?'

'There's always a question mark over foreign nationals

from Eastern Europe, especially now. We went to his place to see if we could find any documents that established exactly where he was from, but someone had been there and cleared out all the paperwork.'

'So naturally you thought of us.'

'That did occur to me,' said Coburg. 'It was all done very neatly.'

Hibbert shook his head.

'Sorry, it means nothing to me. Someone else? Let's face it, at this moment London is so full of spies and undercover agents I'm surprised they don't bump into one another on a regular basis.'

'Who are you thinking of particularly?' asked Coburg.

Hibbert gave him a look of despair. 'No one in particular, all of them. Do you realise how many foreign countries have set up governments in exile here?' He ticked them off on his fingers, and Coburg was reminded of Superintendent Allison doing the same thing. 'Czechoslovakia, Poland, Norway, Belgium, Holland, Yugoslavia, Greece, Luxembourg – all have governments in exile based in London, with their respective presidents and prime ministers and cabinets. And their monarchies.'

'Yes, that's one of the problems we've got with our investigations. Most of the exiled royal families are staying at Claridge's.'

'And every one of them has its own secret service agents here. It's like a spies' convention. And then, to make it worse, you've got that pain in the arse, General de Gaulle and his Free French lot in exile at 3, Carlton Gardens.'

'Why do you say he's a pain in the arse? Surely he's an ally?'

'He doesn't see it that way. As far as he's concerned, Britain is stopping him from being seen as the rightful French government because they still recognise the Vichy mob. That's put his nose out of joint. Not that it wasn't already, because as far as he's concerned, he wants to be seen as the saviour of France, not the British.'

'Even though we took what – a hundred thousand French troops off the beaches at Dunkirk?'

'Yes, well, don't expect gratitude from him if you meet him. Are you going to meet him?'

'I'm not sure. Only if we come across something that suggests a connection to the murder with the French.'

CHAPTER ELEVEN

Rosa walked into Claridge's, aware that there were still enough streaks of dust in her hair to raise eyebrows in such an exclusive place. But then, she reflected, places like Claridge's, the Ritz and the Savoy were used to eccentricities among their guests. The rich could afford to be odd.

The tall concierge at the reception desk, Georges LeGrosse, recognised her because she'd been in a few days before to get used to the grand piano in Claridge's tea room where she'd be performing.

'Ah, Miss Weeks,' he beamed. 'Good to see you again.' Then he became aware of the dust on her and asked tentatively. 'Are you all right? Has there been an accident?'

'Yes, I'm afraid so, but I'm all right. I've come because I was told my husband was here.'

'Ah, of course. DCI Coburg. He was here, but I'm not sure if he still is. I know he went down to the kitchens, but also there was a mention of someone on the second floor.'

'I'll try there rather than get mixed up in the kitchen,' said Rosa. 'Thank you.'

She made her way up the carpeted stairs to the second

floor. The corridor was empty. If Edgar was here, there was no way of knowing where.

This is a wild goose chase, she told herself unhappily. I'll go home and see him later.

She was just turning to make her way back to the stairs, when a door near to her opened and a young man wearing a dressing gown leered at her.

'Ah, you're here,' he said. 'I was expecting you ages ago.'

'I beg your pardon,' said Rosa, bewildered and at the same time affronted by the young man's attitude towards her.

'Are you Stella?' he asked, momentarily taken aback. 'Looking for Joss?'

'No to both questions,' said Rosa coldly, giving him a look of deep discouragement, at which he sneered and went back into his room.

Inspector Lomax and Sergeant Potteridge followed Jessie Peters through the narrow corridor of the terraced house behind King's Cross railway station to the small kitchen at the back of the house. She sat down at the bare wooden table and the two policemen sat down with her. They could see she'd been crying. At first, she'd been reluctant to let them into the house and had tried to shut the door on them, but Lomax had forced the door open.

'We're the police,' he'd told her firmly.

'I know that,' she said, but all her defiance and resolve had been taken out of her, and she led them into the house.

'We're investigating the death of your husband, Terrence,' said Lomax.

'Patch,' she said. 'Everyone called him Patch.'

'Very well, Patch. He was shot and his body dumped at

73

a bomb site over in Mayfair. Who did he know in Mayfair?'

She shook her head.

'No idea. I didn't know he knew anyone in Mayfair.'

'What about Roly Fitt?'

'Who?'

'Did Patch ever mention a man called Roly Fitt?'

'No. He didn't talk about people.'

'What about Hooky Morton?'

She looked at the two policemen, and Lomax thought he saw a glint of anger in her eyes, but it could have been tears.

'What about him?' she asked defensively.

'Do you know Hooky Morton?'

'Everyone in this area knows Hooky Morton,' she said.

'Your husband worked for him.'

'Did he?' she said flatly.

'Did Morton kill your husband?'

'Why would he?' she asked.

'Because we've been told that your husband was thinking of working for another mob over Mayfair way. Hooky wouldn't like that.'

'Then talk to Hooky.'

'You think he killed your husband?'

'I'm not saying that,' said Mrs Peters guardedly.

'Look, Mrs Peters, we're investigating a murder. Your husband was a low-level crook, hardly worth the bother of anyone shooting him, unless there was something going on with him. What was that? Was he selling out Hooky Morton?'

She glared at them, and now her gaze was steely and unflinching. 'My husband's dead. Someone killed him. I don't know who. What I want to know is, when will I get his body back so I can bury him? Because he's going to get a proper funeral.'

Lomax shifted uncomfortably on the chair.

'You'll get his body back when our medical people have finished with it. There could be clues there that will tell us who shot him.' He stood up, as did Sergeant Potteridge. The inspector put his visiting card on the table. 'There's my number at Mayfair police station, if you remember anything.'

With that, the two policemen walked along the passageway and back out into the street. Jessie Peters watched them walk to where their police car was waiting for them. Then she shut the door and walked back to the kitchen.

'I'm gonna get him for you, Patch,' she muttered angrily. 'He ain't gonna get away with it. I don't know how, but I will.'

When Coburg arrived back at their flat it was to find Rosa slumped over the kitchen table, her head resting on her arms. As soon as she heard his footsteps, she leapt up and rushed to him, throwing her arms around him, and he realised as her cheek touched his that she'd been crying.

'What's happened?' he asked, worried.

'Derek Peers, my crewmate, was killed today,' she said. 'We went out on a call to St John's Wood to pick up a woman with a suspected heart attack. Her house had been bombed and there wasn't much of it left standing, and as Derek walked towards it, the whole lot came down on top of him.' At the awful memory, she began to cry again.

'My God!' said Coburg. He held her away from him and studied her tear-streaked face. 'What about you? Were you injured?'

'No. I'd gone to get the stretcher from the back of the ambulance. Derek only had one arm, you see, so he went to see how Mrs Hibbs – that was the patient – was, while I fetched the equipment.' Her body shook with sobs again. 'It was awful. The dust when the house collapsed, it was everywhere, and when it cleared, where Derek had been was just this . . . rubble. A pile of it almost as high as the first floor.'

'You should have come and found me,' said Coburg, holding her tight.

'I tried. I phoned Scotland Yard and they said you were at Claridge's. I went to Claridge's, but you'd gone. So I came home.'

'Oh, my poor love!' said Coburg. He led her to the settee and settled her down on it, sitting beside her, keeping his arm around her and cuddling her close to him. 'Sit there and I'll get you a whiskey.'

'I've already had two,' she said. 'I don't want any more or I'll be sick.'

Coburg hugged her closer. 'Tell me about Derek,' he said.

He could tell that Rosa was still in a state of shock and often the best way to deal with that was to get the shocked person to talk – about the trauma that had happened, or sometimes about anything, just to talk. He sat, his arms around her, and listened as she told him about Derek, how he'd been with St John Ambulance for so many years. She told him about how he'd lost his arm.

'It was during the First War. He was a conscientious objector operating an ambulance in the trenches when he was blown up. He may have been a conscientious objector, but he wasn't a coward. He was a Quaker, and he was brave. The way he walked towards that building before

76

it collapsed. He went into places where he'd been warned there was an unexploded bomb, but it didn't stop him. And now he's dead.' She pushed herself slightly away from him and looked at him. 'He had a wife, Elsie. I thought I might call on her sometime and tell her what happened and how brave I thought he was.'

'That would be a nice thing to do,' murmured Coburg.

She wiped her eyes, then said: 'What made it worse was when I came to find you in Claridge's and you weren't there.'

'Yes, I'm so sorry about that,' said Coburg guiltily.

'No, it wasn't that, it was this awful, unpleasant encounter I had.'

'Who with? One of the staff? Let me know and I'll sort them out.'

'No, it was a guest. Some horrid young man. I was walking along a corridor when the door of this room opened and this odious and very superior young man, wearing what seemed to be just a dressing gown, said to me: 'Are you Stella, looking for Joss?' She gave a shudder of disgust at the memory. 'He thought I was a prostitute! For God's sake, I was wearing my St John Ambulance uniform! All right, I had my outside coat on over it, but—'

'This is interesting,' said Coburg, suddenly alert.

'Interesting? It's disgusting!'

Coburg explained to her about the alleged prostitution ring operating at Claridge's. 'So far, we haven't been able to get any concrete information, like names. A constable caught one of the girls, but she did a runner before we could talk to her. And the two men we think were involved have disappeared. Do you remember which room this man was in?'

77

Rosa thought, bringing the scene in the corridor to her mind and recalling looking at the room numbers as she walked. '224,' she said at last.

'You're sure?'

'Fairly sure. The trouble is all the doors look alike, but I'm pretty certain I saw number 224 when he shut the door.'

Coburg leant back from her, and asked her as gently as he could: 'My darling, do you mind if I leave you for a minute or two?'

'If you're planning on going to Claridge's and punching him in the mouth that's not a good idea. You'll only get in trouble.' She looked unhappy as she added: 'As he's staying at Claridge's, I just hope he's not in the audience on Sunday evening. Every time I look out and see him, I'll remember that incident today.'

'No, I wasn't planning to punch him,' Coburg assured her. 'Well, not at first, although that may come later. I want a word with him because it strikes me that this odious young man may be our way to find out what's going on with this prostitution ring. I'll also have a discreet word with him about Sunday evening.'

'You can't ban him. Claridge's won't like that.'

'No, but I can advise him to keep a very low profile if he's got tickets for Sunday. A table near the kitchens.'

'He won't talk,' said Rosa. 'He'll just deny it even happened.'

'Oh, he'll talk,' said Coburg grimly. 'Believe me, he'll talk.'

CHAPTER TWELVE

Leaving Rosa at the flat trying out pieces on the piano in preparation for Sunday, Coburg drove to Claridge's, where reception told him that room 224 was where the Honourable Jocelyn Walbrook-Staines was staying.

'Is he in at the moment?' asked Coburg.

The receptionist checked the keys.

'He is, sir. Do you want me to ring through to him?'

'No, thank you,' said Coburg with a friendly smile. 'I'll surprise him.'

A short time later he was standing outside room 224. When the door opened to his knock Coburg found himself confronted by a tall, thin, moustachioed young man elegantly dressed in casual clothes, his hair parted in the middle and sleeked back.

'Mr Walbrook-Staines,' said Coburg, producing his warrant card and showing it to the young man. 'I am Detective Chief Inspector Coburg. I understand you accosted a young woman earlier today who was walking past your room, and asked her if she was Stella.'

The young man glared indignantly at Coburg.

'Absolutely not!' he said, his tone one of controlled anger. 'Whoever told you that is lying.'

'I'm afraid I have this report on very good authority,' pressed Coburg.

Walbrook-Staines scowled, drew himself up, and then demanded haughtily: 'Do you know who you're talking to? I am the Honourable Jocelyn Walbrook-Staines, son of the Earl of Staines.'

'And I am the Honourable Edgar Walter Septimus Saxe-Coburg, brother of the Earl of Dawlish, and also a detective chief inspector from Scotland Yard and I am investigating a murder that took place here. Now, are we going to trade competing titles and relatives, or will you answer my questions here and now? Unless you would prefer to accompany me to Scotland Yard?'

The young man stared at Coburg, stunned, his mouth opening and closing, but no sound coming out until finally he managed a strangled: 'I'm sorry, I didn't realise who you were.' He gulped. 'But I had nothing to do with any murder.'

'I'm not suggesting you did, but the information you have might well lead us to the person we're looking for.'

'What information?'

'May I come in?' asked Coburg. 'It will be easier than talking out here in the corridor.'

'Of course,' said the young man, and he opened the door for Coburg to enter.

'We believe the murder that happened here this morning in the kitchens may be connected to a prostitution ring that's operating here at this hotel, and other top hotels in London,' said Coburg once he was in the room.

'I didn't even know there had been a murder here,' said Walbrook-Staines.

'That's understandable, the hotel is hardly likely to

want news like that broadcast. But if we are to get to the bottom of it, we need to know how the appointments with these women are arranged.' As he saw the young man hesitate, he added in a firmer tone: 'We can make this an easy conversation, or we can conduct it at Scotland Yard, with your solicitor present, and the risk of any newspaper reporters who might be hanging around getting hold of your name, which is from a very respectable family and just the sort of thing they like to spice up their column inches with.'

'No, no,' said Walbrook-Staines hastily. 'I'll tell you. What happens is, I telephone a number, and a man arrives to collect the money. It's always money in advance. And we make an appointment, and the girl arrives.'

'Do you know the name of the man you telephone?'

'No. It can be a different voice every time. But it's generally the same man who calls to collect the money.'

'Tell me more about the procedure. Do you use a code or anything?'

'Only the first time. You say that Hercules Evans has given you the number.'

'Hercules Evans,' nodded Coburg. 'And then?'

'They ask you for your name and the address, then tell you how much. After that they tell you what time their man will be calling to make the arrangement and collect the money.'

'They don't ask for references? Who gave you the number?'

'No, just Hercules Evans. But I'm pretty sure they check you're who you say you are, because the first time I did it a man phoned me here. He must have gone through the switchboard at Claridge's, asked for me by name and been given the number of my room.'

Coburg passed the young man a pencil and a piece of paper. 'The phone number you called, if you please.'

The young man took the pencil and paper, but once again hesitated. 'Will my family have to know about this?' he asked.

'Not if you give me that number.'

The man nodded and wrote down a telephone number, then passed the paper and the pencil back to Coburg.

'One last thing,' said Coburg getting to his feet. 'I'd be very careful of how you talk to women you don't actually know in the future. The woman you accosted and referred to as Stella was actually my wife.'

The man's face went bright red and he began to stammer: 'I didn't realise. I didn't know.'

'Well, now you do,' said Coburg. 'You may know her better by her stage name of Rosa Weeks.'

'Rosa Weeks!' exclaimed Walbrook-Staines. 'Oh my God. I've booked a table to see her when she's appearing here on Sunday. I didn't recognise her. She was in a uniform and had grey powder in her hair.'

'Dust from a collapsing building where a friend of hers was killed.'

'Oh my God!' said the man again, and now he began trembling. 'I'd better cancel my table, don't you think?'

'That's entirely up to you. But if you do come on Sunday, we'd both prefer it if you took a less prominent table. I'm sure you understand.'

'Absolutely,' burbled the young man. 'Do give her my apologies.'

'I will,' said Coburg. And he left.

CHAPTER THIRTEEN

Hooky Morton sat in his favourite chair at his favourite table in the Dark Horse and looked around him at the pub interior with a sense of great satisfaction. This was his very own fortress in London. Out on the streets there was always danger for him: rival gangsters intent on bumping him off so they could take over his businesses, but here in his own pub he was safe. He always had a couple of men standing outside, ostensibly manning a newspaper stand – which was a genuine newspaper stand which made a profit, because no one would dream of setting up a rival stand selling newspapers close to the Dark Horse – who would warn of any impending trouble. In the early days of his reign in King's Cross, there'd been rivals who tried to firebomb his pub, lobbing a milk bottle filled with petrol through one of the pub's windows. No real damage had been done, except to Hooky's reputation – which had been dealt with when the body of the would-be firebomber had been found in a burnt-out car with five bullets in him. But since that attempt the newspaper sellers were there, on guard.

'Penny for 'em, Hooky?' asked Dobbin, who was sitting at the same table watching his boss.

'I was just thinking that we've come a long way since the old days,' smiled Morton. 'Remember when the Murphy boys tried to force us out of business?' He chuckled. 'The canal has always been good for us.'

'What are you gonna do about his Sirship?' asked Dobbin. 'Braithwaite? Do you want me to have a word with him?'

Morton shook his head, genially.

'No, I'll deal with him. With all respect, Dob, you'd stick out like a sore thumb walking into a posh hotel like Claridge's. They'd have you marked straight away and questions would be asked. Questions which might be further looked into as soon as you opened your mouth. Luckily, I've learnt to do the walk and talk the talk. They see me as a rough diamond, but one of their own.'

'What are you gonna do?' asked Dobbin. 'Same as Patch?'

Again, Morton shook his head. 'You don't shoot a Sir without causing a whole load of trouble. Also, at the moment the only people who know about Braithwaite and his little fiddles are you and me. None of our blokes know, they don't even know that he's handling the money for the posh lot. Patch, on the other hand, was indiscreet. Roly Fitt's people knew he was talking to Fitt, and word spread on the street. That couldn't be allowed. I'd have been seen as weak, and weak people get trodden on.'

'D'you think Roly Fitt's got the message?'

'I would think so,' shrugged Morton. 'But, just in case, maybe we ought to reinforce it. Just so everyone else knows what happens to people who mess with me.'

* * *

Rosa was running through Rodgers and Hart's 'My Funny Valentine' when Coburg returned to their flat, and he stayed in the hall for her to finish before walking into the living room.

'That was absolutely lovely,' he said. 'I hope you're going to play that on Sunday.'

'Is that a request?' she asked.

'It is indeed,' he said. 'Actually, I thought it would be nice to book a room at Claridge's for Sunday night. That way we wouldn't have to worry about the Blitz or the blackout, we could just relax afterwards.'

'That's a lovely idea,' she said. 'Did you see him? The pest?'

Coburg nodded.

'And?' she asked.

'I got the information I wanted, thanks to you. If you hadn't told me about the Honourable Jocelyn Walbrook-Staines, we'd still have been groping around in the dark and getting nowhere. And, in answer to your unspoken question: no, I didn't punch him. I was tempted to, especially the first time I laid eyes on that superior smirk of his, but once I'd wiped that off his face and got down to the business of getting names from him, which he gave up very easily, I decided we didn't want a headline like "Aristo cop beats up aristo in posh hotel". It won't do the investigation any good, and I could end up facing a disciplinary panel. But I did mention that the woman he'd leered at was my wife, and advised him not to do it again.'

'Or else you'd punch him.'

'Precisely, but said without those exact words. I also suggested that we'd both prefer it if he wasn't a prominent

85

member of the audience on Sunday.'

'How did he take that?'

'He agreed. He also asked me to pass on his apologies to you.'

'Well, that's a relief,' she said. 'So, what's your next move?'

'To lay a trap to catch the big fish behind all this.' He reached for the phone. 'And for that I need Magnus's help.'

Coburg got the operator to connect him to Dawlish Hall, the Saxe-Coburgs' ancestral family home.

'Dawlish Hall,' announced the sombre tones of Magnus's elderly factotum.

'Good evening, Malcolm,' said Coburg. 'Is my brother there?'

'He is indeed, Mr Edgar, and may I say what a pleasure it is to hear your voice and know that you are safe and well.' He paused, then asked tentatively: 'I trust you and Mrs Coburg are safe and well?'

'We are indeed, Malcolm. How are things at Dawlish Hall?'

'We survive, Master Edgar. If you'll hold on, I'll bring the Earl to the telephone.'

There was a lengthy pause, then Coburg heard the voice of his elder brother.

'Good evening, Edgar. I trust you and Rosa are well.'

Coburg smiled to himself as he heard Malcolm mutter in the background, 'I've just asked him that.'

'Well now I'm asking him,' snapped Magnus. There was a brief pause, then Magnus said: 'The damn fool's gone off in a huff now. He's been in a bad mood ever since the wireless packed up halfway through Henry Hall. So, what can I do for you?'

'Do you have an account at Claridge's?'

'The Saxe-Coburgs have always had an account at Claridge's, same as we have at the Savoy and the Ritz. Why?'

'I'd like you to book a room, but you don't have to be there.'

'This sounds like some sort of Scotland Yard thing.'

'Yes, it is, but I promise you, you won't be involved.'

'If you're using my name I am involved.'

'Only to book the room. You're to say a friend of yours will be using the room.'

'And who is this friend?'

'Me, but I'll be calling myself the Honourable Peter Clayton.'

'Yes, all right. When do you want it booked for?'

'Tomorrow, from 10 a.m. And just for the one night.'

'Who's paying for this?'

'Scotland Yard.'

'In that case I'll make it one of their smaller rooms. Can't have the police picking up the tab for a suite. Not patriotic.'

'When will you do it?'

'Now.'

'Can you ask them which room it will be?'

There was a sudden burst of distant music from the telephone, and then Magnus groaned and said: 'He's got the wireless working again. You want to know which room it is? Will do. I'll phone you back as soon as it's arranged.'

Ted Lampson sat with a sandwich and a bottle of brown ale at his kitchen table listening to a play on the wireless. It was a play he couldn't make hide nor hair of what it was about, something about the devil and a priest, and he was just fiddling with the dial to find the Light Programme when there was a knock at his door. It couldn't be Terry, his son had a key. If Terry didn't appear soon, he'd have to go out and find him, he didn't want him out on the streets when the air raids began. Reports suggested the night bombing had lessened lately. Lampson wondered if it really had, or were Londoners just becoming used to it. The bottom line was that during September and so far halfway through October, 13,000 civilians had been killed and over 20,000 injured. And those were the official figures. Lampson and most of his neighbours were sure the real number was bigger, but the government preferred to give out good news. Not that 13,000 dead was good news, but it was better than the numbers at the start of the Blitz.

Lampson opened the door and found the caller was his cousin, Ellie Pike. Ellie was in her forties, a short, thin woman who usually had a cheery air about her. Well, as cheery as anyone could be in a war with all the bombing going on. But today she looked worried.

'Ellie? What are you doing in London?'

'I came up because of Ada. She's having problems with Mum, and she wanted me to go and see her, see what I think.'

Ada was Ellie's sister, and their mother, Dolly, was Lampson's aunt, his father's elder sister who lived in Islington. Ada and her husband, Ben, lived near Ashford in Kent. Lampson often thought of them, right in the target zone for the German bombers as the Luftwaffe pounded the Kent airfields in their attempts to put the RAF out of action.

'Come in. The kettle's on.'

As Ellie entered, she asked: 'Where's Terry?'

'He's out with his mates, I guess. I was just going to look

for him. So, what's the problem with Dolly?'

'The other day she left the gas on under the kettle after she'd poured the water into the teapot, and the bottom of the kettle burnt away. And that's not the first time it's happened. She's always been a bit forgetful, but things are starting to get worse.'

'Sounds bad,' said Lampson. 'Has Ada thought of taking Dolly to live with her? They're in the same area.'

'She tried, but Dolly won't go. She refuses to leave her own house. And Ada can't move in with her because she's got Bert and the kids. At the moment she goes round there all the time to make sure the gas has been turned off and the fire's out, that sort of thing.'

'What does she want you to do?'

'Talk to Mum, see if I can't persuade her to move in with Ada.' She hesitated, then said awkwardly: 'Actually, that's not why I came to see you. I wanted to ask you about Ben.'

'What about him?' asked Lampson, as he poured their tea and handed her a cup.

'There's something going on with him.'

'Another woman?'

She shook her head. 'No, that's not Ben's way. He's too honest, I'd spot it a mile off if he was doing anything like that. No, it's something else. Lately he's been off, going to meetings. At first, I thought it was just the air raid warden thing, they have training and all that kind of thing.' She looked pensive as she added: 'We're still getting hammered in Kent. On Tuesday, Wrotham Heath got bombed. Direct hit on the Royal Oak pub. Killed half the people in it. But it's more than just the air raid protection. Ben's been in a different mood when he comes back from these meetings than when he's been to one of the civil defence ones. He's sort of edgier, secretive. When he comes back from the civil defence meeting, he usually tells me what happened, who was there, what they're doing. But when he's been to one of these other meetings he don't say a word about it. And when I ask, he says they're not supposed to talk about it.'

'Maybe he's right. They're very hot on the business of "careless talk costs lives". Word getting out about how we're defending the country, and what we'll do if the Germans invade.'

'Yes, but it's not like Ben. He's always said I ought to know what's going on in order to keep myself safe.' She then opened her handbag, rifled through it, and produced a box of matches, on which was printed 'Claridge's Hotel'. 'And then I found these in his pocket the other day when I was darning a tear in his jacket sleeve. What's he doing at a place like Claridge's?'

'Maybe he was doing some work there,' suggested Lampson, looking at the box of matches.

'He works on the railway. What sort of work could he be doing at Claridge's?' Then her face darkened as she said, worried: 'I think it might be something political.'

'Do me a favour!' laughed Lampson. 'Ben's the least political person I know. You told me once he doesn't even vote.'

'That was just once, and when I had a go at him over it he said politicians weren't interested in ordinary people like us. But lately he's started to read the papers more, and especially about politicians.'

'Anyone in particular?'

She hesitated, then said: 'Mosley.'

'Oswald Mosley? The Fascist bloke?'

She nodded. 'And he's suddenly got interested in the Duke of Windsor. Started reading about him.'

'Another bloody Hitler-lover!' snorted Lampson angrily.

'Exactly,' said Ellie. 'It don't make sense. Not Ben. He's always been a patriot. He wanted to join up, but they wouldn't let him because of the work he does on the railways. Reserved occupation, they called it.' She looked at Lampson, appealing. 'Will you have a nose around, Ted? See what he's up to. I'd hate to find out he's got himself caught up in something he shouldn't have. The thing is, you being in the police could do it without him being looked at, if you know what I mean.'

'Not official.'

'I could never report him. Not my Ben. Whatever he's got involved in he's no traitor, I know that. But I can't bear the thought that someone may have got him involved in something and he doesn't know what he's letting himself in for.' She gave a sigh as she added: 'He's not the brightest, Ted. He can be easily led.'

CHAPTER FOURTEEN

After Magnus had telephoned back and confirmed that room 347 had been booked at Claridge's for the next day, Coburg telephoned the number Walbrook-Staines had given him. It was answered by a man with a working-class north London accent.

'Good evening. My name's Peter Clayton. The Honourable Peter Clayton. I've been given this number by Hercules Evans.'

'Yes, Mr Clayton.'

'I'd like to arrange for a companion for a short while.'

'Certainly. Do you have any particular preferences?'

'No. So long as she's female.'

'Where are you staying?'

'At Claridge's. I assume you know it.'

'We do indeed. When would you like your companion?'

'Tomorrow, in the afternoon. About two o'clock.'

'That should be no problem. Our agent will call upon you tomorrow morning to confirm the arrangements. I assume you know the terms?'

'Indeed. Payment in advance. How much will it be?'

'That depends on the particular companion. Some are dearer than others. But that can be sorted out when our agent calls on you tomorrow. Will eleven o'clock be convenient?'

'Eleven a.m. tomorrow will be fine.'

'What is your room number?'

'347. It's booked in the name of the Earl of Dawlish. I'm a friend of his. I'm not there at the moment, I shall be arriving tomorrow at ten, just in case your man calls early.'

'He won't, he'll be there at eleven.'

Coburg replaced the receiver and looked at Rosa, a broad smile on his face.

'It looks like the trap has been sprung.'

'Thanks to Derek,' said Rosa sadly. 'If he hadn't died, I'd never have gone looking for you and I'd never have had the confrontation with that smirking poppycock.'

'No,' nodded Coburg, wiping the smile from his face. 'But it is a result, thanks to Derek.' He reached for the whiskey bottle. 'I think now is an appropriate time to raise a glass in his memory.'

Rosa nodded. 'I'll drink to that.'

He was just pouring their drinks when they heard the wail of the air raid siren from outside in the street. They looked at one another ruefully.

'We could always take the bottle with us to the shelter?' she suggested.

'And be the most unpopular people there?' asked Coburg.

'Or the most popular?'

'It's your Irish,' said Coburg. 'Do you really want to share it?'

Rosa sighed and put the top back on the bottle and then put the bottle under the table. 'Just in case the ceiling comes down,' she said.

With that, they made their way down to the fortified basement that served as a shelter for the residents of the small block of flats.

CHAPTER FIFTEEN

Thursday 17th October 1940

The roads were pitted with deep holes from the night's bombing as Coburg and Lampson headed for Claridge's the following morning. Rubble was being cleared from the roads, much of it being pushed into the holes. As Lampson drove, Coburg looked at the scene, noticing that quite a few of the buildings they'd passed yesterday were now gone, leaving empty spaces, like gaps in a row of rotting teeth.

'The Germans can't keep this up for much longer, surely,' said Lampson sourly.

'By all accounts, they can,' said Coburg ruefully. 'It seems they've spent the last few years building up their armed forces, especially the army and air force. They now outnumber ours by God knows how many.'

'I thought they were banned from building up their military might after the last war,' said Lampson. 'Wasn't that part of the peace treaty?'

'It was,' said Coburg. 'But no one was enforcing it. And Hitler kept coming up with different statistics to show the terms of the treaty weren't being breached. He claimed that the planes were for civilian use, and the thousands of men in uniform were for civil defence purposes only.'

'And they believed him?'

'I don't think the politicians wanted to take issue with it. They weren't keen on another war starting.'

'Well, they've got one now,' said Lampson. 'Tell me again what we're doing today?'

'It's a sting operation,' said Coburg. 'I've booked a room at the hotel in my brother Magnus's name. I shall be posing as a client. The plan is that when the pimp turns up to fix the date and collect the money, we grab him. And hopefully we'll get details from him of who's running the prostitution ring, and if it's connected to the murder.'

'I've still got my doubts about that, guv,' said Lampson. 'Killing a bloke, and especially that way, just to keep him quiet.'

'I agree,' said Coburg. 'And if it turns out not to be connected, we pass the whole lot over to Vice.'

As they entered Claridge's, Lampson stopped, caught by a familiar face leaving the hotel.

'That was Lord Halifax. Is he staying here?'

'No,' said Coburg. 'As far as I know he's living at the Dorchester with his wife in one suite, and his mistress, Alexandra Metcalfe, in another there.'

Lampson stared at him. 'You're joking!'

'Inspector Hibbert told me when I saw him the other day. He said it's a nightmare for him and the security services because Mrs Metcalfe is also having an affair with Mussolini's representative in London.'

'Does Halifax know?'

'I don't know, and I didn't ask. We've got enough on our plate without concerning ourselves with the marital infidelities of senior politicians.'

'They ought to arrest him!'

'Who?'

'Lord Halifax.'

'On what grounds? I don't think having a mistress is a criminal offence.'

'But she's also banging Mussolini's bloke. And Halifax was trying to set up a peace deal with Hitler through the Italians. Don't that strike you as suspicious?'

'I leave that sort of thing to Inspector Hibbert and MI5, and by all accounts he already is very well aware of it.' He looked at Lampson and noticed that his sergeant seemed very troubled by this latest revelation, so he added: 'Look, Ted, if there's anything wrong, MI5 will be on to it. We've worked with Hibbert before and he's very capable, unlike some in the security services.'

'Yes, guv,' said Lampson, but Coburg could tell he wasn't convinced. Suddenly Lampson blurted out: 'Guv'nor, could I tell you something in confidence, but this is between you and me only, right? It's not for passing on to Inspector Hibbert, or anyone else.'

Coburg frowned.

'This sounds very mysterious, and also slightly concerning. If you know something that the security services ought to know about . . .'

'No, I don't,' said Lampson. 'But I'm guessing about something.'

Coburg looked at his sergeant intensely. 'You don't just guess about things. You think about things and put two and two together, and that's why you're a good detective. What's happened?'

Lampson looked around him, uncomfortable.

'Can we talk somewhere where we can't be overheard?'

'As I said, I've reserved a room for catching our pimp. We'll go there.' He looked at his watch. 'We've got time before he arrives. But before that, I have to reserve a room for Sunday night.'

'Ah, of course. The missus is appearing here, ain't she.'

'She is indeed.'

Coburg went to the desk and made the reservation, then he and Lampson headed for the room that Magnus had reserved for him. Once there, Lampson told Coburg about the visit from his cousin the previous evening, and her worries about Ben.

'She's worried he might have got mixed up with some of Mosley's Fascist lot.'

'Is that likely? Has he ever shown leanings towards Hitler, or the Nazis?'

'No, never. But this morning when I saw Halifax leaving, it set me thinking. The Duke of Windsor was staying here at Claridge's earlier in the year, wasn't he?'

'Yes, I remember seeing the photo of him standing outside the front entrance in the newspapers.'

'Well, now he's been sent abroad, along with that Mrs Simpson, because they were too friendly with Hitler and his crowd.'

'To be the Governor of Bermuda,' nodded Coburg.

'And well out of the way. But the rumour, as I heard it, was that Hitler was planning to put the Duke and herself on the throne of England and send our King and Queen and their two princess daughters to Canada, get them out of the way. And Mosley's Fascists were part of it, ready to take over as the government if Hitler's armies moved in.'

97

'Yes, I heard the same,' agreed Coburg.

'Now the thing is, Halifax was pally with the Duke, wasn't he? And he was part of the crowd trying to do this deal with Hitler through the Italians.'

'I'm not sure if there was actually talk of Halifax being part of a conspiracy to install the Windsors on the throne,' said Coburg doubtfully. 'And Mosley is currently locked up in Holloway.'

'No, but it's possible, ennit,' Lampson pushed on. 'Ellie showed me a box of matches she found in Ben's pocket that had Claridge's Hotel printed on them.'

'That's pretty standard,' said Coburg. 'Most of the top hotels do that to promote themselves. I, myself, have boxes of matches from the Ritz and the Savoy.'

'Yes, you might, but not Ben. He doesn't move in those circles. He'd never even dare set foot in a place as posh as this . . . unless he was meeting someone.'

'Who? Lord Halifax?' Coburg smiled. 'If he wanted to do that he'd go to the Dorchester where Halifax is actually staying.'

'Unless there's someone else here that's acting as some kind of intermediary, someone who was here earlier in the year when Windsor was here and is still here and acting on his behalf. Someone who meets up with fellow sympathisers.'

'And you're suggesting that Halifax and your cousin Ben . . .'

'I don't know!' burst out Lampson. 'All I'm saying is what Ellie passed on to me about her worries about Ben.' He paused, then added: 'And he's taken to reading about Mosley and the Duke of Windsor, so Ellie tells me.'

'That's not necessarily suggestive of treason,' pointed out Coburg.

'He was never interested in him before,' said Lampson.

They were interrupted by the ringing of the telephone.

'Is that 347?' asked a man's voice.

'It is,' said Coburg.

'Can I speak to the Honourable Peter Clayton?'

'Speaking,' said Coburg.

'Good morning, Mr Clayton. Just checking it's convenient for our man to call on you at eleven as arranged.'

'It is,' said Coburg. 'I look forward to seeing him.'

Coburg hung up and looked at Lampson. 'Double-checking, as I thought they would, that I am who I claim to be, and staying at the hotel as I said I was. So now I suggest you go and station yourself at some convenient hiding point not far away. I noticed a small storeroom next to the lifts where they keep brooms and things.'

'I saw it,' nodded Lampson. 'I'll have a word with the cleaner who does this floor, and get the key to it off her.'

'Good,' said Coburg. 'My plan is to invite the messenger in, but just in case it might be someone who recognises me . . .'

'And they do a runner, I'll be there,' said Lampson grimly.

'So, what are you planning to do about your cousin Ben?' asked Coburg as Lampson headed for the door.

'Cousin-in-law,' Lampson corrected him. 'I thought I'd tail him. Ellie told me when he's got another meeting coming up, although he hasn't said who with. But it's near enough for Ben to get there on his bike. So I thought I'd put my bike on the train and ride from Ashford to their cottage and keep an eye on it, and when Ben sets out, I'll follow him.'

'You need to be careful,' Coburg warned him. 'If he is mixed up with a bunch of Fascists, they don't take kindly to people spying on them.'

'I'll be careful,' Lampson assured him.

'Are you sure you don't want me to come with you and watch your back?'

'No,' said Lampson. 'Thanks for the offer, guv, I appreciate it, but a Metropolitan Police car driving through those lanes is bound to attract attention. I don't want Ellie – or Ben – to think I've turned him over to the law.'

'All right, but if you change your mind, just let me know,' said Coburg. 'When is this meeting? Just in case you're not in the following morning and I can start to worry.'

Lampson hesitated before telling him: 'It's this evening. I shall be picking up my bike and heading for Victoria to catch the train to Ashford as soon as we've finished. But I'll be fine. Honest.'

CHAPTER SIXTEEN

Sergeant Potteridge replaced the telephone receiver and looked at Inspector Lomax with a smug smile. 'Got it, boss,' he beamed. 'That was an old mate of mine who's at King's Cross. The word on the street there is that Hooky Morton's boys got stitched up on a couple of raids recently. They were going to do a butcher's and a warehouse, but a rival mob had done the job a bit before. Rumour says that the rival mob was Roly Fitt's.'

'Moving off their own patch and into Hooky's.'

'And the fact they knew when these jobs were going down means that someone leaked the details to Roly. And Patch Peters was one of Hooky's boys.'

'So Roly was tipping us the wink that Hooky had Patch killed because he was leaking inside stuff to Roly, and had Patch's body dumped on Roly's area to send a message to him: back off, or this is what'll happen to any other of your snitches.'

Coburg was in the hotel room reading a newspaper when the knock at the door came. He opened it and smiled as he saw a short wiry man he recognised. 'Well, well, Soapy Jackson,' he said.

Jackson stared at Coburg in horror, then turned and ran off along the corridor, making for the stairs, but before he could get there the door to the storeroom opened and Lampson stepped out and grabbed the running man by the collar, bringing him skidding to a stop with a strangled sound.

'Soapy Jackson!' beamed Lampson. 'Well, this is a surprise.'

As Jackson began to struggle and tried to throw the sergeant's grip off, Coburg appeared. 'Let's have none of that, Soapy,' he said. 'Be a good boy or we'll have to overpower you for resisting arrest, and then take you to Scotland Yard in handcuffs. Let's do it in a gentlemanly manner, shall we? Avoid the nastiness.'

Defiantly, Jackson thrust out his hand towards Coburg. 'Put the cuffs on me,' he said. 'I don't want people to see me coming out like I'm a grass.'

'Oh, so someone's with you, waiting outside,' said Coburg. 'Sergeant, put the cuffs on him and then I'll take him to my room, where I'll keep an eye on him while you take a uniform and see if there's anyone we recognise hanging around outside.'

'There isn't!' exclaimed Jackson.

'Thanks, Soapy, but we'd prefer to take a look for ourselves.'

When he got Jackson back to the room, he transferred one half of the handcuffs to the stout brass rail at the end of the bed. 'Just in case you have any idea of making a run for it.'

'This ain't right,' scowled Jackson. 'I was just knocking on doors because I didn't know which room this pal of mine was in.'

'Which pal would that be?'

'I'm not saying anything more until I've got my solicitor with me.'

'Suit yourself,' shrugged Coburg.

After a short delay there was a knock at the door, and Coburg opened it to find Lampson and a uniformed

102

constable standing either side of a glowering, tall man in a neat blue suit.

'Look who I found outside,' said Lampson. 'None other than Harry Podge, who is – as we say in the trade – a known associate of one Soapy Jackson. What a coincidence.'

'I was just standing there minding my own business,' grunted Podge sullenly.

'Of course you were,' said Coburg airily. 'Right, let's get you both back to Scotland Yard where we can continue this conversation in more formal surroundings.'

'We ain't done nothing!' insisted Jackson.

'In that case, you've got nothing to worry about,' said Coburg.

Benny Green stood at the foot of the stairs that led down from the street to Roly Fitt's club. He was smartly dressed, a dark shirt and tie, a natty blue suit and with a shiny pair of two-tone shoes on his feet. With his muscular build and broken nose he looked every inch the doorman-cum-bouncer. Usually, one of the waiters was here, acting as a receptionist to welcome the punters; but after the body of Patch Peters had been found on a nearby bomb site, Roly had selected Benny for this particular role.

'The fact that Patch's body was dumped near us was deliberate,' Roly had told him. 'Hooky's letting us know he knows how and why some of his raids went wrong. So I'm expecting him to reinforce it in some way.'

'Ain't killing Patch enough?' asked Benny.

'For most people, yes. But Hooky Morton isn't most people. He's like a mad dog. Really. So I'm thinking it would be a service to society to deal with him the way you would a mad dog.'

'Put him down.'

'Exactly. But it's got to be done in a way that don't set off a whole turf war. The last thing we want is Dobbin and the rest of Hooky's crew pouring down those stairs, all armed to the teeth. No, it's got to be done clever. But in the meantime, I'm expecting Hooky to try something.'

'What sort of thing?'

'Who knows? With Hooky, anything's possible. But my money's on a firebomb attack. He's done it to people before, and he's had it done to him.' He gave a sarcastic chuckle. 'Hooky's never had much in the way of imagination. So that's why I want you here, ready to handle it if it happens.'

Benny had nodded in agreement, and took his place at the foot of the stairs. When a bloke he didn't know appeared at the top of the stairs, it was the way the man had sneaked in, all shifty, that alerted all Benny's senses. And when Benny saw him pull a bottle from beneath his long coat, then flick a lighter to set flame to the cloth stuffed into the neck of the bottle, Benny acted. He pulled a sawn-off shotgun from under his jacket, levelled it at the man and fired.

There was the sound of glass breaking and a scream from the man, which got louder and more panicky as the petrol from the broken bottle splashed over him. The next second the man was engulfed in flames, screaming, his cries being cut short as he fell and tumbled down the stairs.

Benny moved aside surprisingly quickly for a large man, and the still burning man crashed onto the bottom stair.

Benny strode to the bucket of water he'd kept ready for such an occasion. He waited, watching the jerky movements of the man as he burnt; then he threw the water on him, dousing the flames. That done, he dropped the bucket and hoisted a fire extinguisher from the bottom step, aimed the hose, and then sprayed foam up the stairs where the spilt petrol was starting to catch light.

Roly Fitt came hurrying from his office, brought by the sound of the shotgun blast. He stood there, taking in the scene, his face grim and angry.

'Bastard!' he said.

'You were right, boss,' said Benny. He gestured at the charred body of the man. 'Hooky was sending us a present.'

'So I guess it's our turn to send him one back,' grated Roly.

At Scotland Yard, Jackson and Podge were handed over to the custody sergeant to be put in a cell while Coburg and Lampson made a few phone calls. The first was Lampson to DS Vic Fortune.

'You know this prostitution ring at Claridge's I was telling you about? Well, we've picked up Soapy Jackson and Harry Podge. I remember they used to run bets for a bookie called Manny but they've obviously moved on.'

There came a chuckle from the other end of the phone.

'They have indeed. Do you know Jimmy Mussels?'

'Only from the days when he was an enforcer for Mickey Dodds.'

'Well Jimmy moved on after Mickey died. Went into call girls. Less dangerous and more lucrative. Officially it's called a mobile massage service. Jackson and Podge are part of his mob.' There was a pause, then Fortune said: 'I suppose, by rights, this ought to come under Vice?'

'And it will. That's what my guv'nor says, provided it's nothing to do with the murder we're looking into.'

'In that case, I'll alert my boss. It might be nice if your

guv'nor gave mine a call to fill him in. Inter-department co-operation and all that.'

'I'll see that he does,' Lampson assured him.

As he hung up, Coburg asked: 'You'll see that I do what?'

'Give DCI Harcourt a ring and tell him we've collared Jackson and Podge, and what we're planning. It doesn't do any harm to keep in Vice's good books.'

'No, good point,' nodded Coburg. 'What did Vic Fortune tell you?'

'Do you know Jimmy Mussels?'

Coburg shook his head. 'Not that I can recall. What is he, a strong man-type?'

'It's not muscles as in strength, it's mussels as in shellfish,' said Lampson. 'His grandad farmed mussels in the Thames estuary in north Kent. Jimmy worked for him when he was a kid. He used to be an enforcer for Mickey Dodds.'

'I remember Mickey,' said Coburg. 'He got shot in Soho about a year ago.'

'Right. Well after Mickey bought it, Jimmy moved into call girls, although he calls it a mobile massage service. So the ring at Claridge's must be his.'

'In that case, I think we'll bring in Mr Mussels, and I'll have a word with him while you talk to Soapy and Podge separately.' He picked up the phone. 'But first, I'll do the courtesy call to DCI Gerry Harcourt. It always helps if colleagues are working together pleasantly.'

'Unlike Inspector Arsehole Lomax,' commented Lampson.

'Yes,' groaned Coburg. 'I'm going to have to talk to him sooner or later, especially if this lead to Jimmy Mussels turns out to be a dead end.'

CHAPTER SEVENTEEN

When Rosa walked into the ambulance station the following morning, she noticed that Chesney Warren was wearing his St John Ambulance uniform rather than his usual civilian clothes, and a boy of about fifteen was sitting at Warren's desk.

'Good morning, Mrs Coburg,' the supervisor greeted her.

Something's up, realised Rosa. Aloud, she asked: 'Who will I be crewing with today?'

'Me,' said Warren. He gestured toward the teenage boy. 'This is my son, Ian, he's volunteered to answer the phones today. He's done it before so he knows the drill.' He picked up two slips of paper from the desk. 'We've got two calls which are quite close together, one a suspected fractured shoulder, the other a suspected broken hand. We'll pick them both up and take them to Accident and Emergency.' He turned to Ian. 'If anyone else calls, Ambulance 3 should be back in about twenty minutes.'

Ian nodded, and Warren headed out of the building and made for where Rosa's ambulance was parked, Rosa hurrying after him.

'There's no need for you to come out, Mr Warren,' she said. 'I know how busy the phones get.'

'There is,' said Chesney, climbing into the cab's passenger seat. 'I know what I was like after my crewmate had been killed on a shout we were on. I told everyone I'd be fine, but the next day it caught up with me and I crashed the ambulance. My head was too full of what had happened. I kept seeing the image in my head.'

Rosa had to admit that image of the building falling on Derek kept filling her mind, no matter how much she tried to keep it at bay.

'You may be right,' she admitted.

'Trust me, I am,' said Warren.

Rosa climbed behind the steering wheel, started the vehicle up, and then headed towards the street.

'Turn left at the top,' said Warren. 'We're going to Market Court, our first stop. It's about fifteen minutes away.'

'What happened?' asked Rosa as they drove. 'To your crewmate?'

'He was walking round to the back of the ambulance when he got hit by a car. A drunk driver. It was two years ago, but I still remember it like it was yesterday.' He was silent for a moment, then he said, his voice tentative: 'Actually, Mrs Coburg, I've been thinking.'

He's going to tell me he thinks I'm not cut out for this, thought Rosa, and her heart sank and she could feel a cloud of depression descending over her. Then: No! she thought fiercely to herself. He's wrong. I am cut out for this!

'I think you're not using all your talents.'

He's going to suggest I work the phones instead of driving an ambulance. Well, I won't! This is what I want to do.

'Mr Warren—' she began.

'Chesney, please,' he said. 'The thing is, I wondered how

you felt about doing a concert for us?'

For a moment she was so thrown that she had to slow down and recover her thinking.

'A concert?' she repeated, bewildered.

'St John Ambulance is a charity. We get no money from the government, every penny we have is raised from the public. Collecting boxes. Stalls at garden fetes. You have a great talent, people would come to hear you sing and play. A fundraiser. I know you're appearing at Claridge's on Sunday evening, it was in the papers. The famous Rosa Weeks, appearing in concert to raise funds for St John Ambulance. I know it's a bit of a cheek asking a famous star like you, but we'd pay expenses . . .'

'I'm not a famous star,' she protested.

'To lots of people you are. You've been on the radio. You've made records. You've appeared at most of the major venues. You're a good driver, but your real and best talent is music. What do you say?'

Sergeant Lampson sat in the basement interview room in Scotland Yard and faced Stewart Jackson, aka Soapy Jackson, across the bare wooden table. Lampson had already interviewed Harry Podge in this same room and the range of answers he'd received to his questions varied from muttered grunts to 'I don't know nothing'. It was said that Harry Podge was just muscle, a former boxer who'd suffered too many blows to the head, which had scrambled his brain. This made him good for hitting people and putting other sorts of physical pressure on them, but not much else. But it was obvious to Lampson that one thing had been drummed into what passed for a brain in Harry

Podge's head: 'Don't say anything to the coppers. Just your name, that's all they're allowed to know.' So, after twenty minutes of fruitless questioning, Podge had been returned to the holding cell and his place taken by Soapy Jackson.

Unlike the taciturn but grumpy man mountain that was Harry Podge, Soapy Jackson was small and nervous to the point of jitteriness. He had difficulty sitting still on the wooden chair, and the two uniformed constables in attendance seemed on the point of moving to grab him with every sudden twitch.

'Tell me about the girls,' said Lampson.

'What girls?' demanded Jackson.

'Like the one you called on my guv'nor in his room at Claridge's to collect payment for.'

'I didn't know he was your guv'nor.'

'But you ran off as soon as you saw him.'

'Natural reaction,' said Jackson. 'I've been wrongly accused of things before.'

'Like earning money from prostitution?'

Jackson shook his head vigorously.

'I have nothing to do with prostitution,' he said.

'So the girls you arrange for people at Claridge's, and I assume at other hotels . . .'

'Masseuses,' cut in Jackson quickly.

'Masseuses?'

'Yeh. They give massages.'

'In hotel rooms? I thought most top hotels have their own massage service.'

'Yeh, well, some people prefer to choose their own.' He gestured around the interview room. 'This place is disgusting, you know.' He sniffed. 'It smells of disinfectant.

What does that say about it? I tell you, it says people with infections have been here.' He glared accusingly at Lampson. 'I shouldn't be here. I've got a delicate chest. Bronchitis. I could catch something horrible here and die.' And he gave a wheezy cough and slumped forward. Lampson watched him impassively, saying nothing, then turned his attention to the clock on the wall opposite. One minute passed. Two minutes. All was silence in the room, broken by Jackson suddenly jerking himself upright and glaring venomously at the sergeant. 'You're a cruel bastard!' he spat. 'I could be dying here!'

In another of the interview rooms, DCI Coburg sat at an identical table and watched calmly as Jimmy Mussels was ushered in by a uniformed sergeant and sat down on a chair on the other side of the table from Coburg. Mussels was a fleshy man in his mid-fifties, his thinning hair combed across his skull from one side to the other in an attempt to hide the fact. He wore a camel-haired coat, opened to reveal a suit of a loud, highly coloured, checked material beneath. He reminded Coburg of the comedian, Max Miller.

'What's all this about?' demanded Mussels. 'I was brought here under protest from my own home, leaving my poor wife in turmoil as to what's happening. What's going on? Have we suddenly got Gestapo tactics operating in this country? And who are you, anyway?'

'I'm Detective Chief Inspector Coburg and it's about murder. That's why you're here with me instead of being quizzed by Vice. Although they're talking to two of your boys right now, so I'm sure they'll get to you in good time.'

'Murder? What murder?'

'At Claridge's. A kitchen porter there, and we found

by coincidence that two of the kitchen staff are on your payroll to let your girls come through the back door of the kitchen into the hotel.'

'What do you mean, "my girls"?' demanded Mussels indignantly. 'What are you implying?'

'Prostitutes,' said Coburg.

'How dare you?' said Mussels angrily. 'We are talking about legitimate masseuses engaged in a lawful occupation.'

'But who come into the hotel the back way and through the kitchens.'

'What's wrong with that? There's nothing illegal in that.'

'Rather than through the front entrance?'

'It's because of client confidentiality,' said Mussels stiffly. 'Many of our clients don't like people to know that they have hired a masseuse. That's because of the rumours and slander that go with the profession. Allegations of immoral behaviour, which may happen with some masseuses, but certainly not with ours. As a result, we instruct our masseuses to go through the back door and then direct to the client's room.'

'Why do you send someone to collect the money beforehand?'

'Business protection,' said Mussels. 'You'd be surprised how many people hire someone for a service and then refuse to pay afterwards. Painters. Decorators. Builders. Masseuses. All of them have got stung at some time, so our policy is payment in advance. Our clients understand and appreciate that.'

'And the business of giving a code name when arranging a visit from one of your . . . masseuses?'

'Again, business protection. There are a lot of dodgy people out there who hear the word "masseuse" and leap to all sorts of wrong conclusions. We only deal in legitimate people. The code word is to ensure that we are dealing with people who are legitimate. It's only passed on by satisfied clients to legitimate people.'

'So your business is legitimate and only supplies bona fide masseuses to people.'

'That's correct.'

'And, as a legitimate business, I assume you're registered and pay tax.'

For the first time, Mussels look discomforted. 'Tax?'

'Yes. That you do a tax return showing the proceeds from your business, along with a list of the legitimate costs you can claim. And a list of your employees.'

'My masseuses are freelance, not employees,' said Mussels.

'But your man collects the money in advance,' pointed out Coburg. 'So you must pay them, which means having a payroll that can be examined.'

Mussells shifted on his chair.

'That's a matter between my accountants and the tax people,' he said.

'Yes, it is,' agreed Coburg genially. 'And I'm sure the tax people will be keen to talk to your accountants, and your lawyers, and some of the people who work for you. But right now, my concern is why a man who worked in the kitchens at Claridge's was murdered. The suggestion I've heard whispered is that he was silenced to stop him talking about what was going on with your girls. It seems the murdered man was very righteous and far from believing that the girls traipsing through the kitchen where he worked were masseuses, he was convinced they were prostitutes. So convinced, that he was about to complain to the hotel management. Sounds like a valid motive for murder to me.'

CHAPTER EIGHTEEN

When Coburg and Lampson met up in their office after the interviews were over, they were both of the same opinion.

'They're running girls, all right, but I can't see them as murdering the kitchen porter,' said Lampson. 'Especially not how it was done. That's not their way. A beating, yes, and maybe a shooting, but not a wire garrotte.'

'I agree,' said Coburg. 'We need to look into Janos Mila's life to find out why he was killed. In the meantime, we'll keep Jimmy Mussels and his two men in the holding cells and pass them on to Vice. I'll give Gerry Harcourt a call and let him know where they are. Let's hope he has better luck with this masseuse stuff.' He smiled. 'But I think I may have unsettled Jimmy Mussels with my talk about the tax people. Remember, it was the tax people who were the only ones who were able to put Al Capone away.'

He looked at his sergeant as Lampson got up and collected his hat and coat from the hook. 'You sure you don't want me to go with you tonight?'

'Certain, guv. Thanks anyway, but this is something I've got to do privately.'

Lampson left Coburg making the phone call to DCI

Harcourt, while he made his way to his parents' flat in Somers Town. They lived in a block that had been put up in the twenties, but instead of it being in art deco style favoured by many architects in the twenties and thirties, this block had been created by the council as an economic way to house the poor. It was of drab grey concrete, four storeys high, with balconies that served as walkways along the front of the block. Mr and Mrs Lampson lived on the second floor, and the arrangement was that Terry would go to their flat when school finished to be looked after by them until his father arrived to collect him. At least, that was the arrangement in theory. Lately, Lampson knew that Terry often hung around the street with his mates instead of going to his parents' place, something that especially worried Lampson's father.

'Is Terry with you?' Lampson asked when his father opened the door to his knock.

'No,' said his father, and there was no mistaking the heavy disapproval in his voice.

'What's he been up to?' asked Lampson, concerned.

'He's been hanging around with the Purvis brothers,' said Mr Lampson. 'I don't like it. And nor does your mum.'

'They're a bad lot,' added his mother as she appeared from the kitchen, wiping her hands on her apron.

'They're always in trouble, especially that older boy, Jake. Mrs Henderson caught him nicking a packet of cigarettes from her shop, and when she took them off him, he swore at her. The dirty little toerag.'

'I'll have a word with him,' promised Lampson.

'He needs more than just a word,' said Mr Lampson sternly. 'He needs to be taken in hand. Me and your mum can't manage him.'

'Maybe if I have a word with Mrs Purvis?' suggested Lampson.

'Ha!' snorted Mr Lampson derisively. 'She's just as bad as her two boys. Ever since her husband went into the navy, she's been swanning around like she was a free woman, going out with all sorts of who-knows-what blokes.' He scowled in disgust.

'I will have a serious word with Terry,' Lampson assured his parents. 'But right now, I've got a favour to ask. I've got to go to Kent.'

'Why?' asked his mother.

'It's a sort of mission,' said Lampson. 'Something's come up. Part of the job. Can Terry stay here overnight with you, just in case I get caught up in something and don't get back?'

Mr Lampson gave his son a sour look.

'That's just the sort of thing I'm talking about,' he said sternly. 'You're losing control of him.'

'I will talk to him,' Lampson repeated. 'But this is something I've got to do. It can't be avoided. I'll be back first thing in the morning.'

Feeling their disapproving looks on his back, Lampson left for his own home, where he picked up his bike. He cycled to Victoria Station and put himself and his bike on the train to Ashford.

All the way on the train journey he thought of this latest disturbing news about Terry and the Purvis brothers. Deep down, Lampson felt his son wasn't a bad kid. The trouble was he often got into scrapes, depending on who he was with. Most of the scrapes were innocuous because the majority of Terry's friends were just like him, high-

116

spirited, excitable with overactive imaginations; but the Purvis brothers were a different kettle of fish. Jake Purvis was fourteen and already had a bad reputation around Somers Town as a foul-mouthed thief. His brother, Jud, ten years old and in the same class at school as Terry, was the more dangerous of the two, always eager for a fight. And Jud didn't fight fair. Someone had seen him carrying a bike chain, someone else a chisel.

Yes, determined Lampson, I've got to do something about Terry. But what? Have a warning word with his son, but he knew it would just bounce off the boy. Terry liked exciting things happening, and that was certainly true where the Purvis boys were concerned. He needed to get Terry involved in something that would take him out of the Purvis brothers' orbit and influence. Before the war it had been football, and especially Spurs. Tottenham Hotspur. Most Saturday afternoons Lampson had taken Terry on the long bus ride to White Hart Lane to watch a match, just as Lampson's dad had taken him. Spurs were the family team. It was upsetting that in the last season before the war they'd languished in the Second Division, while their hated north London rivals, Arsenal, rode to success in the First Division, but there was always the promise that Spurs would make their way into the top flight, where they deserved to be. This ambition fired Terry up just as much as it did his father and grandfather. Lampson knew this because when Terry wasn't watching Spurs, he was reading about them and collecting the cards with pictures and information about the players. But with the coming of the war, all that had changed. Most of the players had joined up, so there were no teams left to watch or play against.

Yes, there was a London League of sorts involving Spurs, Brentford, Charlton, Chelsea, Fulham, Millwall, West Ham and the despised Arsenal; but somehow it wasn't the same. The schedule was erratic, most of the top players had gone, and the demands of his job meant that too often Saturday afternoons were taken up with work. It wasn't the same, and Terry's enthusiasm for football had waned, to be replaced with activities like identifying the planes flying overhead, both British and German, and looking out for potential fifth columnists, or German spies. And now he'd taken up with the dreaded Purvis brothers.

I've got to come up with something for him to do to get him away from them.

He was aware that the train was slowing down. Ashford. Lampson off-loaded his bike and cycled to Ellie and Ben's small cottage in a small village outside the town, and then took cover in a small copse from where he could keep watch on the cottage. It was just starting to get dark when he saw Ben emerge from the cottage, wheeling his bike. Lampson waited until he was sure which direction Ben was heading, then waited a few minutes more before setting off after him. Fortunately, the area was quite open so Lampson could keep Ben within sight without getting too close to him. It was a narrow country road and there was no other traffic, mainly because the blackout rules kept most cars off the road at night. Because it was a moonlit night, Lampson was able to see when Ben took a turning off the road they were on and follow him. Finally, after about half an hour's cycling, Ben pulled up outside a pair of gates made of iron railings set in a high wall. Lampson kept back. Ben said something to someone on the other side of the gates, and the gates were opened and Ben cycled through, whereupon the gates were shut again.

Lampson cycled past the gates, looking out for a nameboard, and saw a plate with the words 'The Garth' fixed to one of the pillars beside the gates. The high wall continued, suggesting a sizeable estate. Lampson pulled up and leant his bike against the high wall. There was a tree near the wall, which he used to help him climb up and reach the top.

By now the evening had turned darker, there was no light at all coming from any buildings behind the wall. Whoever was there was observing the blackout rules religiously.

Lampson lay on the top of the wall, listening. There was no sound. The area immediately beyond the high wall was thick with trees, which would make it easier for him to get back over the wall. He assumed Ben had cycled deeper into the grounds. He'd have to drop down and find a way to the drive, then follow that until he came to some sort of building. Lampson dropped down onto the soft ground and the cover of the trees. He was just moving forwards when he heard a noise behind him. He half-turned, and then an explosion of pain smashed into his head and he felt himself falling.

CHAPTER NINETEEN

Over supper, Rosa told Coburg about Warren's suggestion of her giving a concert for St John Ambulance. 'I'm sure he's only suggesting this to help me get over Derek's death,' she said, concerned.

'No, he's doing it as a way of raising money for the cause,' said Coburg. 'But even if that was one of his motives, I approve of it. If it helps you cope with it – and I think it will because it'll give you something concrete to do as well as driving the ambulance – then I think it's a good idea. With most of the nightclubs and jazz clubs closed, at the moment you're only doing occasional gigs, albeit at the top hotels.'

'Yes, that's true,' she said. 'So, you approve?' When he didn't respond, she repeated her question: 'So, you approve?'

He looked at her, momentarily bewildered, then smiled and nodded approvingly and said, 'Absolutely.'

'What's the matter, Edgar?' she asked.

'The matter?'

'You responded, but you seemed to have drifted off for a moment. And it's not the first time this evening. You've got that look on your face you get when you're worried. Is it the business at Claridge's?'

'No, it's Ted Lampson,' admitted Coburg.

'Ted? What's he been up to?'

'Nothing, yet. But he's worried about his cousin's husband. She thinks he might be caught up in something unpleasant.'

'In what way unpleasant?'

'Some kind of Fascist conspiracy. Apparently, he's been going to meetings, which he won't tell her about. And there have been a few other things that have set alarm bells ringing for Ted. So he's decided to follow Ben – that's his name – to find out where he goes and what happens at these meetings.'

'Sounds dangerous.'

'That's what I told him. I offered to go with him, but he refused my help.' He gave a worried sigh. 'The trouble is, he's doing his spot of following tonight.'

'Where?'

'His cousin lives near Ashford in Kent, and Ben rides to these meetings on his bike, so it can't be far from there.'

'Why don't you phone the local police station and ask them to put a watch on Ted?'

'No, I can't bring the police in. Ted would never forgive me.'

'You want to go and check up on him?'

'I do,' admitted Coburg. 'The trouble is, I don't know where his cousin lives.' Then a thought struck him. 'But I know someone who might.'

Bert Lampson was surprised to open the door of his flat in Somers Town and find DCI Coburg standing there.

'Mr Coburg!' he exclaimed, his startled tone bringing his wife to the door.

'Good evening, Mr Lampson; Mrs Lampson,' said Coburg.

'If you're looking or Ted, I'm afraid he's out,' said Lampson.

'Yes, so I understand,' said Coburg. 'Actually, I've come here because I understand Ted has got a cousin in Ashford?'

'That's right. Ellie. Married to Ben Pike.'

'Do you have their address?'

'Why?' asked Mr Lampson, suspiciously. 'What's wrong?'

'Nothing,' said Coburg. 'But Ted mentioned he might be going there, and there's something I need to tell him.'

Mr Lampson regarded him with suspicion. Fortunately for Coburg, before Mr Lampson could start asking more questions, Mrs Lampson said: 'I'll get it for you. I've got their address on my Christmas card list.'

She hurried indoors.

'Is Ted in any sort of trouble?' asked Lampson, concerned.

'Good heavens, no!' said Coburg firmly, inwardly thinking, I certainly hope not. 'It's just something personal I have to tell him, something about my situation, in case I'm not in the office tomorrow.'

'Not health, is it?' asked Lampson.

'No, no,' said Coburg.

He was relieved when Mrs Lampson returned with a slip of paper.

'There you are,' she said, 'And if you see him, tell him Terry's all right, he's being a good boy.'

When Lampson returned to consciousness he found himself in a kitchen, tied to a heavy wooden armchair. It wasn't just any kitchen, it was the kitchen of a big house to judge by the size of it, the very large black kitchen range, the long wooden table with benches on each side, the large red tiles on the floor. His head throbbed painfully where he'd been struck. Two muscular men stood by him watching him grimly, while a tall, elegant man leant against the wooden table, studying his warrant card.

'Detective Sergeant Edward Lampson,' recited the man. He frowned, thoughtfully and muttered, 'Lampson. Lampson.' Then he turned to Lampson and said: 'You're DCI Coburg's man.'

'I'm saying nothing,' grunted Lampson. 'But as you know that much, let me tell you we're on to you. You're not going to get away with it.'

'Get away with what?' asked the man.

'The plot to destabilise this country. Help Hitler.' He shook his head. 'It ain't gonna happen.'

'I certainly hope not,' said the man firmly. 'Is that what you think we're doing?'

'Well, ain't it?' demanded Lampson angrily.

'Certainly not,' said the man, his tone calm but angry. 'In fact, the exact opposite.' He turned to the two men standing by Lampson's chair. 'Untie him.'

'But he sneaked in!' protested one of the men.

'I'm sure he had a reason, and it wasn't what we were thinking. He's not a fifth columnist, he's on our side.'

As the two men set to work to untie the ropes that held Lampson to the chair, the tall man asked. 'What brought you here? Have local people been talking, worried about what's going on here?'

'No. I came to see what was going on because someone was worried.'

123

'DCI Coburg?'

'Yes, he knows, so if you're thinking of bumping me off, you'd better think again. If I turn up dead, he'll come looking for you.'

The tall man glared at Lampson in annoyance. 'Didn't you hear what I said? We're on the same side.'

'Well that's what you would say,' said Lampson obstinately. 'Let me lower my guard. But I'm not that big a fool.'

'No, but you're pig-headed. I know about you because you were badly injured in that Russian business Coburg and my brother were involved in. You were stabbed, as I recall.'

Lampson looked at the man suspiciously.

'Who are you? And who's your brother?'

'Ian Fleming. My name's Peter Fleming. It seems only polite to introduce myself as I know who you are, and also because I know what a tenacious person Coburg can be, and unless I tell you what's going on, and you pass that on in turn to Coburg, he'll start ferreting around and that could mean a disaster for this operation, which is supposed to be top secret.' He gave a short, sarcastic laugh. 'Which is obviously not the case, or you wouldn't be here. What brought you here?'

Lampson looked at the man suspiciously. Yes, he'd ordered the ropes removed, but that could be just a ruse to gain Lampson's confidence.

'You say you're Peter Fleming, but I don't know you from a hole in the ground. You say you know my guv'nor, DCI Coburg, but loads of people know him because he's often in the papers. I grant you that business with the

Russians wasn't, but you could have heard about it from anyone.'

'I heard about it from my brother, Ian.' Fleming produced a military ID card from his pocket and handed it to Lampson. Lampson looked at the photograph, which was of the man standing in front of him: Captain Robert Peter Fleming, Grenadier Guards.

'Did you meet my brother, Ian?'

'No, I was in hospital when that business happened.'

'I ask because people say we look alike, so I was hoping that might also convince you.'

Lampson gave him back his ID document. 'Okay, let's say I believe you're who you say you are. But what's this all about?'

'Before we go into that, let me ask you what brought you here.' When he saw Lampson hesitate, he added: 'It will help us tighten up our security, which was obviously lax in some way, otherwise you wouldn't have come all this way to spy on us. How did you find out about The Garth?'

'I didn't, not till I got here. I was following someone and that led me here.'

Fleming smiled.

'Ah yes. The man following Ben Pike. Ben reported that he felt someone was following him, so I asked my men to keep a special watch, just in case anyone tried to break in.' He nodded to one of the men, who disappeared and returned a short time later accompanied by Ben Pike, who stared in shock at Lampson.

'It was Ted who was following me?' he said, stunned.

'Apparently,' said Fleming. 'How do you know Detective Sergeant Lampson?'

'He's my wife Ellie's cousin, sir.'

'Ah,' nodded Fleming. 'The old concerned-wife syndrome. Is that right, Sergeant Lampson?'

'She was worried, that's all.' He looked at Ben accusingly. 'Going off to meetings and not telling here where you were going.'

'Those were my instructions, Sergeant,' said Fleming stiffly. 'Absolute secrecy. Not even close family members should be told.'

'Then you don't know my cousin, Ellie, Mr Fleming. She's like all of the Lampsons. Fiercely loyal and protective of our own. And it wasn't just the meetings. She found that box of matches from Claridge's in Ben's pocket, and we all know what's going on at Claridge's.'

'A murder that you're investigating, along with DCI Coburg, according to the newspapers,' said Fleming.

'I'm talking about the politics. People who should know better consorting with people who have no loyalty to this country.'

'In that case, Sergeant, you're wrong. Yes, Ben went to Claridge's, but not to consort with any traitors but to report back to me on possible meetings that might be happening there.'

'Lord Halifax, and whoever the Duke of Windsor asked to take care of things,' said Lampson.

'Very good,' said Fleming. 'Not quite accurate regarding the actual personnel, but in the right area.'

'Ellie should never have said anything to you!' burst out Pike angrily. 'Reporting me to the police was a dreadful thing for her to do!'

'She didn't report you to the police, she told me as her

126

cousin,' retorted Lampson, equally angry. 'And she did it because she didn't want you getting into any trouble. If you were doing something with people you shouldn't, she wanted me to stop you.'

'Which is very commendable,' said Fleming. He gave a rueful sigh. 'You're going to have to tell her something, Ben. Not everything, just that it's a matter of national security, which is why you can't tell her.'

'It'd need to be better than that,' said Lampson. 'Ellie's not stupid.'

Fleming nodded. 'I'll think up something. And now, Sergeant, I think we need to have a talk, just to reassure you that what's going on here is vital to the war effort, and all very official, and sanctioned by none other than Winston Churchill himself. But I need your word that you won't pass any of what I tell you to anyone else. With the exception of DCI Coburg. I assume he knows you've come here?'

'Yes.'

'In that case, you'd better let him know, but no one else. Are you married, Sergeant?'

'I was, sir, but my wife died.'

'My sympathy. But, apart from Coburg, no one else must be told. Is that agreed?'

Lampson nodded. 'Agreed.'

'Some months ago, I was instructed to assemble a guerrilla force of selected men from the Local Defence Volunteers, as they were known at that time.'

'The Home Guard,' said Lampson.

'Exactly. I started with Kent because we're the closest to the German invasion force moored off the coast of northern

127

France, and if Hitler decides to invade – which everyone seems to think he will – then there is a great possibility that his forces will overrun our defences, in the same way they did at Dunkirk. The plan is simple. To train selected men in ways to kill and carry out sabotage. Fortunately, my place here has extensive grounds and a high wall around it, so we can do the training here in relative secrecy. If the Germans invade, we will have a secret army, highly trained, to offer resistance. If we can't stop them by a conventional defence, we'll demolish them bit by bit, taking them out in ones and twos. We also have the weapons necessary for larger attacks, tommy guns, explosives.'

'And Churchill knows about this?'

'It was set up on his authority. So, Sergeant Lampson, are you convinced that what we are doing here is a patriotic endeavour?'

'I am,' said Lampson. 'And thank you for telling me.'

'Remember your promise. This goes no further than DCI Coburg, and only then because I know and trust Edgar Coburg implicitly. And you must tell him he can't pass it on to anyone.'

'I'll make sure I tell him,' Lampson assured him.

'In that case, I believe our business is finished. How did you get here?'

'By bike.'

'From London?'

'Train to Ashford, then bike to here.'

'In that case, I'll leave you to locate your bicycle and return. One thing.'

'Yes?'

'It might make sense for you to cycle back to Mrs Pike and make some reassuring noises so that she won't poke around any further.' He looked at Pike. 'That all right with you, Ben? After all, you'll be here for a bit doing your training, and the less time she has to worry about you, the better.'

'Fine by me,' nodded Pike. He looked at Lampson. 'Just tell her it's Home Guard stuff, Ted, but extra security is involved. Careless talk costs lives. That sort of thing.'

'Leave it to me,' nodded Lampson.

'And I'm sorry we had to hit you on the head,' apologised Fleming. 'But we can't be too careful. It was either that, or slit your throat.'

Lampson gave a wry grin.

'In that case, thank God for the bang on the head.'

CHAPTER TWENTY

It took Coburg longer than he'd hoped to find Ben and Ellie Pike's cottage. His search was made more difficult because road names and signposts had been removed to confuse the enemy should they invade. The absence of location points certainly confused Coburg. Finally, after many false turnings, he found the small cottage, and knocked, then smiled politely at the small woman who answered the door.

'Mrs Pike?' he enquired. 'My name's Coburg and I'm a colleague of your cousin, Ted Lampson.'

'Ted!' she called. 'It's for you.'

Lampson appeared from inside the cottage and stared at Coburg, stunned. Coburg saw that he wore a broad bandage around his head.

'What are you doing here, guv?' he asked.

'I came in case you needed help. And, by the look of that bandage, I was right.'

'Dreadful. He hit his head and they didn't even bother to look after it,' complained Ellie Pike. She held the door open wider. 'Come in. We don't want the warden reporting us for letting light out.'

Coburg followed them through to the small kitchen.

'I tripped and bashed my head,' explained Lampson.

'You'd have thought that Ben would have done something about it,' insisted Ellie. 'Lucky I took a look at it when I saw the dried blood.'

'Ben had things to do,' said Lampson. 'Like I told you, Ellie, he's busy with what's going on at the Home Guard.'

'Did you see him?' asked Coburg.

'I did, and everything's fine.' He looked at his cousin. 'Actually, I need to get off, Ellie. With the trains the way they are.'

'That's all right, I'll run you back to London,' said Coburg.

'So you've got time for a cup of tea,' said Ellie.

'Thank you, but I need to get back,' said Coburg apologetically. 'I'm sorry it's such a short visit, but I needed to bring Ted up to date on something before we go to work tomorrow. Where's your bike, Ted?'

'Round the side of the cottage.'

'Fine. We'll put it in the back of the car.' He smiled at Ellie. 'Nice to meet you, Mrs Pike. I'm sure we'll meet again.'

When they were in the car and motoring, Coburg said: 'So you got hit on the head.'

'Yes,' said Lampson ruefully. 'I followed Ben to this big house with walls all round it. I climbed over the wall and wallop! Bang on the head. They were protecting this secret army they've got going on.'

'Secret army?'

'But official. Churchill himself is behind it. At least, that's what this bloke Fleming told me.'

'Fleming? Ian Fleming?'

'No, his brother Peter. I got the impression he knows you.'

'Yes, he does. He's the elder brother of Ian Fleming, who we got caught up with in that Russian business. What's he up to with this secret army?'

Lampson told Coburg what Fleming had told him, about having a guerrilla force ready to fight the Germans if they invaded. 'But it's all very hush-hush.'

'Yes, it would be,' said Coburg.

'So this Peter Fleming is another action hero then, like this brother.'

'But less obvious in the way he goes about it. To be honest, Ian's always been a bit envious of Peter. Peter's the older brother, an achiever in every way. Won all the major prizes at Eton, and then went on to get a first-class degree in English at Oxford. He's always been a bit of an adventurer and earns his living writing about his exploits. I read a book he wrote about an expedition he led in the Brazilian jungle. Exciting stuff. He writes well.

'I'm not surprised that Churchill asked him to organise this secret army to fight the Germans if they invade. That's right up his street. He spent some time in China, and I heard that he'd been there training the Chinese in guerrilla techniques after the Japanese invaded. I lost track of him after that, I didn't even realise he was back in England. What was your impression of him?'

'A gentleman, very polite, well educated, but you know that if push comes to shove, he'd kill without a second thought. The sort of bloke you'd want on your side, rather than against you.'

'I agree. And you can stop worrying about Ben, if he's being trained by Peter, he'll be in the safest possible hands.'

CHAPTER TWENTY-ONE

Friday 18th October

Lampson slept till six the next morning, then walked to his parents' flat.

'I've come to pick up Terry,' he said.

'I was just about to make breakfast for him and get him ready for school,' said Mrs Lampson.

'I can do that,' said Lampson.

His father looked with suspicion at the bandage around his head. 'What've you been up to?' he demanded. 'You become a Sikh, or something?'

'I fell over and banged my head,' said Lampson.

'Doing what?'

Luckily, Mrs Lampson interrupted with: 'Did you see your boss last night? DCI Coburg? He came round looking for Ellie's address.'

'Yes,' said Lampson.

'Was it he who hit you?' asked Mrs Lampson.

'No one hit me. I fell over.'

'Great, clumsy lummox,' grunted his father.

'He's a nice man, that Mr Coburg,' said his mother. 'Very genuine.'

'Yes, he is,' agreed Lampson.

It took another half an hour before Terry was up and dressed and they made their way to their own home.

'What's that bandage on your head for?' asked Terry as they walked along the street.

'I had an accident last night.'

'Someone hit you?'

'No, I fell over and banged my head and it bled. And as soon as we get in, I'm taking it off. I'm fed up with people asking me about it.'

Once they were home, Lampson asked: 'What do you fancy for breakfast this morning?'

'Have we got any bacon?' asked Terry.

'We have,' said Lampson. 'And there's a sausage if you'd like it.'

'Yes please!'

'Right, wash your hands while I get the frying pan on.'

'I already washed 'em at Gran's.'

'When?'

'Last night.'

'Well wash 'em again.'

'What's the special occasion?'

'Just because you're washing your hands doesn't mean it's a special occasion.'

'No, but having a sausage is. You're always talking about rationing and how we have to watch how we use our food.'

'Well, today is special.'

'Why?'

'Go and wash your hands and when we're eating, I'll tell you.'

Fifteen minutes later, father and son were sitting at the table, Terry with bacon and a sausage, and Lampson with a bacon sandwich.

'So, what's special about today?' asked Terry through a mouthful of sausage.

'I've got an idea I'd like to run by you. How do you fancy playing football?'

'Who with?'

'A team.'

'What team?'

'A team of our own. A Somers Town boys' team.'

Terry looked at him, puzzled.

'There isn't one,' he said.

'Not at the moment. I was thinking of starting one. We could practise in the park. We could play other teams.'

'What other teams?'

'School teams. The Boy Scouts. Local boys' clubs. They've all got football teams. We could go in for their cup competitions.'

Terry looked at his father, stunned.

'What do you think?'

'I think it's a great idea, but . . .'

'But what?'

'Will you have the time, Dad? You're always at work.'

'I'll make the time,' said Lampson.

'Where will we get the players from?'

'I reckon we could make a start with some of your mates from school. I thought I'd pop in and see your teacher, Miss Bradley, and see what she thinks.'

'I don't know,' said Terry doubtfully. 'She's a hard one. A real dragon.'

'She seems all right to me.'

'Yeh, but you ain't in her class.'

* * *

Yvette Corot frowned when she heard the doorbell of her flat ring. Seven o'clock. Who could it be calling at this early hour? The postman didn't arrive until eight o'clock, and it was rare for her to receive any post. And any that did come was usually addressed to the previous tenant of the flat, a Martin Maidstone.

It could be her contact in England, but they'd arranged for their meetings to be on neutral ground, a park, the Embankment, somewhere where two people could sit as apparent strangers and exchange comments on the weather before going their separate ways. She had no friends in England. No one knew her and she knew no one outside of work, except for her contact. So her caller could only be someone from work. But why would they be calling on her? She was just a clerk at the Free French headquarters in London. She kept her profile low, as she'd been instructed. Do nothing to arouse interest in you. That way, when the moment came for her to act, her target – her victim – would suspect nothing until it was too late.

The bell rang again. She called out *Attendez!* in case it was one of her colleagues from the office, then made for the door. She took a small pistol from the drawer of the small chest of drawers in the hallway and dropped it in her pocket, just in case. It was important to be ready.

She opened the door and found a young man standing there, holding a small parcel. Beneath his arm was a clipboard with papers on it.

'Miss Corot?' he asked.

'Yes,' said Yvette. She was puzzled. Who would be sending her a parcel?

'Parcel for you, to be signed for,' said the man.

He held out the parcel to her, and as she took it, he took the clipboard from under his arm and held it out to her. A pencil was attached to the clip at the top.

She took the clipboard and unclipped the pencil. She was just about to sign the paper when there was a slight flurry behind her, and a wire loop dropped over her neck and was pulled tight. Frantically, she reached into her pocket for the pistol, but everything started to go black before her eyes as the wire tightened, and then she stopped and fell.

The two men dragged her body into the flat, closed the door, and then set about their systematic search, removing every item of paper and putting them in a small bag. When the job was complete, they left, leaving the door of the flat slightly ajar.

'Now we phone Mayfair police station,' said one as they left the small block of flats and made for the nearest telephone booth.

'Mayfair?' queried the other. 'Not Scotland Yard?'

'Scotland Yard would mean DCI Coburg. Mayfair means Inspector Lomax. Which would you rather have investigating?'

The phone call came through to Mayfair police station at half past seven, reporting a disturbance at a flat in Mayfair.

'I heard screams,' the caller said. 'A woman. I think she was being attacked. Perhaps murdered.'

The sergeant on duty sent a constable to investigate, and he in turn telephoned the station within minutes of his arrival.

'It's murder sure enough, Sarge,' he said. 'A young woman. It looks like she's been strangled with something sharp. Her body's lying in the hallway of her flat.'

'Did you have to break the door down to get in?'

'No, Sarge. It was ajar. Whoever did it didn't pull the door to.'

Half an hour later Inspector Lomax and Sergeant Potteridge pulled up outside the block of flats in their police car and joined the constable in the flat.

'It's the same,' said Lomax. 'Garrotted.' He smiled. 'You know what this means, Sergeant?'

'Yes, boss. The same killer.'

'Which means they'll have to give us back the one at Claridge's.'

'It could be a serial killer,' said Potteridge, concerned. 'They're the hardest to solve.'

'Even better if it is,' said Lomax. 'When we solve it, the publicity will be even bigger. Our names in the papers. Commendations from the commissioner.' He grinned broadly. 'This will be one in the eye for DCI bloody Coburg. There's no way he can take this one away from me.'

After breakfast, Lampson made sure Terry got to school on time, where he noted that the two Purvis brothers, Jake and Jud immediately made a beeline for Terry and were soon in a huddle.

They're planning trouble, he thought, even more determined to intercede, but without appearing to.

Coburg arrived and as Lampson drove them to Scotland Yard, he told him about his concerns over Jake and Jud Purvis. 'They're real nasty. And crooked. Most of the kids around here are scallywags, nothing really nasty about them. But the Purvis brothers are bad news, just waiting to be unleashed.'

'And they've got their hooks into your Terry?'

'That's the way it looks to me. Nothing I can put my fingers on, they haven't done anything wrong – yet. But they will. And when it all goes wrong, they'll scarper off and leave Terry to carry the can. That's why I thought I'd do something to divert his attention away from them.'

'What have you got in mind?'

'Terry loves football. Mad about it. Not just Spurs, but all football. Trouble is, with the war on, there's not a lot of football about to hold his interest. So I thought I'd start a boys' football team, here in Somers Town. Get some of the boys together.'

'Can you do that? You've got a lot on your plate already, with work.'

'I'll see if I can rope in some other local dads to help. My dad will come in, I'm sure. See if I can get the school involved.'

'It sounds a good idea, if you can manage it.'

'I feel I've got to, at least, try. I know what kids like the Purvis brothers are like, and Terry's easily led. If I want to keep him on the straight and narrow, I've got to do it in a way that doesn't look like I'm being the heavy father. My old man was always heavy with me, and all it did was make me do the opposite to what he told me.'

'Well, I think it's a great idea,' said Coburg. 'And if I can help in any way, just ask.'

'You're offering to give a hand?'

'No,' said Coburg. 'I've definitely got enough on my plate to keep me occupied. I meant that if you need time off or anything, I'll cover for you.'

'Thanks, guv. I thought at lunchtime I'd go to Terry's

school and see if his teacher would make an announcement about it, find out who's interested. If there's enough, maybe we can make a start tomorrow afternoon.'

'By all means. By the way, I see you've got rid of that bandage. How's the head this morning?'

'It's all right. I've been told I've got a thick skull. Or was it a thick head?' He frowned. 'I'm surprised at Ben getting involved in something like this guerrilla army business. I never thought secret warfare was his thing.'

'It isn't, if he caused his wife to get suspicious,' commented Coburg drily.

'You know what I mean. I've always thought of him as a quiet sort of bloke. Kept himself to himself.'

'That sums up most of the commando types I've met,' said Coburg. 'I've often found that people who tell you how brave and fearless they are, are usually the ones who run away first and fastest.'

Inspector Lomax stood in Superintendent Moffatt's office, his mouth open and a look of absolute outrage on his face.

'No, sir!' he bellowed angrily. 'Absolutely not! This is my shout. The call came to us here at Mayfair. You can't take this away from me!'

'It's not my decision, Inspector.'

'Whose is it then, sir? Because I'm going to take this up at the highest level. This is my shout, and because it's the same method – the exact same method – by rights the Claridge's murder should be handed back to us here at Mayfair as well. Taking that from us was a slap in the face, but to take this one as well . . . !'

'The powers that be feel, as you do, that both cases are

connected, and as Scotland Yard and DCI Coburg have been given the first one, then he should also look into this one.'

'It isn't fair, sir!' burst out Lomax.

'It may not be fair, but it's the way it is. I have explained to the commissioner, and indeed to Superintendent Allison at Scotland Yard, that by rights, logically and by protocol, both these murders should be allocated to this station and to you. But unfortunately the powers that be feel that as the victim was working for the Free French in London, politics will be involved.'

'I can deal with politics, sir!' exploded Lomax. 'I deal with it all the flipping time!'

'I'm sorry, Inspector, but that's the way it is.'

Oh no it isn't, thought Lomax vengefully as he made his way back to his office. I'm not going to take this lying down. I am going to do something.

On Coburg and Lampson's arrival at Scotland Yard there was a message from Superintendent Allison informing Coburg he wanted to see him urgently.

'But not that urgent, or he'd have phoned me at home,' said Coburg.

He made his way along to corridor to the superintendent's office, where Allison gestured for him to take a chair. The superintendent looked worried, which was not unusual.

'We have a problem,' he announced in serious tones.

'Just one, sir?'

'I'm being serious, Coburg.'

'Yes, sir.'

'There was another garrotting last night.'

'At Claridge's?'

'No, she had a flat in a small block in Mayfair. A French woman in her thirties called Yvette Corot. She worked for the Free French at their HQ in Carlton Gardens. The emergency call was answered by officers from Mayfair police station.'

Coburg's heart sank. 'Inspector Lomax?'

'The same.'

'And I assume he insists it's his case to investigate?'

'He does, according to the station superintendent, Jeremy Moffatt.'

'But it's obviously connected with the dead man at Claridge's. If the same method was used.'

'From what I've been told, it is. Thin wire.'

'Then it should be ours.'

'I've told Superintendent Moffatt that, and he's told Inspector Lomax. But I'm advising you because we both know that Inspector Lomax has some kind of vendetta against you.'

'For no reason.'

'That may be, but I thought you ought to know.'

Hooky Morton stood with Dobbin and half a dozen of his cronies on the pavement looking at the wooden crate that had been left outside his pub sometime during the night. The top had been taken off, revealing a jumble of charred bones and cooked flesh, with fragments of cloth still sticking to the mess. A pair of blackened shoes were still on the feet. The remains of a broken bottle had been laid on top of the remains.

'Bastards!' muttered Hooky.

'What are we gonna do with him?' asked Dobbin.

'We bury him of course,' snapped Hooky. 'Tommy was

142

one of ours.' He turned to Jack Parker. 'You know the family best, Jack. You inform 'em. Tell 'em we'll arrange the funeral.'

'There's only his mum and his gran,' said Parker. 'His dad was killed at Dunkirk.'

'Tell her there'll be money to come.' He turned to Dobbin. 'Dob, you fix up with the undertaker.'

'He'll need a death certificate,' said Dobbin.

Hooky turned on him, angry, and pointed at the burnt carcass. 'There he is. Burnt to a bloody crisp. What more does he need?'

'It's for the books, Hooky. The undertaker has to have proper documentation.'

'Bollocks to proper documentation. Sort it out.'

He stormed away from them and into his pub. That bastard Roly Fitt. It wasn't enough for him to kill poor Tommy, he had to rub Hooky's nose in it by sending his remains back.

Well, it didn't end here. If Roly Fitt had declared war, Hooky Morton would finish it.

Ted Lampson was reading the notes of the little they'd been able to find out about Janos Mila when there was a knock at the door. Sergeant Watson, one of Lampson's uniformed pals, looked in.

'Are you on your own, Ted?' he asked.

Lampson nodded. 'The guv'nor's been called to the superintendent's office.'

'Ah,' said Watson. 'It might be to tell him the news about Joanne Nicholson.'

'What news?' asked Lampson.

'I just heard it from a pal at the prison where she was. She smashed the toilet bowl in her cell and used one of the broken bits to cut her wrists. She's dead.'

Lampson stared at him. 'Dead?'

Watson nodded. 'I thought I'd let you know personally, rather than have you hear it over the phone. I know you were hoping she'd get off.'

'She would have, too,' said Lampson. He shook his head. 'Thanks, Ernie. I appreciate it.'

After Watson had left, Lampson sat staring at the written interviews, but not seeing them. He kept thinking of Joanne Nicholson, dead in her cell.

There'd been no need for her to do that.

He was still sitting there when Coburg returned.

'What's up?' asked Coburg, aware that his sergeant looked decidedly unhappy.

'Joanne Nicholson's killed herself,' said Lampson. 'Ernie Watson just came in with the news.' He look enquiringly at Coburg. 'Was that what the super wanted to tell you?'

'No.' He gave a sigh. 'What a bloody awful thing to happen. That poor woman.'

'She said the Angel of Death was upon her,' said Lampson. 'I suppose that's what she meant. I should have spotted it and warned the prison.'

'It wasn't your fault,' said Coburg. 'They couldn't keep watch on her twenty-four hours a day. You did everything you could.'

'But much good it did her,' said Lampson bitterly. 'Anyway, what did the boss want?'

'There's been another murder. Garrotted, same as the other one, by all accounts.'

He related to Lampson what he'd been told by Allison, including the business of Inspector Lomax wanting to claim the right to investigate this latest murder.

'Fortunately, the superintendent has insisted it's connected to the murder of Janos Mila and so is ours.'

'Lomax won't like it, sir. He'll do everything he can to undermine you. Mess up the investigation.'

'He can try!' said Coburg angrily.

'There is one way you can throw a spanner in his works,' said Lampson, suddenly thoughtful. When Coburg looked at him questioningly, he added: 'Bring him in.'

'Bring him in? To the investigation?'

'If you think about it, sir, it makes sense.'

'It makes no sense to have that vengeful dimwit messing up what we're trying to do.'

'With respect, sir, it does. Think of the old Indian saying.'

'I can't see that any of Gandhi's pearls of wisdom have any bearing on the matter.'

'Not India Indian, guv. Native American. The one about "It's better to have your enemy inside your tepee pissing out than outside pissing in". In this case, give him something to do. With two murders, the extra pair of eyes will be a help.'

'Not Lomax's eyes. They'll be fixed on me.'

'Maybe, but mostly they'll be set on solving the murder so he can claim the credit. And he'll be too busy on that to try and screw you up.'

Coburg fell silent, mulling this over. Finally, he admitted: 'There might be something in what you say. While we're trading old sayings, there's the famous one about the battle between the wind and the sun as to who could make a man take his overcoat off. The more the wind blew, the tighter the man pulled his coat around him; but when the sun shone, he took it off.' He nodded. 'Right, Sergeant. Let's give it a try. It's time for me to pay a call on Inspector Lomax.'

CHAPTER TWENTY-TWO

Hooky Morton looked up from his newspaper as Dobbin and young Hopkins entered the bar and sat down at his table. They looked frustrated.

'Well?' asked Morton.

Dobbin shook his head.

'Roly's got guards outside his club. They don't look like guards, but they are. And they're tooled up. There's no chance of doing an attack on the club. If we try it, we'll get mowed down before we can get to the front door.'

Morton nodded. 'So we've got to find another way,' he said.

'Is it worth it?' asked Dobbin.

Morton stared at him, shocked and angry.

'Worth it?!' he echoed, and Dobbin could hear the rage in his voice. 'Worth it? He sends Tommy back to us in a crate, burnt to a crisp, and you ask if it's worth it?'

'We did Patch first,' pointed out Dobbin. 'So it's one all. Maybe we ought to leave it there. If it escalates it could get out of hand, and then we'll have the law really poking it's nose in.'

Morton looked coldly at his second-in-charge. 'I never

thought I'd see the day when you turned yeller, Dob.'

'It's not being yeller. I'd take on Roly Fitt one-on-one any day of the week, and you know it. But this way, by attacking his club, we're making trouble for ourselves.' He leant forward. 'If you really want to get Roly Fitt, why not do it. Take him out.'

'Kill him?' asked Morton.

'Why not? Do it at his home. Or when he's on his way home.'

'Because I want to send a message who did it.'

'His people will know who did it,' said Dobbin. 'That way it'd be neat and clean. All right, you may have to take out his family if you do it at his home, but you could make it look like bomb damage. Start a fire there, let him and his family go the same way as Tommy.'

Morton fell silent. 'You might have something there,' he conceded. 'Let me think about it.' Then a nasty smile appeared on his face. 'In the meantime, I'll make myself feel better by going and having a word with that cheating scumbag at Claridge's.'

Inspector Arnold Lomax sat at his desk filled with righteous anger. Once again, a prime murder case had been snatched away from him by DCI Edgar bloody Saxe-hyphen-Coburg. The old public school network cutting him out. It had been bad enough when they'd taken the Claridge's murder away from him and given it to Coburg, but this one rubbed salt into the wound. There were no kings and queens and prime ministers involved in this one, just a dead French woman.

He had two murders on his books at the moment, but there was no mystery about either of them. A vicar had strangled a prostitute who'd infected him with a sexual disease, which had led to him infecting his own wife, thus blowing his reputation as a person of the highest virtue, a reputation which had been vitally important to him, however hypocritical it may have been. It was an open and shut case, which wouldn't find its way into the pages of the press. Not the respectable press, anyway. The Sunday rags would pounce upon the vicar story.

The other was Patch Peters, part of Hooky Morton's mob who'd been passing inside information to Roly Fitt. To Lomax, that put Morton in the frame for the killing. Everyone knew that Morton didn't have a forgiving approach to anyone who tried to cross him. The trouble was the murder of a low-level crook like Peters was unlikely to give Lomax the high profile he wanted, and felt he deserved. The one at Claridge's would have given him that. Admittedly, it had just been a kitchen porter who'd died, but the high-profile people staying at Claridge's would have elevated the case. And it would have been even more newsworthy because of this second killing, the Free French woman.

There was a tap at his door, then his sergeant, Joe Potteridge, put his head round it.

'Sorry to trouble, you, sir, but there's someone to see you.'

'Who is it?'

'DCI Coburg from Scotland Yard.'

Lomax stared at his sergeant.

'Here?' he asked, stunned.

'Yes, sir. He asked to see you.'

I bet he did, thought Lomax vengefully. Come to gloat.

His first reaction was to tell Potteridge to tell Coburg to get lost. Then he thought about it. No, he decided, this would be a good time to give that snob a piece of his mind. Put him in his place. Remind him what being a real policeman was about.

'Okay. Send him in.'

Potteridge nodded, then disappeared. A short time later there was a further tap at his door, and Lomax called 'Come in!'

The door opened and Coburg entered.

'Good morning, Inspector,' he said.

'If you've come to gloat over the fact that you've stolen another of my cases from me—' snarled Lomax, getting to his feet.

'No,' said Coburg. 'The exact opposite. I've come to suggest we work together on both cases.'

Lomax stared at him, at first bewildered, then suspicious. 'What's going on? What's your game?'

'Exactly as I said.'

'They should have been mine,' said Lomax aggressively. 'Both of 'em!'

'I agree,' said Coburg. 'Trust me, I didn't ask for the one at Claridge's, that was forced on me by the owner of the hotel pulling strings. But I think you'll agree that the two murders are connected.'

Warily, Lomax nodded. 'Both garrotted by what looks like the same weapon. A noose of thin wire.'

'So find the killer of one, we find the killer of both.'

Lomax hesitated, still unsure if he was being duped. Then he said, 'Superintendent Moffatt told me he'd been ordered to pass the case to Superintendent Allison at the Yard.'

'Yes, so I've been told,' said Coburg. 'But I feel this is a case of credit where credit's due. You took both shouts. It wasn't my fault the first was taken from you, but this way you can have both.'

'For my own?'

Coburg gave a rueful sigh. 'I'm afraid Rupert D'Oyley Carte won't allow that. He wants me to be the one asking questions of all the kings and queens and assorted royalty staying at Claridge's.'

'I bet he does,' sneered Lomax.

'But there's nothing to say that you can't do it with me,' added Coburg.

Again, Lomax looked at Coburg with suspicion.

'Why?' he asked.

'Because we need to catch this murderer before he kills any more people, and I believe we've got more chance of doing that if we work together.'

Lomax watched him, still dubious; then he asked: 'And if we catch him, who gets the credit?'

'When we catch him,' Coburg corrected him. 'And the answer is: we both do.'

'My name will be in the paper as well?'

'It will,' Coburg assured him.

Lomax weighed this up, then asked: 'So, what's our first move?'

'What have you done so far?' asked Coburg.

'The usual. Went to the small block of flats where her body was found.'

'Where was it found, inside or outside?'

'Inside, but whoever did it left the front door open. What happened, a neighbour who was passing saw the door was open so she knocked to check if everything was all right. When there was no answer she looked in, and saw the dead woman lying there, just inside the door.'

'No attempt to hide it?'

'No. So whoever did it wanted the body found. Sergeant Potteridge and I went there when we got the shout. We called in the duty medico, and after he'd confirmed cause of death, we had the body taken to the Middlesex. While we were there the landlord arrived, in a panic. One of the other tenants had heard about what had happened and telephoned him. It was he who told us she worked at the Free French place in Carlton Gardens.'

'Did you search the flat? Talk to the neighbours?'

'Of course,' retorted Lomax indignantly.

'And?'

'I was about to write it up as a report when I got the call telling me I was off the case,' he said, his tone bitter and resentful.

'Did you find any papers in the flat? Letters? Addresses?'

'No. Not a thing. Either she didn't have any papers there, or someone had cleared everything out.'

'Same as at Janos Mila's room,' said Coburg. 'Someone had been in and cleared out everything that might have given us a clue as to him and the sort of life he led. What did you find out about the dead woman?'

'Nothing. We didn't have time. All we've got is her name, her address and the fact she worked for the Free French at the London HQ at Carlton Gardens.'

Coburg nodded.

'As you've already started with the latest victim, the dead woman, I'd like you to carry on with that, if that's all right with you, while I carry on looking into the other victim, Janos Mila. As Yvette Corot worked for the Free French in London, perhaps you could talk to them, find out who she was and what she did there.'

'That would have been my first move,' said Lomax, still annoyed. Then he asked: 'Do you think it's political?'

'I don't know. I've got an open mind. Later we can meet up and compare notes, see if any similarities come up in the two murders, apart from the fact they were killed the same way.'

The first two calls Rosa and her crewman, Stanley Robinson, attended were both for the same reason: in the first a car had driven into a huge bomb crater in the road, in the second a lorry had done the same thing, leaving both drivers badly injured.

'I don't understand it,' said Robinson as they drove back to the St John station after delivering the lorry driver to the hospital. 'How come both of them did that? Couldn't they see there was a bloody great hole in the road right in front of them?'

'I think some people go into automatic when they drive,' said Rosa. 'They drive the same route day after day. One day there's a big hole in the road but they're not aware of it because it wasn't there yesterday.'

'People like that shouldn't be allowed to drive,' grumbled Robinson. 'It's busy enough with us having to pick up war casualties and genuine accident cases, without having these nitwits adding to the load.'

Stanley Robinson was in his sixties and retired from the fire brigade, although he still volunteered for the Auxiliary Fire Service, fighting the fires that dominated London at night. He coped with the demands of being a St John volunteer during the day and a fireman at night by sleeping in the afternoons. 'Mornings only on the ambulance for me,' he'd told Rosa the first time they crewed together.

'Did you do your medical training in the fire brigade?' asked Rosa.

'Mostly,' said Robinson. 'We had to because you never know what condition people are going to be in when you go to a fire. With that, and the courses I've done with St John, I hope I've got enough knowledge to be able to cope with someone, keep them all right until we can get them to hospital.'

'I'd like to do that,' said Rosa. 'I know driving an ambulance is important, but sometimes I feel useless when we get to somewhere and there are quite a few injured people around and I haven't got the training to help. I can try, but I'm worried that I might do something wrong and make them worse.'

'You've done the St John training?' asked Robinson.

'Yes, but I don't think it's enough. I want to do more.'

'That's what doctors are for,' said Robinson. 'Our job is to keep them alive until we can get them to a doctor.'

'Yes, but sometimes we don't keep them alive because we don't know enough,' said Rosa. 'Derek said there used to be doctors in the crews, but all that changed with the war because they were needed in the hospitals.'

'They weren't exactly doctors. More like medical students who volunteered.' He looked at her inquisitively. 'Are you thinking of doing something like that? Studying to be a doctor? If so, it ain't easy. And it takes a long time. This war'll be over by the time you finished.'

'I don't know,' admitted Rosa. 'I just feel I could be doing more. I want to be doing more.'

Inspector Lomax was still feeling puzzled as he approached the large white building at 3 Carlton Gardens, the base for the Free French, accompanied by Sergeant Potteridge. Why had Coburg brought him in to the investigation? And, more than that, let him be the lead on the dead French woman? This murder was high profile, more so than the dead kitchen porter at Claridge's. What was Coburg playing at?

He pulled on the ornamental bell pull by the side of the doorway and heard the sound of the bell inside. Shortly after, the door opened a crack and an unshaven man looked out at him suspiciously.

'*Oui?*' he asked.

Just my luck, thought Lomax bitterly. I bet he talks English well enough but he's being French.

'Detective Inspector Lomax from Mayfair police station,' announced Lomax, and he produced his warrant card and held it out so that the man could see it. The man didn't look impressed, he certainly didn't open the door any wider. Instead, he just gave Lomax a quizzical look.

'I am here investigating the death of Yvette Corot who was killed at her residence. I understand she worked here.'

The man looked sourly at Lomax for a few moments, then muttered a grudging '*Oui.*'

'I need to look at her desk and the room where she worked,' said Lomax, and he stepped forward, but was stopped by the man pushing the door further closed.

'*Non,*' said the man.

Lomax scowled.

'You don't seem to understand. I am the police and this is my sergeant. We are investigating a murder.'

The man shook his head.

'This building is French territory,' he declared. 'You cannot enter without permission.'

'I have permission,' grated Lomax. 'I am the police.'

'Permission from the authorities of the Free French government,' insisted the man.

Lomax stared at him, then spat out, 'Bollocks! This is Britain. Now open this bloody door and let us in.'

Instead, the man slammed the door shut and Lomax heard a security chain being drawn inside. He turned to look at Potteridge in indignant astonishment.

'Did you see that?!' he said, stunned.

Potteridge looked uncertain. 'Maybe he's right, sir. There's a lot of these buildings where foreign governments and ambassadors and the like are a rule unto themselves. Sergeant Nicholls was telling me about the Dutch—'

'Never mind about the bloody Dutch!' burst out Lomax angrily. He stared vengefully at the closed door. 'Right,' he said determinedly. 'DCI Saxe-bloody-Coburg has landed us in this. He can sort it out.'

CHAPTER TWENTY-THREE

Once Stanley Robinson had finished for the day and gone home to bed, Rosa went to the office to seek out Chesney Warren.

'Anything in?' she asked.

'Fortunately not,' said Warren.

'Good,' said Rosa. She sat down in the chair opposite him. 'How long does it take to qualify as a doctor?'

'A doctor?' he echoed, puzzled.

'Yes.'

'It takes a long time,' said Warren. 'Years of study, and that's just to be a junior doctor. After that, there are even more years. Why?'

'I want to do more,' said Rosa. 'I'm very grateful for the training I've been given here, it means I've been able to make the patient comfortable when putting them in the ambulance. But I want to do more than just that. I want to save them. Save their lives. Sometimes they're just about hanging on, but by the time we get them to the hospital it's just too late.'

'That's very commendable,' said Warren, 'but, as I said, it takes years to qualify to be a doctor. Have you thought of training to be a nurse?'

'A nurse?'

'Nurses these days are trained in medical disciplines to a very high standard. The training is far better than it used to be in the old days, it's about medical treatments, not just caring as it was. That shows in the training. But it's far less than you'd have to do to become a doctor. Three years for a state-registered nurse, two years for a state-enrolled nurse. And you'd have the medical knowledge to really help people, not just basic first aid.'

Coburg hung up the receiver and turned to Lampson with a weary sigh. 'That was Inspector Lomax. Apparently, the French have refused him permission to enter their premises at Carlton Gardens. They claim it's the headquarters of the French government in exile and, as such, French territory.' He picked up the phone and asked the operator to put him through to Sir Vincent Blessington at the Foreign Office.

'DCI Coburg,' said Blessington. 'How are you? Well, I trust?'

'I am, but I'm in need of some professional diplomatic advice.' He related what he'd heard from Inspector Lomax about being refused entry to Carlton Gardens as it was French government territory.

'I hate to cause dissension between us and our French allies, but in this case, whoever refused Inspector Lomax entry was quite wrong to do so,' Blessington told him. '3 Carlton Gardens is the headquarters of the Free French Armed Forces under General Charles de Gaulle, which is quite separate from the French government. Britain still recognises the French government in Vichy.'

'A government allied to the Nazis,' said Coburg.

'In practice, yes, but our official position is that we will

157

continue to recognise the Vichy regime, led by Marshal Pétain, as the official government in France for two reasons: the first is that when the Nazis are defeated we will already have the French government as our allies in the rebuilding of Europe. The second is that we're going to need the French colonies on our side, and at the moment they're still officially ruled by Vichy.

'At the same time, we are happy to give a home to General de Gaulle and his Free French forces because we will need their military assistance in the war. But we cannot recognise them as being the French government in exile while we continue to recognise the Vichy government. We cannot recognise two opposing bodies both claiming to be any country's official government.'

'Can you let me have that in writing on Foreign Office headed notepaper?' asked Coburg.

'It will be with you within the hour,' said Blessington.

Coburg then telephoned Inspector Lomax.

'Right, Inspector. I've checked with Sir Vincent Blessington at the Foreign Office, and he says the French can't refuse us entry.' He told the inspector the legal position regarding the British government's continuing recognition of the Vichy regime.

'So they can't keep us out?' said Lomax, but Coburg could tell he was still doubtful.

'They can't,' said Coburg. 'Sir Vincent is putting the official legal position in writing for me. I've been promised that within the hour. When that arrives we'll take it to Carlton Gardens, along with some muscular police constables, and if they resist, we'll just force our way in.'

'It could cause an international incident,' Lomax cautioned.

'We have the law on our side,' said Coburg. 'I'll gather a couple of constables and we'll meet you at Mayfair station, then go en masse to Carlton Gardens.'

Coburg hung up the phone and turned to Lampson.

'Right, Sergeant. I can deal with this. I suggest you take this opportunity to go to Terry's school and put your football team idea into operation.'

'Are you sure, guv?'

Coburg nodded. 'From what you've told me about the Purvis brothers, the sooner you get this off the ground, the better. I'll see you back here.'

Lampson's arrival at Terry's school coincided with breaktime, so Lampson was able to talk to Miss Eve Bradley, Terry's teacher. He'd met her before, but that had been during a parents' evening when there'd been a whole crowd of people. Today, he was able to talk to her one-to-one in her classroom, and for the first time he became aware of what a really nice person she was. Terry had told him that she was very strict – 'she's a right dragon' – and Lampson was sure she was like that with the children because many of them were tough and confrontational, a rough area like Somers Town bred that kind of kid, but sitting with her, Lampson liked her. She was in her early thirties, short, slightly plump, her blonde hair tied back with ribbon. When Lampson outlined his idea for a local boys' football team she responded with a broad, enthusiastic smile.

'What a wonderful idea!' she beamed. 'The boys, particularly, have got quite edgy. At first, I thought it was worry about the Blitz, we're so much at the heart of the bombing being so near to Euston Station, but then I realised it's actually boredom. All the things they used to do, most of them can't any more. And for many of them, their fathers and elder brothers are away in the services, so they're at a loose end. When do you plan to start?'

'I was thinking of having the first meeting tomorrow afternoon,' said Lampson. 'I'm off duty on Saturdays and that will give me time to rope in some helpers.'

'You can count me in as one,' she said keenly.

'You, training football?' asked Lampson doubtfully.

'Why not?' she asked. 'My father played for West Ham first team, and my mother played for West Ham Ladies during the First War. My fiancé played for Millwall.'

'Your fiancé?' asked Lampson, and although he didn't like to admit it, the news that she was engaged to be married came as a disappointment.

'Wilfred. He was killed at Dunkirk.'

'I'm sorry,' said Lampson.

'It's sad, but everyone knows someone who's lost someone. I understand that you, yourself, are a widower.'

'Yes, but she died before the war.'

'Anyway, I'm telling you about my footballing background to let you know that I do know the game inside and out. If the stupid Football Association hadn't banned women from playing football on their grounds in 1921, I'd have loved to have played it at the top level, just as my mother did. You know why they banned it, don't you?'

'They said the game was unsuitable for women.'

'Poppycock!' she said scornfully. 'They were jealous because of the large crowds women's football garnered. One match my mother played in had an attendance of 40,000! So, when would you like to come in and tell the children about the idea? This afternoon?'

'Well, that's a bit difficult,' said Lampson awkwardly. 'You know I'm a detective at Scotland Yard?' She nodded. 'At this moment we've got a couple of complicated cases that are keeping me at work. I only managed to get away now because my boss suggested I come here. I need to get back. What I was wondering is if you'd mind telling them about it, and saying if anyone's interested they can come to the local park tomorrow afternoon at two o'clock?'

'No problem!' she smiled brightly. 'What are you going to call the team?'

Lampson thought it over. 'I was thinking of Somers Town Hotspur.'

She gave a doubtful frown.

'You don't think that might put boys off who are Arsenal fans?' she said. 'We all know about the deep rivalry between the Gunners and Spurs.'

'That's a good point,' he admitted. Then, tentatively, he asked: 'So, what team do you support?' dreading she might say Arsenal.

'Isn't it obvious?' she asked. 'West Ham, of course. My parents' team. I would suggest Somers Town United. Isn't that what this is about, uniting the boys and bringing them together?'

With Sir Vincent Blessington's typed and signed authority on the legal position, Coburg and two burly constables drove to Mayfair police station. They then followed Inspector Lomax and Sergeant Potteridge, along with a constable of their own, to Carlton Gardens. This time it was Coburg who led the way to the front door. As well as ringing the bell, he pounded on the front door with his fist. The front door was opened a crack and a man peered out at him suspiciously.

'Detective Chief Inspector Coburg from Scotland Yard,' announced Coburg, showing his warrant card. He produced the letter from Sir Vincent Blessington and held it out so the man could see it. 'I am authorised by the British government to enter these premises.'

'No,' said the man, and started to close the door, but Coburg put his foot in the gap, preventing the door from shutting. He then pushed the door inwards, pressing the man back, and strode into the house, gesturing for the others to follow him.

Another man appeared from the depths of the building, looking angry, and launched into a tirade in French aimed at Coburg, at which Coburg responded with equally strong words expressed in fluent French. A man and two women appeared, brought by the sound of raised voices. The new arrival seemed to be a man with authority, because as soon as he started talking – also in rapid and angry French – the others shut up and left it to him. Coburg, for his part, did not let himself be intimidated, and thrust the authority from Sir Vincent at him, accompanying it with a verbal explanation in fluent French.

The man read the letter, then scowled and gave the sheet of paper back to Coburg with a haughty glare and a reluctant nod of agreement.

'Thank you,' said Coburg, putting the letter back into his pocket. 'We can continue in French, if you wish, but I wish my colleagues to be aware of what will happen now. One of your staff will take Inspector Lomax here to the desk where Mam'selle Corot worked.' He turned to Lomax and asked: 'Do you or Sergeant Potteridge speak French?'

Lomax scowled as he grunted, 'No.'

'In that case we'll leave you to inspect whatever she was working on, and anything else you might find in her desk, while I talk to all those who worked with Mam'selle Corot, or who had anything to do with her.' He turned back to the angry Frenchman. 'I'm sure you can arrange that.'

The man gave a surly and very reluctant nod. Coburg gave an appreciative smile and said: 'We thank you for your co-operation. Is there an office we can use to talk to these people?'

'Follow me,' grunted the Frenchman, and he made to lead them down a corridor.

'Perhaps you'd show Inspector Lomax which was Mam'selle Corot's desk first,' said Coburg. 'I'll wait here for you to return and show me to the office.'

The Frenchman gestured for Lomax and Potteridge to follow him into the main building.

'You wait here, by the front door,' Coburg told his uniformed officers. 'We'll call you if we need you.'

The angry Frenchman returned, having taken Lomax and his sergeant to Yvette Corot's workstation, and gestured for Coburg to follow him down another corridor. He stopped by a door and opened it to reveal a small room, its walls lined with box files on shelves. A table and two chairs were the only furniture.

'Here,' he said.

'*Merci*,' said Coburg. 'Who was Mam'selle Corot's immediate superior? Her boss?'

'Captain Dupont,' said the man.

'I'd be grateful if you could ask him to come and see us.'

The man nodded and left. After a few moments, a man in French military uniform appeared. He was stiff-backed and regarded the chief inspector with undisguised hostility. Coburg noted that he walked with a limp and he kept his left hand in his tunic pocket. A livid scar ran down the left side of his face.

Coburg rose to his feet and gave a slight bow.

'*Bonjour, Capitaine,*' he said. And then in French he explained why he was there. The fact that Coburg spoke in French seemed to mollify the captain slightly and he accepted the chair that Coburg offered him.

Coburg began by asking which of Corot's co-workers she'd had most to do with; and which of them she'd socialised with outside of work. According to Dupont, Yvette Corot had had no social contacts with anyone at the office outside of work. Further, she did not appear to encourage talk about her life.

'She was all about work,' said Dupont. 'Which is as it should be. We have a war to win.'

'How long had she been working here?' asked Coburg.

'She started work in July.'

'How did you come to engage her? Did she write applying?'

'No. She arrived in person and volunteered her services. From talking to her I could tell she was a patriot, passionate about the freedom of France.'

Coburg got to his feet and said: 'Would you excuse me for a moment, *Capitaine*? I need to talk to my colleague, Inspector Lomax.'

Leaving Captain Dupont, Coburg made his way to

where Inspector Lomax and Sergeant Potteridge were engaged in going through the papers in Yvette Corot's desk.

'They're all in bloody French,' hissed Lomax as Coburg appeared.

'Nothing in English?'

'If there is, we haven't found it. There's stuff in German and Italian.'

'I'll have a word with Captain Dupont and arrange for you to take it to the station. Once I can get him to agree, we'll fix up a translator for you. When you saw Mam'selle Corot's landlord, did you ask him how long she'd been living there?'

'I did. He said she moved in during July.'

'Did he know where she'd been living before?'

'No.'

'He didn't ask for references?'

'He had the only reference he needed, money paid up front. These are unusual times. The old rules don't apply.'

'Thank you,' said Coburg.

He was about to leave, when Lomax gestured at the contents of the desk and said irritably: 'I can't see the point in us doing this. Not here. Like I said, it's in languages we don't understand.'

'And I'll do my best to get Captain Dupont to agree that you can borrow them. I'll be back shortly.'

Coburg returned to the small room and resumed his seat, asking Dupont: 'Her landlord told us she only moved into her flat in July, the same time she started to work here. Where had she been before?'

'I do not know. It did not seem a relevant question to ask. There are many French people here in Britain who

165

have been forced to flee France.'

'But crossing the Channel has been virtually impossible for civilians since the Battle of Britain began.'

'There are still ways for people desperate to escape from France, if they are prepared to take the risk. Small planes. Small boats.'

'But you didn't ask her how she came here?'

'No,' said Dupont. 'To ask would be demanding she give us information about her journey, and those answers could put brave people at risk. Secrecy is vital.'

'So you have no idea where she lived or worked before she came to work for you?'

'No,' said Dupont.

Realising he wasn't going to get much more from the captain, Coburg then asked his permission to borrow the papers from Yvette Corot's desk for translation and examination. This met with a firm refusal, and eventually a compromise was arrived at: Dupont would arrange for English translations of the documents to be made.

'You may take those.'

'Very well,' said Coburg. 'How soon will they be available?' He then added pointedly: 'We are intent on finding out who murdered your colleague, and if it relates to anything in those papers, the sooner we can have them, the better.'

'Very well,' said Dupont. 'I will arrange for the translations to be ready tomorrow morning.'

Coburg nodded and shook the captain's hand, then set off to find Lomax.

'I've arranged for translations of the documents to be available tomorrow morning,' Coburg told him.

'Huh! Better than nothing, I suppose,' grumbled Lomax.

'Can we trust the translations will be right?'

'If you like, I could insist that you bring your own translator into the Free French offices and examine them properly there,' suggested Coburg.

Lomax shook his head. 'No,' he said. 'I can't see we're going to get much from them, anyway.'

'In that case, I suggest you call back tomorrow and pick up the translations. In the meantime, you continue to look into Yvette Corot, while Sergeant Lampson and I dig into Janos Mila. Talk to the neighbours again. Then we'll meet up and see if there's any common ground for both of them that can give us a clue as to why they were killed, and by whom.'

Sergeant Potteridge looked at the venomous look on his boss's face as he glared at Coburg as the DCI walked away.

'So what do we do now, boss? Go to the dead woman's flat and start digging around?'

'Do we hell!' grated Lomax. 'You saw what happened today. He sent me to the Free French place first knowing I'd be refused entry, so he can come along like the great hero and walk in. He did it deliberately to humiliate me in front of the Frenchies! And he's still trying it on! This business of giving me the job of looking through her papers. He knew full well most of them would be in French. Bastard! Who does he think he is ordering me to go here and there. I'm a bloody detective inspector, for God's sake! We know from before it'll just be another dead end to make me look small.'

'So what will we do?'

'We'll do what we're supposed to do, proper policing. We've got our own caseload. As soon as we pin the killing of Patch Peters on Hooky Morton, that'll be the one all the papers will talk about. One of London's top gangsters, nicked and sent to the gallows, by me. All this penny-ante stuff, a kitchen porter and some French bird killed!' He snorted. 'Let DCI Saxe-bloody-Coburg stumble around in the dark for a bit on his own. We'll come to his rescue soon enough, but once we've got Hooky Morton off the street.'

CHAPTER TWENTY-FOUR

When Coburg arrived back at Scotland Yard he found Lampson in the office.

'You're back,' he said. 'How did it go at the school?'

'Really good,' said Lampson. 'I saw Terry's teacher and she's all for it. She's going to make an announcement that we're having our first meeting tomorrow afternoon. At this stage it'll be just a kickabout and some training, and looking out for the ones worth having in the team.' He added hastily. 'I only chose that because I'm off tomorrow afternoon.'

'I know you are. I do keep a check on the rota.' Coburg and Lampson alternated their Saturday afternoons off.

'How did you get on with the French?' asked Lampson.

'Better than expected, after their initial reluctance to talk to us.' Then he frowned. 'However, there's something wrong there, Sergeant. I feel it in my bones. We need to find out where Yvette Corot was before she moved into the Mayfair flat and started working at Carlton Gardens. But if we find nothing, then it might indicate she only came to England in July.'

'But how could she have when there's no civilian traffic

crossing the Channel, only military?'

'Captain Dupont said people can get across the Channel if they have the right contacts. Secret agents from both sides are doing it all the time, but it's very risky.'

'Maybe she was a secret agent for the French.'

'But if that was the case, why didn't anyone at the Free French offices know about that? No, there's more to her than meets the eye. One thing we did find out – that she and Janos Mila had something in common: they didn't have much in the way of social contacts with their fellow workers. So who did she socialise with? And if no one, why not?'

'So what do you want me to do?'

'I'd like you to go back to Janos's lodgings and talk to everyone in the house and see if you can find out what sort of life he led – any visitors, his friends, his interests. I'll go and poke around at Claridge's, see if I can find anyone there who knows something about him and who might have wanted him dead. Meet me at Claridge's after you've finished.'

Inspector Lomax pushed open the door of the Dark Horse on King's Cross with such force it sent it crashing against a wall.

'Oi!' barked Hooky Morton in protest. 'Careful, that's antique glass in that door, that is!'

Lomax stood with Sergeant Potteridge just inside the doorway, scowling at Morton who was sitting in his usual chair, a motley crew of villains gathered around him who eyed the obviously angry inspector warily. Lomax strode to Morton and looked down at him.

'Antique glass?' he sneered. 'Scum like you wouldn't know what antique is. The only thing you've got that's antique is your missus.'

At this there were definite looks of concern on the faces of Morton's cronies. It was well known that Hooky had married a woman, Lorna, ten years older than him. It had been a marriage of genuine love and affection, not convenience, and Hooky had been known to break the arm of anyone who said anything detrimental about his wife. Morton got to his feet and glared menacingly at Lomax.

'I'd watch your tongue if I were you, Inspector,' he said threateningly.

'Why? What you gonna do?' jeered Lomax. 'Hit me? Do that and I'll have you in so fast your feet won't touch the ground.'

Morton stood, clenching and unclenching his fists, then he managed to say: 'Is there a purpose in your visit, Lomax? Or are you here just to show what a thick, ignorant shit you are?'

Lomax growled and moved towards Morton, fists bunched, but Sergeant Potteridge put a hand on his arm, restraining him.

'Careful, boss,' he murmured.

'No, let him go, Sergeant,' said Morton. 'Then we'll see how big a man he really is.'

'I'll show you how big a man I am, Morton,' snarled Lomax. 'I'm taking you in for the murder of Patch Peters.'

'On what evidence?' demanded Morton.

'On the fact that he was grassing you up to Roly Fitt,' said Lomax.

'You'll have to prove that, Inspector. And I can also tell

171

you that when Patch got shot, I was here, with my business colleagues.' He smirked and shook his head. 'You've got nothing, Lomax.'

'No?' said Lomax angrily. 'Well let's see what you say when I've got you in a cell somewhere tied to a chair.'

'Threats of police brutality?' queried Morton. 'In front of witnesses? Tut-tut, Inspector. That won't do at all.'

And he laughed, as did his cronies.

It was the laugh that did it for Lomax, pushing him over the edge. He'd had a very bad day of it: the humiliation of having the latest murder taken away from him and given to Coburg, being held up to ridicule at that Free French place, and now this scumbag laughing openly at him. Before Potteridge could stop him, Lomax had rushed at Morton and punched him hard in the face, sending him reeling backwards into a table laden with half-filled glasses, which turned over, sending glass and liquid spilling everywhere.

Morton sat among the wreckage, surrounded by broken glass, his clothes saturated with beer and spirits, and glared vengefully at Lomax. A trickle of blood came down from his lips.

'I'm going to have you, Morton!' snarled Lomax. Then he turned and stormed out of the pub, Potteridge following.

'No, I'm gonna have you,' vowed Morton.

CHAPTER TWENTY-FIVE

Questioning the other residents of the house where Janos Mila lived was deeply frustrating for Lampson. There were five other households in the tall house, all of them foreign nationals. A Polish couple with a six-month-old baby lived in two rooms on the ground floor. On the other side of the passage on the ground floor was Josef Malic's room, next to the bathroom and toilet. Lampson checked, but there was still no sign of the Romanian.

On the first floor lived an American writer in his thirties who had come to England just before the war in order to write a novel. 'It's set in England so, of course, I had to come here to get the right feeling for it.' Also on the first floor lived an Irish woman with two young children whose husband had been at Dunkirk but was now classed as 'missing'.

'They say that so the bastards don't have to pay me a war widow's pension,' she told Lampson bitterly. To make ends meet she took in clothes that needed repairing, sewing up torn jackets and shirts and dresses.

On the top floor were two attic rooms. One had been occupied by Janos Mila. The other a Russian woman in her sixties, a refugee from Soviet Russia who claimed to be a member of the Russian Royal Family. 'They will kill me if I go back,' she told Lampson. 'The Communists want to wipe out all traces of the Romanovs.'

He'd heard their individual stories of financial worries, privations, tragedies, but none of them could tell him anything about Janos Mila.

'I never saw him,' was the most usual comment. Along with: 'He was no trouble. He didn't play music or the wireless like some people. He never had people come to visit him. He never got drunk. As far as I know, he went to work and came home.'

No one reported ever seeing him with anyone. To all intents and purposes, Janos Mila had no acquaintances or social contacts outside of work.

Lampson trudged down the steps from the house to the pavement with an overwhelming sense of failure. He'd expected there to be something to give them a clue as to Janos Mila's life, but as far as the house was concerned it was all a dead end.

He was just turning to walk away, when a sixth sense kicked in and he jerked to one side, aware of a sudden movement close behind him. Shocked, he was aware of a knife thrusting close by him, ripping into his jacket. Automatically, he slammed his hand down on the wrist holding the knife, at the same time spinning round, coming face to face with a frightened-looking man in his thirties. The knife had fallen to the pavement. Lampson reached out to grab hold of the man, but the man suddenly kicked out at him, catching him painfully just below the knee. Lampson swore in pain. He tried to move but his leg gave way, and he was forced to just watch as the man turned and ran away.

Lampson scooped up the knife from the pavement and dropped it in his jacket pocket.

Coburg had had a frustrating time at Claridge's, failing to find anyone who could give him any insight into the social life or interests of Janos Mila. He'd started with Alexandru Hagi, but got the same story from him as previously: he only knew Mila from working with him in the kitchens. There was no time for social chit-chat, it was all work work work. And even when they'd taken their breaks, Janos hadn't talked, except about work. He'd never told Alexandru where in Romania he came from, and he'd expressed no interest when Alexandru had started to talk about his own family.

Coburg had then moved on to everyone else in the kitchens, from the chefs downwards. Most of them said they'd never exchanged more than a basic greeting, hello or goodnight, with Mila. It wasn't that he'd been unfriendly, he just hadn't been friendly. The general consensus was that he was a private man. He didn't talk about himself and seemed to have no friends or interests outside of work.

Coburg then tried the rest of the hotel staff – waiters, chambermaids – but none of them even knew who Janos Mila was.

It was as he was coming up the stairs from the sluice, where he'd been quizzing some of the laundry staff – again, with no result – that he was approached by a young woman in her late twenties.

'Excuse me. Are you the detective investigating the murder here?'

At last! thought Coburg. Someone who knows something!

'I am, madam. Detective Chief Inspector Coburg. Do

175

you have information that may be of help?'

'Possibly. I was wondering if it might be connected with a man who's staying here. He killed my brother, Ronald.'

'Killed him?'

She nodded.

Coburg looked up the stairs towards the reception lobby, then said: 'It might be better if we continued this somewhere more private, Mrs . . . ?'

'Farnsworth. Mrs Linda Farnsworth. My brother was Ronald Kemp.'

Coburg led her up the stairs and into the reception area. He approached Georges LeGrosse at his concierge's desk and asked if there was an office or a room he could borrow for a few moments. 'This young lady has information that could be of value.'

'Of course,' said Georges. 'Please, use my office.'

Coburg led Linda Farnsworth towards Georges LeGrosse's small but very well-ordered office just off the main reception.

'You say this man killed your brother?'

'Yes, and I thought there might be a connection with the murdered kitchen porter.'

'Why?'

'If I tell you what happened, I'm hoping you'll see. There's a man claiming to be a titled person who's staying here at Claridge's. He's selling army commissions to young men who want to join the army and fight in the war as officers. I have to admit, when Ronald told me about it I had my doubts, but Ronald was so excited. He said the man was called Julian, and had contacts at the top level of the military. The man told him it would cost £600 because there were lots of people to be paid, but at the end he would be a commissioned officer.'

'And your brother paid?'

'He did, but because he didn't have the funds himself, he borrowed it from a friend of his. But as time went by and nothing happened, he became suspicious. And then this Julian told him that he'd been let down by certain people, they hadn't come through as they'd promised and there was no chance of getting his money back.

'Ronald was desperate. He said he was going to sue to recover his money, but this Julian warned him against that. He said that as it would involve naming and shaming some of the hitherto most respected figures in the military it was unlikely his case would succeed. And such a case being mounted would lead to awful publicity for Ronald. He'd be depicted in the press as someone using his name and money to gain an unfair advantage over other brave young men eager to sign on and go through the regular channels.

'It was then that Ronald realised he'd been cheated. The shame at what had happened, how stupid he'd been, and how he would be letting his friend down, it was all too much for him. He killed himself.'

'So this Julian didn't actually kill him.'

'As good as. He was responsible. He should at least be charged with fraud. If he did this to my brother, he must be doing it to other young men, taking money for commissions he can't supply. Those other young men may be able to afford losing that kind of money, Ronald couldn't.'

'Did your brother tell you this man's name?'

'No, just that he was called Julian and that he had a title and he seemed to know top people inside the military.'

'And he was staying here, at Claridge's?'

'Yes. Ronald said he had a suite here in the hotel. It occurred to me that perhaps this man who was murdered found out who he was and what he was doing, and perhaps was blackmailing him; so this Julian killed him.'

'Forgive my asking, but why did your brother feel it necessary to arrange some kind of private purchase of a commission? It must have struck him that something underhand was going on. Why didn't he simply enlist?'

She gave a sad smile of weary resignation. 'Ronald had an image of the person he wanted to be. A hero. In command. The trouble was he was terribly short-sighted. He had attempted to get on to the officer's pathway, or whatever they call it, but he'd been turned down because of his eyes. This Julian had told him he could fix it. Grease the right palms and anything was possible.' She gave Coburg a look of heartfelt appeal: 'I know nothing you can do will bring Ronald back, but if you could arrest this man and put him away, I'd feel some sort of justice has been done. At least it would stop other young men being caught the same way.'

'I'll see what I can do, Mrs Farnsworth. I assume you're not staying here?'

'No, too expensive for me. Unlike Ronald, I do my best to live within my means.' She produced a visiting card which she gave Coburg. 'This is my address and telephone number.'

'Thank you,' said Coburg. In return, he gave her one of his cards. 'You can usually find me at Scotland Yard. If I'm not there, ask for Detective Sergeant Lampson.' He stood up. 'And now, I must resume my enquiries, but I do promise you we'll do our best to get justice for your brother.'

CHAPTER TWENTY-SIX

Once Mrs Farnsworth had left the hotel, Coburg went to the reception desk. He waited while LeGrosse dealt with a guest, then moved to talk to the concierge, keeping his voice low.

'I'm afraid an allegation has been made against one of your guests, Georges.'

'An allegation, Mr Coburg? Concerning what?'

'It seems to be some sort of financial fraud.'

'Who is the guest who's accused?'

'That's what I'm trying to find out. All I know is his name is Julian, he is apparently titled, and he is said to have connections to top military figures; although this last may be false. Oh, and he has a suite, not a room.'

The concierge took his list of current guests and began to go through it.

'There are four Julians with a title and a suite. Lord Julian Danley, the Honourable Julian Huxtable, Julian Porter, Duke of Maxwell, and Sir Julian Braithwaite, a baronet.'

'Out of those four, can you imagine any of them selling commissions in the armed services to eager young men?'

A slight smile crossed LeGrosse's face.

'As you know, Mr Coburg, in my position it is never

done to pass on information about a guest. However . . .'
He stopped and he turned the register, opened at a page, so that it was facing Coburg, and his index finger hovered over the name Julian Braithwaite. 'Let us say that I had begun to think that the young men who came to this desk asking for Sir Julian, who were always allowed up to his suite, were calling for a different purpose.'

'I can imagine,' said Coburg, returning the smile.

'You mentioned a possible fraud,' said LeGrosse.

'That is what has been alleged.'

'It would be most unfortunate if our hotel was caught up in any unsavoury publicity,' said LeGrosse, his face showing his concern. 'Mr D'Oyly Carte would be extremely upset if he felt I was in any way responsible.'

'I can assure you he will not even consider that. In fact, I will tell him that an allegation was made to me by someone outside the hotel, which is true, and I was forced to order the security forces to install a listening device in his suite, but I did so without informing anyone in the hotel in order to ensure that secrecy was guaranteed. So we have not had this conversation.'

'What conversation?' asked LeGrosse blandly.

Coburg smiled.

'It's possible that an electrician may arrive later today following reports of a flickering light bulb in one of your suites. It was reported by someone outside who saw it flickering and was worried it might be someone sending signals to the enemy.'

'I will ensure that when your electrician arrives, he is admitted to the suite to fix the offending article,' said LeGrosse.

'Out of curiosity, is the room next to Sir Julian's occupied?'

LeGrosse checked. 'No, sir.'

'Good. In that case, I will be sending two of my plain-clothes officers to take up residency here for a couple of days. I would be grateful if they could be accommodated in that room.'

LeGrosse made an entry in the register.

'Consider that done, sir.'

'Thank you, Georges.'

Coburg was moving away from the reception desk when he saw Lampson enter through the main entrance. The unhappy expression on his sergeant's face told him that all had not gone well.

'So, Ted, I assume you came away empty-handed.'

'I came away with something,' scowled Lampson. He showed Coburg where the knife had ripped his jacket.

'What on earth happened?' asked Coburg, alarmed.

Lampson pulled the knife from his pocket. 'This,' he said. 'I was just walking away from the house when some bloke had a go at me with a knife. Luckily, I dodged. If I hadn't, I'd be on a mortuary slab.'

'Did you see who did it?'

Lampson nodded. 'No one I recognised. He was in his thirties. Scrawny. Nothing special about his clothes, they looked old and worn.'

'Nationality?'

'No idea. He could be English, but there's so many foreigners in that area he could have been anything. Polish. Romanian. He didn't say anything. The knife's English, but that don't mean much. I can only think he did it because I was asking questions about Mila.'

'If it was our killer, I'd have expected him to garrotte you.'

'To be honest, guv, he looked a bit feeble. Garrotting takes speed and skill. Drop the wire over and pull tight quick. He didn't look the type.'

'Maybe it's not connected with our killer?'

'What else? It's the only big case we're working on where if we catch them, they'll hang.'

'True,' admitted Coburg. 'Did he have gloves on? Your attacker?'

'No.'

'Then we'll get the knife to the Yard and have it checked for fingerprints. If we're lucky it might turn out to be someone in the files. And I need to get back to the Yard to arrange for some listening equipment to be installed.'

'Where?'

Coburg waved a hand airily at the reception area. 'Here,' he said.

As he led the way out of the hotel and towards the car, he filled Lampson in on the story he'd been told by Mrs Farnsworth. 'We've got a con-artist operating in Claridge's. Name of Sir Julian Braithwaite, Bart.'

'Bart?'

'Baronet. Or, so he claims, although I have no reason to doubt he is who he says he is. There are as many crooks in the pages of Debrett's as there are in the boozers of Wapping.'

'What's his con?'

'He passes the word around wealthy young men – or, at least, those with access to money – that those who've been unsuccessful in getting into the armed forces in officer rank for whatever reason, bad eyesight, a prison record, for example, can still gain entry for a certain sum. I've been told the going rate is six hundred pounds.'

'Six hundred quid! To get in the army!'

'As an officer, Sergeant. Without all the bother of exams and boards.'

They got in the car and Coburg started it up, as Lampson asked: 'What does he do? Bribe the examining boards?'

'As far as I can make out, he tells the applicants that's what he's going to do, but instead he just pockets the money and keeps them dangling on a string, until he's forced to tell them it won't be happening.'

'At which point they demand their money back, obviously.'

'And Sir Julian tells them, sadly, that it's all gone, paid to people who promised him everything would be fine, but who have reneged on that promise and absconded with their money. He tells the unfortunate young man that he can always sue to try to recover his money, but that as it would involve naming and shaming some of the hitherto most respected figures in the military it is unlikely his case would succeed. And such a case being mounted would lead to awful publicity for the young man, where he would be depicted in the press as someone using his name and money to gain an unfair advantage over other brave young men eager to sign on and go through the regular channels.'

'What a bastard!' snorted Lampson indignantly.

'I agree,' said Coburg. 'Which is why we're going to put a stop to his activities. I've arranged for a listening device to be placed in Sir Julian's suite, with a couple of our men in the room next door who'll take down everything that's said when the next young man arrives to discuss the arrangements with the rather bent baronet.'

Lampson gave another snort of derision. 'It could be weeks before another pigeon turns up.'

'It could, but such a young man will be in contact with Sir Julian tomorrow.'

'Who?'

'The son of a friend of mine. He's been unable to get into the army as an officer through the usual route because of some previous trouble.'

'What sort of trouble?'

'Prison, I think.'

Lampson looked doubtful.

'It could be seen as entrapment, guv.'

'And it will be, but once I get Sir Julian in a room and tell him what his options are, I'm fairly sure he'll want to make a clean breast of his activities.'

When they got to Scotland Yard, Lampson took the knife to the forensics department to be checked for fingerprints, and for those fingerprints to be checked against the files, while Coburg made arrangements for listening equipment to be installed surreptitiously in Sir Julian Braithwaite's suite. He also arranged for two detective constables to take up residency in the room adjoining Braithwaite's suite. The two detective constables, Peter Wemyss and Eric Arkwright, listened attentively as Coburg outlined what he wanted them to do.

'Are either of you any good at shorthand?' he asked.

'I am, sir,' said DC Wemyss. 'I was considering a career in newspapers, so I did shorthand and typing at night school.'

'He was the only male in a class of women,' grinned DC Arkwright.

'An advantage in getting to know members of the fair

sex, I imagine,' smiled Coburg.

'True, sir,' said Wemyss. 'I met my fiancée there.'

'Well for the next few days you will be staying at Claridge's, sharing a room. Your job is to transcribe any conversations the man in the next room, Sir Julian Braithwaite, has.'

'All conversations, sir?'

'Just those when someone is visiting him. I'll be arranging for a young man to visit him sometime tomorrow.'

Arkenshaw looked uncomfortable. 'When you say, a young man . . . ?' he asked awkwardly.

'It's all right, Constable, I'm not asking you to listen to two men engaged in sexual activity. This is about a suspected fraud. We suspect that Sir Julian Braithwaite is selling commissions in the armed forces, commissions which he cannot fulfil.'

'The bastard!' burst out Wemyss. 'He's taking advantage of people's patriotism.'

'That's the allegation, Constable. I look to you two to get the proof. Although it shouldn't start until tomorrow, I suggest you take occupancy this afternoon, and use that time to get used to the equipment, and to practise your shorthand.' He handed them a slip of paper with his home telephone number on it. 'If anything happens that requires my assistance, ring me at home. While you go home and pack, I shall telephone Georges LeGrosse the concierge at Claridge's and give him your names.'

'Thank you, sir,' they both said. As they left his office, Coburg heard Arkwright murmur excitedly to Wemyss: 'We're going to be staying at Claridge's!'

Coburg was just going through the reports he and

185

Lampson had made on their investigation into the murder of Janos Mila when the door opened and Sergeant Lampson entered. He had a broad smile on his face.

'Got him, guv!' he announced. 'The prints on the knife. According to records they belong to a bloke called George Wiggins, a very minor criminal. All small-time. Petty theft, vagrancy, nothing big.'

'So why would he want to kill you?' asked Coburg.

'I thought I'd go along to his address and ask him,' said Lampson.

Coburg got to his feet.

'Not without me, you don't,' he said firmly. 'If he tried to kill you once, he might try again.'

CHAPTER TWENTY-SEVEN

Sir Julian Braithwaite frowned when he heard the knock on the door of his suite. He wasn't expecting anyone. There was a prospect he was lining up, a young man from a titled family who unfortunately was forced to wear a calliper on one of his legs due to a childhood illness, which had so far prevented him from going through the usual channels to get a commission in the armed forces. Braithwaite had heard about this unfortunate young man and his ambition and had decided to seek him out when the time was right. He knew the clubs the young man was a member of, and his plan was to pop in casually one day when he knew the young man was there. They'd get into cheerful conversation, with Braithwaite mentioning his time in the navy, and Braithwaite was confident things would move on from there. But, at this immediate moment, he didn't have anyone on his hook.

The knock came again, more insistent this time, and he opened the door to find a man wearing overalls and with a toolbox in one hand. His other hand gripped a tall standard lamp.

'Maintenance,' said the man. 'We've had reports of a lamp flickering.'

Braithwaite looked at the man, puzzled. 'I never reported any lamp flickering.'

'No, the report came from someone in the building opposite. It took us ages to work out which room she was talking about.'

Again, Braithwaite gave him a puzzled look. 'There's nothing wrong with the lamp,' he said. 'I was reading by it yesterday evening with no trouble.'

'That often happens,' said the maintenance man. 'Intermittent fault. They're the worst to correct. This one will do you while we check it out.'

'Is that really necessary?'

The man looked shocked.

'It's vital!' he said. 'There's a war on. Flickering lights that go on and off could be thought of as signals to the enemy. You don't want the police and Special Branch knocking on your door.'

'No, absolutely not,' agreed Braithwaite. He gestured at the standard lamp. 'By all means, change it.'

George Wiggins lived in a small terraced house, the street door opening directly into the tiny living room. He opened the front door to the knock and looked inquisitively at Coburg on his doorstep. Then his face changed to one of fear when he saw Lampson behind the detective chief inspector and he turned and ran for the back of the house, but Coburg was too quick for him. He grabbed Wiggins by the shoulder and hauled him back.

'Guilty conscience, Mr Wiggins?' he asked. He led him to an armchair and pushed him gently down onto it. All the time Wiggins looked at the bulky Lampson with a mixture of panic and loathing.

'I'm DCI Coburg from Scotland Yard. I believe you already know my sergeant, Sergeant Lampson, as you tried to kill him earlier today.'

'I didn't!' burst out Wiggins.

'We have the knife you used,' said Coburg. 'You should have worn gloves, Mr Wiggins. As it is, your fingerprints were all over it. Attempted murder, assault with a deadly weapon. Not to mention the damage to my sergeant's jacket. You'll be going away for quite a few years. Is there anyone you want us to contact after we've taken you in? Family?'

'The only family I had is dead, and he killed her!' exclaimed Wiggins suddenly, pointing angrily at Lampson.

Lampson stared at Wiggins, bewildered. 'What are you talking about? I ain't killed anyone!'

'You killed my sister, Joanne!' raged Wiggins, and now he pushed himself up from the armchair and leant towards Lampson, his face contorted in anger.

'Joanne Nicholson?' asked Coburg. 'She was your sister?'

'She was.'

'She killed herself,' said Lampson. 'In her cell.'

'Only after you bullied her and had her locked up!'

'I never bullied her!' protested Lampson. 'The exact opposite. I tried to offer her a way out. I told her we'd arrange for a good lawyer for her, and it wouldn't be a charge of murder. At worst it would be manslaughter, and we'd make sure the court knew it was self-defence from that pig of a husband of hers.'

'Sergeant Lampson is telling you the truth,' confirmed Coburg. 'There was no bullying. He did everything possible to try and ensure she was freed once she came to trial.' Then

189

Coburg said, his face grim: 'If you were so upset about your sister, why didn't you protect her from her brute of a husband? You must have known he was beating her black and blue. And it had been going on for years.'

Wiggins dropped back into the armchair, hanging his head and mumbling something.

'What?' demanded Coburg.

Wiggins looked up at them, shame and embarrassment on his face.

'Because I was scared of him. Eric wasn't the sort of bloke you faced down.'

'So instead you decided to kill the one person who'd shown her compassion and was trying to get her freedom.'

'I didn't know that!' shouted Wiggins defensively.

'Well, you do now,' said Coburg curtly. 'George Wiggins, I am arresting you on a charge of the attempted murder of Sergeant Edward Lampson. You don't have to say anything, but anything you do say will be noted down and may be used in evidence. Now get your coat.' He turned to Lampson. 'Handcuff him, Sergeant. I don't want him causing mayhem in the car.'

Detective Constables Wemyss and Arkwright watched, curious, as the men in overalls set about installing a wooden box containing a wireless receiver on the table in their room at Claridge's.

'This will pick up everything that's said or done in the suite next door,' said the one in charge. He pointed at a row of switches on the front of the wireless receiver. 'They're going to be set to be on, all the time,' he said. 'Don't tinker with 'em.' He pointed to a speaker, which had a knob next

190

to it. 'That's where the sound comes out. If someone starts shouting right next to the microphone we've put in there, turn the knob to lower the volume. Luckily the walls between the rooms at this hotel are nice and thick, but we don't want to take the chance of someone next door hearing their own voice.' He put out a finger and flicked the switches to 'on'. Immediately, they heard the sound of Sir Julian Braithwaite humming a tune. The engineer turned the knob, lowering the volume. 'That should be about right,' he said. 'If he moves too far away from the microphone, turn it up so you can hear him. You can always lower it again later.'

The men put their tools and other pieces of equipment in cases. The man in charge looked around the room, sounding impressed as he commented: 'You blokes have landed on your feet with this one. Comfortable surroundings. The best food in London. We had one lately where we were in a freezing rat-infested shed by the Thames for three days, and we got nothing. The bloke wasn't even there.'

'We all got stinking colds,' put in another, his face unhappy at the memory. He, too, looked enviously around the luxurious room. 'You lucky bastards!'

After they'd booked Wiggins into a custody cell at Scotland Yard, Coburg told Lampson his duty was over for the day.

'Grab some time with Terry,' he advised.

'Thanks, guv, I will,' said Lampson.

After Lampson had gone, Coburg picked up the phone and asked the switchboard to get him a number of an old friend of his in Kensington, Ian Anderson, a former comrade-in-arms of his.

'Edgar!' boomed Anderson when he heard Coburg's

voice. 'Long time no see!'

'Unfortunately,' said Coburg apologetically. 'The two curses, war and work, have interfered with everything.'

'Not everything,' said Anderson. 'I saw in the paper you got married. Rosa Weeks, the jazz singer. Lucky man!'

'I am indeed,' said Coburg. 'Actually, Ian, I'm phoning to ask a favour.'

'Of course you are!' chuckled Anderson. 'What is it? Ask and it shall be given.'

'It's not you so much as your son, Martin, I'm hoping will be able to help me.'

Martin Anderson was twenty and an actor who'd appeared in a couple of films, as well as onstage. And a very good actor, Coburg had thought when he'd seen him on the screen.

'It's an unofficial acting job, although Scotland Yard are happy to pay him for it.'

'Scotland Yard? What is it, some kind of re-enactment where he plays a criminal?'

'No, simpler than that. I'd like him to visit someone we've got our eye on. This man is staying at Claridge's and we have reason to believe he's illegally selling fake army commissions to young men who want to join up as officers, but can't get through the regular system because of personal issues.'

'Bad cheques. Fornication with a superior's wife. Robbery.'

'That sort of thing,' said Coburg. 'What I'd like Martin to do, if he agrees, is to phone this man and arrange to go and see him at his suite in Claridge's sometime tomorrow. I'd like him to pretend to be someone who is desperate to become an officer, but can't because of some issues in his past. A term in prison, for example. The man will say he can fix it, for a price. I'd like Martin to agree and say he'll sort out the money, and fix up to see him later to make arrangements. Do you think he'd do that?'

'He'd love it!' boomed Anderson.

'In that case, if he can make an appointment with this man – his name is Sir Julian Braithwaite – for some time around eleven tomorrow, I'll alert my men who will be listening in to be ready.' Coburg gave Anderson the telephone number of Claridge's, along with the suite number where Braithwaite was staying. 'Thanks, Ian. I appreciate this a great deal.'

'Selling fake commissions,' growled Anderson. 'The man deserves to go away for a good, long time.'

Arnold Lomax checked his watch as he got off the bus. Half past six. He'd be home in ten minutes. He wondered what Muriel had prepared for their evening meal. She was amazing, his wife, how she produced such good, tasty meals in spite of rationing. There wasn't much meat to be had at the butchers, but she was always able to make a little go a long way. People talked about stretching sausages, well his Muriel could stretch them better than anyone else he knew, and they still looked plump when they were on his plate.

Lately, Muriel had started to suggest he should apply for an official police car. She was worried because of all the reports lately of buses being hit by bombs. He pointed out that if a bomb came down on a road full of traffic, it didn't matter if you were in a bus or a car.

Another, more practical, reason, which Muriel was perfectly well aware of, was that he couldn't drive. When he was growing up, cars were a novelty for the rich. Living in central London as he did, there'd been no need to learn to drive. Buses were plentiful, and there was always the Tube. For the moment, he was happy being driven by his sergeant, Joe Potteridge, when they were going anywhere on official police business. Joe had learnt to drive when he was in the army, like many other working-class men of his age.

The other thing was that he felt it wasn't right for police officers to be driving official cars around on private business. People like DCI Saxe-bloody-Coburg. Yes, he'd had his own car, which he drove around in at the start of the war, a Bentley, but official sanctions on private vehicles being used for official purposes had put a stop to that. So instead, Coburg had snaffled himself a police car for his own use. It wasn't fair

But then, nothing in this life was fair. The people at the top, the Saxe-Coburgs with their public school backgrounds and their money, had one sort of life, while the less well-off, people like Arnold and his wife Muriel, had to make do and mend.

I bet Coburg isn't sitting down to stretched sausages this evening, he thought angrily. Some posh restaurant where expense is no object.

He heard a car door shut, then felt rather than saw a movement just behind him, and something hard jabbed into his back.

'What's going on?' he demanded, startled.

'You're the detective, you work it out,' grated a voice.

Then the gun went off, the sound only partially muffled by being pressed against his body, and Lomax tumbled to the pavement.

CHAPTER TWENTY-EIGHT

Saturday 19th October

Rosa put the two bowls of porridge on the table.

'I thought we'd have porridge every other day for breakfast, and ration the sausages and bacon,' she said. 'According to our local butcher, things are going to get more difficult.'

'I'm very happy with porridge,' said Coburg. 'Have you got your programme worked out for tomorrow night?'

'I have,' she said. 'I thought I'd go to Claridge's after I've finished ambulance duty and have another practice on their piano.'

'An excellent idea,' said Coburg.

Rosa watched him spooning up his porridge for a short while, then said: 'You look particularly thoughtful this morning.'

'I am,' admitted Coburg. 'Remember I told you about the murder at Claridge's?'

'The man in the kitchen who was strangled.'

'To be exact, garrotted. Someone dropped a noose of thin wire around his neck and pulled it tight.'

Rosa shuddered. 'How awful!'

'And yesterday we had an identical killing, this one a woman who worked for the Free French at their London

HQ. She was killed in her own flat in Mayfair. Same method, by all accounts. A garrotte made of thin wire.'

'So, the same killer?'

'I hope so. I'd hate to think there were more than one going around doing this.' He hesitated, then said: 'I've brought Inspector Lomax in to work on the investigation with me.'

'Inspector Lomax?!' she said, indignant. 'The one who tried to get you sacked? Who made up those lies about you?'

Coburg nodded. 'The fact is, he got the initial shout on both victims, but just like as with the first victim, this latest was taken away from him and given to me.'

'No wonder he hates you.'

'It's not my fault!' Coburg said defensively. 'It's the people at the top making these decisions. Anyway, it was Ted who suggested I bring Lomax in. He said it would be a good way to keep an eye on him and stop him messing up the investigation to try and make me look bad.'

'That's good thinking,' said Rosa approvingly. 'Your sergeant's very clever. By the way, I've been thinking about something as well.'

He looked at her quizzically, and she asked him: 'How would you feel if I decided to train as a nurse?'

He frowned, doubtful. 'What about your singing career?'

'I love doing that, but who knows how long it will last?'

'For ever,' said Coburg. 'You're good. People want to hear you. Look at someone like Bing Crosby. He's been around for ever, but there's no talk of him retiring.'

'It's not just that,' said Rosa. 'Ideally, I'd like to be a doctor . . .'

'A doctor?' echoed Coburg, bewildered.

'Why not? The thing is it would take about ten years of study to get qualified. Mr Warren suggested nursing because it takes about two or three years, depending whether you go for state-registered or state-enrolled. But it's a way in.'

Coburg nodded, his expression he hoped showing approval. But inside he had major doubts about this idea of Rosa's. It sounded like a whim, but he didn't want to say that at this stage. Instead, he used Chesney Warren to change the subject.

'Talking of Mr Warren, has he said anything more about the concert he wants you to do?'

'He's suggested a week today, next Saturday, in the afternoon. He says there's more chance of getting a reasonable audience.'

'Makes sense,' nodded Coburg. 'And fortunately, next Saturday afternoon is my half day off, so I'll be there.' He finished his porridge and took his bowl to the sink to rinse it. 'Can I give you a lift this morning?' he asked.

'Yes, please,' said Rosa. 'At least I know I'll get there on time. Sometimes the buses have to find alternative routes because of bomb craters.'

After Coburg had dropped Rosa off at Paddington, he made for Somers Town where Ted Lampson was waiting.

'I thought we'd go to the Middlesex Hospital first and take a look at Yvette Corot's body,' he told Lampson as his sergeant slid behind the steering wheel.

'I thought Lomax had already done that, guv.'

'He has, but I like to take a look myself.'

'In case he's missed something?'

197

'Let's say it's a double-check.'

As they made their way down Tottenham Court Road, Lampson said: 'I'm not sure about putting Wiggins on trial.'

'Why? He tried to kill you,' said Coburg.

'Yeh, but he was upset about his sister.'

'Not upset enough to do anything to stop her from being beaten regularly by her husband. And it was only good luck that you weren't killed by him.'

'It wasn't luck, it was me dodging.'

'It was luck you were aware of a movement that made you dodge.' He shook his head. 'No, Ted, he's going to trial. I'm not having someone who almost killed my sergeant walking around free. The next time he loses his temper with someone over something, they might not be so lucky. Some time in jail should help him learn his lesson.'

Their visit to the Middlesex Hospital mortuary was brief. Coburg wanted to examine the marks on Yvette Corot's neck and compare them with those they'd observed on Janos Mila. They were the same, caused by the same thin wire.

'So what is the common point between a kitchen porter at Claridge's and a clerk working for the Free French in London?' asked Coburg as they walked back to their car.

'They're both foreigners,' said Lampson.

'So are a quarter of the people in London at this moment,' sighed Coburg.

They returned to Scotland Yard and found Detective Constable Arkwright waiting to see Coburg.

'I thought you'd like to see this, sir,' he said excitedly, brandishing a few handwritten sheets of paper. 'It's a transcript of a conversation the target had with a visitor yesterday evening.'

Coburg frowned, puzzled.

'It must be another mark,' he said. 'I've arranged for a young man to visit Sir Julian about eleven this morning. Unless he went to see him earlier.'

'No, this is about something completely different, as you'll see from the transcript. It was a man called Hooky Morton. Isn't he a gangster, sir?'

'He is indeed, Constable.'

Arkwright looked at his watch. 'I'd better leave the transcript with you and get back to Claridge's if your young man is arriving at eleven.' He gestured at the handwritten pages. 'We haven't had time to type it up yet. I wanted to get it to you straight away.'

'And this is exactly what was said?'

'Word for word. DC Wemyss is brilliant at shorthand. He wrote it down as they spoke, then he read it to me and I put it down in longhand.'

'Excellent work, Constable.'

Once the young detective constable had left, Coburg read through the transcript, passing each sheet to Lampson as he finished them. It made for interesting reading. Although there was no indication of the manner in which Morton and Braithwaite had spoken to one another, the words spelt out the tension between the two men: Morton angry and aggressive, Braithwaite defensive.

M: Now you listen here, Braithwaite, I don't like people who short-change me. Try to fiddle me. When that happens, I get upset, and when I get upset bad things happen to people.

B: I have no idea what you're talking about.

M: Oh no? Well I've been looking at the books, and what you say you've collected from your people is different to what they say they've paid.

B: Have you been checking up on me with my friends?

M: To you they may be friends, to me they're business associates and you're just the intermediary.

B: Now look here—

M: No, you look here!

B: (Yelp of pain.)

M: We got an agreement, you and I. Your rich mates get deliveries of petrol and diesel with no ration problems, but it comes at a price. Because you know 'em I agreed you'd collect the money from them. It saves me doing it and solves the problem of either them not being there when my drivers turn up, or them not having the money at that time to pay. And for that you get a collection fee: two quid for every customer you collect from. Very generous, in my book. But you've been getting greedy.

B: Now look here, Hooky—

(Sound of a slap. Cry of pain from Braithwaite.)

M: Mr Morton to you, you thieving scum. My drivers make a note of exactly how much they deliver to every customer. When I noticed that some of your customers seemed to be paying less than what they'd had delivered, I sent out one of my blokes to double-check with a couple of them. Because I didn't want to upset the applecart and have them wondering, I got my bloke to simply ask them if they were happy with the product and the service, all very amenable. And then my blokes asked them what price they were paying because we were looking to maybe introduce a discount system depending on the amount they took, which could save them money. Well, there's nothing like offering someone the chance to save money to get them talking. And they confirmed what I'd already spotted, that you weren't content with my very generous two quid a customer, you were skimming off your own take on the money you collected.

B: I swear, Mr Morton, it only happened twice.

M: Ten times. I've got the figures. Do you think I'm a mug?

(Sound of punch. Cry of pain.)

M: I want it back, Braithwaite. Every penny. And if I don't get it from you, I'll have it in kind. A finger here, a finger there until you've repaid it. And if you still don't turn up with the money by the time you've run out of fingers, then you're dead.

Morton added: And I'm not joking. I've recently had to deal very severely with a couple of people who thought they could mess me around. Bear that in mind.

'Well, we set a trap for one criminal and it looks like we've netted an even bigger one in Hooky Morton,' said Coburg.

'It would be great to take him off the streets,' agreed Lampson. 'For a long time he's been able to get away with it because everyone's too scared to give evidence against him. Do you think this bloke Braithwaite might?'

'Somehow I doubt that,' said Coburg. 'But we might be able to pressurise him to get Morton to incriminate himself more.'

They were interrupted by the phone ringing. Lampson picked it up.

'DCI Coburg's office.'

'Switchboard here,' said a voice. 'There's a Mrs Farnsworth calling for DCI Coburg.'

Lampson looked at Coburg. 'A Mrs Farnsworth calling for you?'

Coburg took the receiver.

'DCI Coburg,' he said. 'Put Mrs Farnsworth through.'

A second later he heard Linda Farnsworth's voice. 'I'm sorry to trouble you, Chief Inspector, but as I hadn't heard from you, I wondered if there was any news.'

'There is, Mrs Farnsworth. We've identified the man who you claim defrauded your brother . . .'

'He did defraud him,' she said firmly. 'It's not a claim.'

'No, I know, but legally we can't say that until we have the evidence we need. At the moment we have him under observation.'

'Until when?' she asked, obviously impatient.

'Until such time as we are able to move against him.'

There was a pause, then she asked plaintively: 'At least can you tell me who this man is? I deserve to know that, at least.'

Coburg hesitated before saying: 'His name's Sir Julian Braithwaite. And I can assure you he is under constant observation.'

'He should be under arrest!' she said, her voice full of despair.

'He will be once our enquiries are complete. I promise you, as soon as we have anything concrete I shall let you know.'

He hung up and went back to his seat.

'The con-artist at Claridge's?' asked Lampson.

'The sister of one of his victims,' said Coburg. 'Hopefully, once we've got firm evidence we can move against him.'

The phone rang again, and once more Lampson picked it up.

'DCI Coburg's office. Sergeant Lampson speaking.'

'Is he there?' came the voice of Superintendent Allison.

'Yes, sir,' said Lampson. He handed the receiver to Coburg. 'It's the superintendent.'

'Yes, sir?' said Coburg.

'Inspector Lomax has been shot dead,' said Allison crisply.

'What? When?'

'Yesterday late afternoon. His body was dumped on a bomb site in King's Cross. It was only discovered this morning. Someone shot him in the back, up close, the bullet went straight into his heart. I'd like you to meet Superintendent Moffatt and Lomax's sergeant, Joe Potteridge, at Mayfair police station. This is a police officer been murdered. We need to move on this straight away.'

CHAPTER TWENTY-NINE

Today Rosa found herself paired with a bubbly, talkative woman in her fifties, Doris Gibbs. Doris was a nurse who worked at Paddington Hospital. 'But I wanted to do more. I'd see these people come in, their bodies broken, and lots of the time they died, and I thought, if I could have got to them earlier they might still be alive.'

'You don't think you're doing too much?' asked Rosa. 'I mean, you're already working at the hospital and here you are doing the same on your day off. And I know you volunteer in the evenings because I've seen you arrive sometimes when I've been leaving.'

'Bless you, no!' chuckled Doris. 'There's a war on and we all have to do as much as we can. Look at the auxiliary fire crews, out every night fighting fires after they've done a full day's work.'

'True,' admitted Rosa.

The two women were sitting in the rest room, waiting for a shout, taking the chance to grab a cup of coffee. On the wall was a poster advertising Rosa's forthcoming concert the following Saturday afternoon. Chesney Warren had obviously got hold of the poster of a previous concert of hers she'd done earlier in the year in Croydon. She recognised the typography, the photograph of her at the piano, and the promotional wording: 'Rosa Weeks, star of stage and radio, with all the songs you love.' The change to it was where a piece of paper had been stuck over where it had previously said 'Bassett Hall, High Street, Croydon' and it gave the venue as St Mary's church hall, Paddington, with the additional information 'all proceeds to St John Ambulance'.

Doris gestured at the poster. 'It's like you, doing this concert. There you are, a famous star, and here we are drinking coffee together, and you're giving up your time on your day off to raise money for St John Ambulance.'

'I don't see myself as a famous star,' said Rosa.

'Plenty of people do, though,' said Doris. 'I saw in the paper you're appearing at Claridge's tomorrow night. They're saying it's already sold out. That sounds famous to me.'

'Yes, but what I'm doing at this concert is nowhere near as important as what you do.'

Doris shook her head. 'Don't you believe it. At times like this, people need entertaining to give 'em a lift. What you do is make 'em feel life's worth living despite all the misery that's going on.'

'But I love doing what I do,' said Rosa. 'It's not hard work, not like you do.'

'Nothing's hard work if you love doing it,' said Doris. 'And I love nursing, and working here. And my kids have all grown up and left home, so I don't have to worry about them. And my husband, Jeff, got killed on the last day of the First War, God rest his soul, so there's only me to think

205

about. So what else am I going to do with my time?'

Chesney Warren appeared in the doorway, holding a piece of paper.

'Building collapsed in Old Marylebone Road,' he said, and handed Doris the piece of paper with the address on it.

'Here we go,' said Doris, putting down her half-drunk cup of coffee, then getting up and heading for the door to the yard and the ambulance.

Collapsed building, thought Rosa as she followed her, and her stomach constricted as she remembered the building collapsing on Derek. Was this going to be another such scene?

The mood at Mayfair police station was deep anger. Not just Superintendent Moffatt and Sergeant Potteridge, but every uniformed officer, the workers in the canteen, everybody associated with the station. One of their own had been killed, brutally shot down and his body dumped unceremoniously.

Coburg and Lampson joined Moffatt and Potteridge in the superintendent's office.

'Is this connected with the joint investigation you and Inspector Lomax are conducting into these garrotting murders, DCI Coburg?' asked Moffatt.

'No, sir. Not in my opinion.'

'Why not?'

'The fact that he was shot, not garrotted. I'm the lead detective on those two murders, so if they wanted to disrupt that investigation, I'd have expected them to target me rather than Inspector Lomax. There's also the fact that Inspector Lomax's body was left in the King's Cross area.

He didn't live there, he lived near Lisson Grove.' He looked at Sergeant Potteridge. 'Did he say anything to you about going to King's Cross, Sergeant?'

'No. He was going home. He always travelled the same route: bus from Mayfair up Edgware Road.'

'So he was either shot on his way home and his body taken to King's Cross; or he was taken to King's Cross and then shot. Why King's Cross?'

'Hooky Morton,' growled Potteridge.

'Apparently, Inspector Lomax had a confrontation with Morton yesterday at his pub in King's Cross,' added Moffatt.

'What sort of confrontation?' Coburg asked Potteridge.

'The body of a small-time crook called Patch Peters was dumped on a bomb site in our area. Peters was part of Morton's crew, but there was talk that he was planning to move to Roly Fitt's outfit, and he'd been giving Fitt inside information about what Morton's mob were up to. Peters was shot. Inspector Lomax reckoned Peter's body had been left where it was found to send a message to Roly Fitt. So he and I went to confront Morton about it.' He hesitated, then said: 'It became a bit heated.'

'How heated? Insults?' asked Coburg.

When Potteridge hesitated, Moffatt came in with: 'Sergeant Potteridge told me the confrontation became physical.'

'A fight?'

'Not so much a fight,' Potteridge admitted. 'Morton made fun of Arnold – Inspector Lomax – and the inspector lost his temper. He'd had a bad day, what with him being upset by the way the Frenchies treated us, and that was like the last straw. He sort of went for Morton.'

'They scuffled?'

'No. The inspector belted Morton one in the face and he went over a table, which was loaded with glasses of beer and spirits.'

'This was in Morton's own pub, the Dark Horse?'

Potteridge nodded.

'In front of his own mob?'

Again, Potteridge nodded.

'There's your answer, Superintendent,' said Coburg. 'Hooky Morton did it. He's always reacted very badly to anyone challenging him, even more so if it's done in public. Punching Morton in his own pub in front of his own gang members and sending him crashing into a table loaded with beer glasses . . .' He looked at Potteridge. 'Was there a lot of mess?'

Potteridge nodded.

'Morton got soaked. And his lip was split.'

'But why leave his body on a bombed site?' asked the superintendent. 'And in King's Cross? He must know that all fingers would point to him. Wouldn't it have made more sense for him to dispose of the inspector's body in the river?'

'Not for Morton. He wants people to know he did it, and that the same will happen to anyone who dares cross him in the same way.'

'Then we arrest him,' said Moffatt.

'We need proof,' said Coburg. 'We need to prove that it was Morton who pulled the trigger. Otherwise, it will be his defence that one of his associates did it without his knowledge.'

'How do we get that proof?'

'For a start we find out where the inspector was either shot or abducted, then we ask questions to see if anyone saw anything. Were there any cars around at that time.'

'I can do that,' said Potteridge. 'I know the route the inspector took. I know which bus stop he got off at to go home. I'll take some men with me, and we'll start tracing the inspector's walk home from the bus stop.'

'We'll do the same with King's Cross,' said Coburg. 'Tell us where the bomb site is that he was found, and what time. We'll talk to people in the area. Sergeant Lampson lives in Somers Town, so he knows the King's Cross area.' He looked at Lampson. 'Is that all right with you?'

'No problem,' said Lampson.

'I assume Mrs Lomax has been told?' asked Coburg.

It was Potteridge who answered. 'I went to tell Muriel myself as soon as we heard the news.'

'She hadn't suspected anything might be wrong when he didn't come home last night?'

Potteridge shook his head. 'She's used to it. The boss was often working late. Sometimes he got into a case and was out all night on it.'

'While Sergeant Potteridge is doing that, and Sergeant Lampson is asking questions in King's Cross, there's another line of enquiry that I'll look into,' said Coburg. 'We've been investigating another case involving fraud at Claridge's, and we put a listening device in the suite being used by our suspect. Quite coincidentally, it picked up a confrontation between our suspect and Hooky Morton when Hooky turned up at Claridge's to threaten him.'

'You're thinking that you might be able to use this suspect to get Morton to trap himself?' asked Moffatt.

'I am,' said Coburg.

'Does this suspect know he was being eavesdropped on?'

'No. But if I can persuade him his life is at risk, I might be able to get him to get Morton talking about Lomax.'

Moffatt nodded thoughtfully, then said: 'Sergeant Potteridge will be doing all he can, but we need a lead officer on the investigation into Inspector Lomax's death. Superintendent Allison has agreed that you will be in overall charge of the case, DCI Coburg. Is that acceptable to you?'

'Very much, sir. But I state here and now that I will bow to Sergeant Potteridge's knowledge of the case. He was Inspector Lomax's closest associate for many years . . .'

'Five years,' put in Potteridge angrily.

'I will pursue the line of enquiry I mentioned, the suspect we've been listening to and see if we can reel Morton in through him. At the same time, I and Sergeant Lampson will be in constant touch with Sergeant Potteridge and with you, Superintendent. The murder of Inspector Lomax has to be top priority.'

CHAPTER THIRTY

Rosa pulled the ambulance to a halt at the kerb beside piles of rubble: heaps of broken bricks, roof tiles, chimney pots, and the debris of shattered windows. The two women jumped down from the cab of the ambulance and ran to where a small group of anxious-looking people were standing beside two unmoving bodies on the ground.

'Were they hit by the building coming down?' asked Doris.

A young woman was kneeling by the bodies and she looked up at them, her face anguished. 'No,' she said. 'They're my mum and dad. We were walking along the street when it came down. Both of 'em have got bad hearts.'

Doris took a stethoscope from her pocket, put it to the man's chest and listened.

'His heart's stopped,' she said. 'Can you do resuscitation?'

'I've practised it, but I've never done it for real,' said Rosa.

'Now's the time,' said Doris. 'You take the man, I'll take the woman.'

While Doris checked the woman's heart and lungs with the stethoscope, Rosa set to work, frantically recalling the training she'd received. Before, they'd practised on dummies. This was a real live person. Well, not alive, she thought bitterly.

After checking the man's tongue wasn't blocking his airway, she knelt down, placing one hand flat on his chest, the other making a fist on top of the flat hand, and began to pump, counting as she did so. Fifteen compressions, rest for two seconds, then another fifteen; then another two-second rest. Check the patient. No response, do it again. And keep doing it until the patient responds.

For how long? Rosa wondered desperately. She'd been pressing and resting for three minutes, and still no response from the man, who lay there, eyes closed, mouth open, unmoving.

Again, she pressed on his chest in the rhythm she'd been taught, fifteen compressions, rest, then compressions again . . .

Suddenly she heard a groan from the man, and then a spluttering sound.

Stop now! she told herself.

She bent down and put her ear to the man's chest. Yes, there it was, a heartbeat!

She went back to the position, hands ready on his chest, her ear now close to his open mouth, listening, ready to resume compressions if his breathing stopped.

'What's happening?' called Doris.

'He's breathing!' Rosa called back. 'I've got a heartbeat.'

'I can't get mine resuscitated,' said Doris. 'Can you take over and see what you can do? I'll keep him stable so we can get him to the hospital.'

Rosa got up, swapping places with Doris and taking over with the woman while Doris took over with the man. He was still unconscious, but breathing, although in a laboured way.

Rosa knelt beside the woman and took up the same position she had beside the man, hands on her chest, and began the compressions. Fifteen, rest, fifteen more, rest again. Her arms and shoulders were aching, but she carried on, sweat blinding her as it came down from her forehead.

'That's it,' said Doris's voice flatly. Rosa looked up at her colleague. 'It's no good, Rosa. She's gone. But he's stable, thanks to you. I'll go and get the stretcher. We'll put them both in the ambulance. I'll ride with them in the back.'

As Doris headed towards the ambulance, the nervous-looking woman approached Rosa.

'My mum's dead, isn't she?' she said.

'She is,' said Rosa, her voice sad. 'I'm sorry.'

'It wasn't your fault,' said the woman. 'She was dead before you came.' She looked at the prone figure of her father, whose chest could now be seen to be rising and falling. 'But you brought him back to life.' And she burst into tears and fell to the ground, sobbing.

CHAPTER THIRTY-ONE

Coburg drove them away from Mayfair police station, ostensibly heading for King's Cross, but after they'd passed Euston Station, Coburg took a left into Somers Town.

'I thought we were going to King's Cross nick, guv,' he said. 'Talk to the people who found Lomax's body. You earmarked me for it.'

'No,' said Coburg, 'I'm going to King's Cross nick. You are going to make proper preparations for this afternoon's football training. It's just gone twelve o'clock. You are officially off duty. I'll see you at the Yard on Monday morning.'

'I'm not sure about this,' said Lampson, concerned. 'Lomax may have been an arsehole, but he was one of ours. We all ought to be looking out for who shot him.'

'We know who shot him,' said Coburg. 'Hooky Morton. It's now a matter of proving it. I'm going to start with King's Cross and see what they've got, which I doubt will be much, and then I'm going to call on Inspector Hibbert at MI5.'

'Why?'

'I want to know if we can get a confession out of Morton through the listening device we've got in Braithwaite's room.'

'Morton's lawyers will contest it, guv,' said Lampson. 'They'll say we made up the stuff.'

'Not if we can get his voice admitting what he did.'

Lampson looked intrigued. 'How?'

'When the Princesses did their broadcast, it was copied by some means and that recording was played later,' responded Coburg. 'Same when the King abdicated. His speech was recorded.'

'You plan to record Hooky Morton admitting he shot Lomax?'

'If it can be done. And, if it can, MI5 are the people who'd know how to do it. At the same time, I'm going to see if Inspector Hibbert can help us find out what Janos Mila and Yvette Corot were up to that caused them to be targeted.'

'You think they might have been spies or something?'

'I know I'm grasping at straws, but I do feel there's something not right about those two.'

He pulled up outside Lampson's house, and they saw that Terry was outside, kicking a ball against the wall.

'See, your striker is already here and eager to play. Have a good afternoon.'

Sergeant Potteridge and two uniformed officers were checking the route Inspector Lomax took to get home once he'd got off his bus. Sergeant Potteridge took the other side to the bus stop, reckoning that there was a greater chance of someone on the opposite side of the road seeing something from their window. The two uniforms canvassed the other side. The first five houses Potteridge knocked at reported hearing a bang of sorts, but none of them had bothered to look out.

'There's a war on,' one man told him. 'There's bangs going on all the bloody time. The last thing anyone should do is go and stand near a window. If a blast goes off all that glass coming in could kill you.'

It was the sixth house that he struck lucky. A Mrs Randall reported that not only had she heard a bang, but she'd looked out of her window.

'It was a sort of bang, but muffled. I thought it was a car backfiring, we get quite a lot of that. My Dave says it's because of the ropey petrol that so many people are using. He says it makes the engine pink. I think that means it goes bang, but I'm not sure. My Dave's a car mechanic, see, so he knows about these things.'

'Did you see anything when you heard it?'

'Well, not then. It was a minute or so after I looked out of the window. I was seeing if our Doreen had got off the bus. She usually arrives home about that time.'

'What time was that?'

'Quarter to six. But she wasn't on that bus, she got a later one cos she had to work a bit later. She's a typist for a firm of solicitors.'

'And when you looked out of the window . . . ?' asked Potteridge patiently.

'There was a car there, just past the bus stop, and two men were lifting a bloke up from the pavement and putting him in it. I reckon he was a pal of theirs and he must have fainted.'

'Did you see the two men who were lifting him up?'

'Not really. They had their backs to me at first, but when they put him in the car, I saw one of them.'

Potteridge took a photo of Hooky Morton from his pocket and showed it to her.

'Might this be the man?'

Mrs Randall took the photo, studied it, and frowned pensively. 'It might be,' she said. 'I didn't see him properly because he had a hat on and the collar of his coat turned up.' She studied the photo again, then shook her head. 'I'm not sure,' she said doubtfully. 'What happened, anyway? Was it an accident?'

'We're investigating the shooting of a man, a police officer.'

'A shooting!' exclaimed the woman, horrified. Hastily she pushed the photo back at Potteridge. 'No!' she said. 'It wasn't him.'

'If you're worried about identifying him, there's no need to be.'

'No,' she said firmly.

'A senior police officer was killed. An honest, decent, hard-working man. He lived round here. Someone shot him and they took his body and dumped it on a bomb site at King's Cross. He was a friend of mine, as well as being my boss.'

'I'm sorry, but I can't help you,' she said, agitated now. 'I didn't see anything.'

'But you said you saw two men lifting another from off the pavement and putting him in a car.'

'I was mistaken,' she said. 'Now, please leave me alone.'

With that, she shut the door. Potteridge knocked at the door, but it remained firmly closed.

At King's Cross police station, Coburg talked to Herbert Proud, the station sergeant who'd received the first report of a body being found on a bomb site.

'It was a shock when I was told he was one of ours. A

217

detective inspector. Arnold Lomax, they said his name was. I never knew him. Let's face it, Mayfair's a far cry from King's Cross. But who'd do that to one of ours?'

'At the moment we're looking into Hooky Morton. I assume you know him?'

Sergeant Proud gave a sour look. 'There's not a copper in and around King's Cross who doesn't know Hooky Morton. Trouble is, we've never been able to nail the bastard for anything. No one's prepared to give evidence against him. If we could catch him red-handed doing something it would be great, but he's too sharp for that.'

'Who found Inspector Lomax's body?'

'Two boys. They were playing on the bomb site, looking for stuff.'

'What sort of stuff?'

'Spent cartridges. Shrapnel. War mementoes. The kids collect 'em and swap 'em with one another.' He opened his ledger and ran his finger down the page. 'Here we are, their names and addresses. I talked to the boys myself.'

'Did they say if they saw anyone leaving the body?'

'No such luck,' said Proud. 'Mind, even if they had done, they wouldn't have said. If Hooky Morton and his mob were involved, people around here stay quiet about them.'

Coburg made a note of the names and address of the boys, thanked the sergeant and left. He had no plans to talk to the boys at this stage, Sergeant Proud had already got all the information from them, and Coburg felt it was more important to follow up his idea of getting Morton to incriminate himself. Accordingly, he headed for Wormwood Scrubs. If anyone would know about covert surveillance it had to be MI5.

Inspector Hibbert was in his office and looking fraught when Coburg entered his office.

'You again,' he complained.

'I'm sorry to disturb you when you're overloaded, but something serious has happened. Detective Inspector Lomax from Mayfair police station has been shot dead.'

Hibbert nodded. 'Yes, I heard. Not the brightest penny in the box, but he was one of ours. We need to catch whoever did it and hang them. Let one get away with it and we'll all be targets. How can I help?'

'We've got our eyes on a north London gangster called Hooky Morton. Do you know him?'

Hibbert shook his head. 'I deal in spies, not gangsters.'

'In the case of Morton, we've got a listening device in the hotel room of someone else we're investigating about a different matter. Yesterday we made a transcript of a conversation our target had with Morton. What I was wondering is: is there a way to get an actual recording of any conversation, not just transcripts?'

Hibbert frowned thoughtfully. 'Not that I know of. At least, not in this country. I've been told that the Germans and the Americans have been working on some sort of covert surveillance equipment, but I don't know how successful it's been. Why don't you have a word with your wife?'

'With Rosa?'

'Yes. She's made records, she's appeared on the wireless. She must know about recordings.'

'That's a good idea,' said Coburg, mentally kicking himself for not having thought of it before. 'The other thing I wanted to see you about are these murders we're investigating.'

'The one at Claridge's and this woman at the Free French HQ?'

'That's them,' said Coburg. He produced Yvette Corot's ID card with her photo on it and put it on Hibbert's desk. 'By all accounts she appeared out of nowhere in London in July and got herself a job working at the Free French offices in London. I can't find any trace of her being in this country before that.'

'That doesn't mean she wasn't. She could have been living anywhere. Bournemouth. Liverpool. Glasgow.'

'And suddenly she gets the urge to work for the Free French?'

'Why not? It takes a while for some people to make that sort of move. Not everyone joined up when the call first went out.'

Coburg shook his head.

'There's something not right about this. If she'd been living somewhere else in the country, you'd expect to find letters from people she knew, but there's no correspondence of any sort in her flat. Nothing personal at all. No address book. Nothing. I've got a suspicion that she just turned up here in London in July and got the flat and at the same time applied to work at the offices of the Free French.'

'Turned up from where?'

'The Continent.'

Hibbert shook his head. 'With the Battle of Britain and the coasts on both sides of the Channel bristling with soldiers and barbed wire, there are no boats or civilian planes.'

'There are small planes and small boats.'

'Covertly,' said Hibbert. 'Are you suggesting the French sent her over?'

'No, because if that was the case the Free French would have been informed. I think she might have been an enemy agent, brought over on a French boat under the command of the Germans.'

Inspector Hibbert looked thoughtful. 'It's possible, but why?'

'To find out what the Free French are up to. You've got a bunch of double agents working for you, haven't you?'

'Everyone's got double agents working for them,' said Hibbert ruefully. 'All you can hope is that they're not triple agents. Espionage is a convoluted business.'

'Can you do me a favour? Can you show these photographs to your double agents, those you've picked up and turned in in the last three months, and see if anyone recognises either of them?'

'Both of them?' asked Hibbert, looking at the photographs.

'Their deaths are connected, I'm sure of that. Both were killed the same way, by garrotting. That smacks of a special agent's technique to me. If I'm right and Yvette Corot was an undercover agent for the Germans, then I think we might find the same is true of Janos Mila.'

'You don't know she was a German agent,' pointed out Hibbert.

'No, but I think I know someone who'll help me make my mind up about that.'

CHAPTER THIRTY-TWO

The football idea hadn't gone badly, thought Lampson, pleased. Twelve boys had turned up, including, Lampson noted, Jake and Jud Purvis. The brothers looked shifty and uncooperative, but seemed to be on their best behaviour. That's because they know I'm a copper, and Miss Bradley is here and she keeps them on a tight rein at school.

The fathers of six of the boys had also turned up, as had the headmaster of the school, the elderly and grim-faced Derek Stern. Stern by name stern by nature, thought Lampson. With the scowling headmaster also present it meant another watchful eye on the Purvis boys helping to keep them in check. Lampson's parents had also come along, delighted to watch their grandson playing football.

Lampson had decided to begin with a match, six-a-side. It would give him a chance to see the boys in action, see who had talent, which ones hogged the ball and which were team players. One of the fathers, Jerry Button, had brought his two sons with him, one who was playing for the same team as Terry, the other on the team with the two Purvis brothers. Lampson had persuaded Jerry Button to act as referee for the game, while he and Miss Bradley were the linesmen. That way there would be no accusations of favouritism by the referee.

Once the game had begun, a small crowd began to gather, curious, and also missing watching football of any type. As the game wore on, the Purvis brothers' innate preference for violence showed itself, with both boys kicking their opponents, tripping them, even punching them when they thought the referee wasn't watching closely enough. But Jerry Button had his eye on them, and despite their angry protests a free kick was awarded against a particularly nasty tackle by Jud, which was brilliantly converted by one of the smallest players on the pitch, and Terry's team led 1-0.

Not all of the players on the Purvis brothers' team shared their malevolence, there were also skilful players in the side, and with ten minutes to go a brilliant shot made the score 1-1.

It was in the final minute of the game, with the scores level, that things changed decisively. Jud Purvis had the ball at his feet and was running at their opponents' goal. Just Terry and the goalkeeper stood between him and the goal. As Terry moved in to tackle Jud, the boy suddenly gave a yelp of pain and fell to the ground, rolling over in apparent agony, clutching his shin.

'He kicked me!' he howled.

No he didn't, thought Lampson angrily. His father was determinedly vocal about it.

'That was a dive!' he shouted. 'Our Terry never touched him!'

Jud Purvis continued rolling about in agony on the ground. Jerry Button looked appealingly at Lampson, and at Miss Bradley. It was obvious that neither Jerry nor Miss

Bradley had spotted the fake 'injury' that Jud Purvis was demonstrating, standing up and then falling over with a cry of pain.

But I can't say what really happened because it would be seen as me being biased on my son's behalf, thought Lampson, so instead he shrugged his shoulders helplessly.

Jerry Button had no option but to point to the penalty spot.

'Rubbish!' shouted Lampson's father, his anger being echoed by his wife who yelled: 'You're a rubbish referee, Jerry Button. You should be sending off that Jud Purvis for faking it!'

Despite their protestations, the ball was placed for the penalty. Instead of Jud taking it because he was still limping about, the penalty was taken by the boy who'd scored the team's earlier goal, and he made certain of this one, his shot evading the helpless goalkeeper's groping hands.

It was 2-1, and Jerry Button blew the whistle for full time.

'We was robbed!' shouted Mrs Lampson, seething.

As the Purvis brothers left the field, Jud – now no longer limping – gave Terry a broad wink as he passed him.

Lampson and his parents went to Terry and saw that he was almost beside himself with rage.

'We were robbed, Dad!' he said. 'You saw it! He dived! I never touched him!'

'Yes, I did,' admitted Lampson, 'but who'd have believed me? Especially as I'm your dad.'

'He's a cheat!' stormed Terry. 'Both of them are cheats. And dirty players. Well, I'm having nothing more to do with either of those Purvis boys. And next time they come knocking for me, you can tell them I said so.'

With that, he stamped off to join the other five members of his team to commiserate with them, accompanied by his grandparents.

'Well, that looked like one angry young man,' said Eve Bradley, coming to join Lampson.

'Furious!' agreed Lampson. 'He says he's never going to have anything to do with the Purvis brothers again.'

Miss Bradley gave a chuckle and a big smile. 'I know I shouldn't be judgemental, Mr Lampson, but that's what I call a good result.'

'Yes,' said Lampson, feeling a surge of relief. 'That really is.'

From Wormwood Scrubs, Coburg drove to the Foreign Office where he found that Sir Vincent Blessington was available.

'DCI Coburg,' Blessington greeted him warmly. 'Was that missive I sent over of assistance in gaining access to Carlton Gardens?' Then his face showed concern as he asked: 'Has another problem occurred? The French can be quite difficult.'

'No, your letter did the trick, and since then the French have been co-operative.'

'Excellent,' beamed Blessington. 'They can be quite touchy. Especially since that unfortunate business at Mers-el-Kébir.'

Blessington was referring to the attack by the Royal Navy on the French naval fleet at Mers-el-Kébir in Oran in which over a thousand French naval personnel were killed and many French ships were sunk. After the French had surrendered to the Germans and Italians in June 1940, the British government had been concerned that the French battleships and destroyers would be used by the Germans. Churchill had asked Admiral Darlan, the commander of the French navy, to move the fleet to the French West Indies so it would be out of the German's reach; but Darlan refused. So, in July, the Royal Navy attacked the French fleet, destroying it.

For many French people, this meant the British were their enemy. In the immediate aftermath, French aircraft bombed Gibraltar.

The French and British may be allies, but we're still at war with one another, thought Coburg ruefully. No matter how much Churchill says it was an attack on Nazi Vichy France, to the French people it was their sailors, their sons, husbands and brothers who'd been killed. Over a thousand of them.

'I'm interested in finding out about how easy it is for someone to get from France to Britain.'

'Now?' asked Blessington.

'Let's say, in July.'

'Safely?'

'Yes.'

'It can be done by someone who's of particular importance. De Gaulle, for instance. He flew to Britain in June, landing at Heston airfield, and was able to do that because we knew he was coming and which aircraft he was on. His wife and daughter came over by boat, smuggled out of France. Again, we knew they were coming so as much protection was given to them as possible to get them to these shores. Sadly, another boat which left France at the same time was sunk by the Germans.'

'But for an ordinary person to make the journey?'

'Extremely hazardous. The danger would be of a small aircraft being shot down, or a small boat being sunk by either side. The only ones that make it are when one side is aware of the importance of such a journey and steps are taken to ensure it succeeds. But that would mean someone special is making the trip, not just an ordinary citizen.'

So, Yvette Corot must have been important enough to receive official assistance in order to reach Britain. But not from the French or British. Which left . . . the Germans.

Coburg returned to his car to hear the radio calling him: 'Control to Echo Seven, come in, please. Control to Echo Seven, come in, please.'

The fact it was being repeated meant they must have been trying him for a while.

'Echo Seven to Control,' he responded.

'Echo Seven, Sergeant Potteridge at Mayfair asks that DCI Coburg contact him urgently. Over.'

'Echo Seven. Tell Sergeant Potteridge that DCI Coburg is on his way to Mayfair station now. Over.'

Sergeant Potteridge was waiting for Coburg on his arrival at the police station.

'We've got a witness, but once she found out it was about a shooting she clammed up. Denied she'd seen anything.'

'Who is she?'

'A Mrs Randall. She lives not far from the bus stop where Arnold used to get off the bus on his way home. At first, she said she heard a bang and thought it was a car backfiring. She looked out of her window and saw two men lifting a man up from the pavement and putting him in a car. I showed her Morton's picture, and at first she said she thought one of the men might have been him. But when I told her about the shooting she got scared and said she'd been mistaken, she hadn't seen anything.'

'It doesn't sound like she'd make a good witness in court,' said Coburg.

'No, but it's evidence about what happened. Arnold was shot and his body put in a car and taken to King's Cross.'

'The trouble is getting that evidence accepted in court. Morton's barrister would tear her to shreds. Even if she turned up.'

'Maybe if you had a word with her?' suggested Potteridge. 'You being a DCI might impress her.'

'It's worth a try,' said Coburg. 'The big problem is that once word gets out about her, Morton and his mob will lean on her, and we know how nasty they can be. We can't afford for that to happen.' He thought it over, then said: 'I think there might be another way to play this, but to make it work, I think I'm going to need my original thought.'

'The eavesdropping stuff you talked about?'

'Yes,' said Coburg. 'Give me Mrs Randall's address and I'll see how I get on with the listening business. We may not need to bring Mrs Randall in personally at this stage, but knowing that we have a witness – however reluctant – could be what we need to nail Morton. If the first part of what I've got in mind pays off. Can I use your phone?'

'Help yourself,' said Potteridge.

Coburg phoned the flat, keen to talk to Rosa about how recordings were made. There was no answer, so he phoned the Paddington St John Ambulance HQ.

'St John Ambulance,' said a voice he recognised as that of Chesney Warren.

'Mr Warren, it's DCI Coburg. Is my wife with you?'

'She is,' said Warren.

'Can I speak to her? I know it's irregular, but this is police business, not a personal matter.'

'She's in the rest room. I'll go and fetch her.'

'Thank you,' said Coburg.

There was a long pause, sounds of people moving around at the other end of the line, and then he heard Rosa's voice, concerned.

'Mr Warren said it was police business. What's happened?'

'Are you busy?' he asked her.

'Not at this immediate moment,' she said. 'I've just come back from a call.'

'How did it go?'

'Good,' she said, but then asked again, impatiently: 'What's happened?'

'Are you able to take time off to meet me?'

'Yes. I was just about to sign off and head for Claridge's, once I've changed out of my uniform. Remember, I said I wanted to check the piano there again?'

'Actually, I was going to suggest we meet at Claridge's anyway.'

'Why? What's happened?'

'I'll tell you when I see you.'

CHAPTER THIRTY-THREE

Coburg had arranged for a pot of tea and a plate of cakes and biscuits for them in Claridge's sumptuous tea room. Rosa arrived in her St John uniform and said: 'You should have said we were meeting for tea. You told me it was urgent. If I'd known it was to have tea here I'd have gone home and changed first. This is a jolly, not police business at all.'

'It's not a jolly,' said Coburg. 'And with a war on, more people are wearing uniforms than civvy clothes.'

She looked at the spread suspiciously. 'If this is police business, why all this?'

'I thought it would be nice to talk about it over tea and cakes. Do you object?'

'No. It's just that it seems more like a skive than anything official. What's it about?'

'Inspector Lomax has been shot dead.'

She stared at him horrified.

'Shot dead?'

'I'm afraid so.'

'But . . . why?'

'That's what I need to find out.'

'Do you think it's connected with these stranglings? You said that you asked him to investigate them with you. And the person who's doing them sounds pretty ruthless.'

'I don't think so. If that was the case, I'd be a target first.'

'Please, don't say that,' said Rosa. 'I don't want you tempting fate.'

'No, it's not to do with the stranglings. In my book, his death was vengeance by a gangster after Inspector Lomax humiliated him in front of his own gang. At least, that's what I intend to prove. And that's where you come in.'

'Me?'

'I need to know about making recordings.'

'In what way?'

'How it's done.'

'You're asking the wrong person,' said Rosa, taking a bite out of a cream and cherry tart. As the taste exploded in her mouth, in the nicest possible way, she said: 'My God, this is exquisite!'

'It's Claridge's,' said Coburg. 'I'd expect nothing less. But why are you the wrong person? You've made records, and broadcasts.'

'Yes, but I don't know the technicalities of it. I play and sing, and what I do is picked up by a microphone. The technicalities happen in a different room from where I am.'

'Have you ever been in one of those rooms to look at the equipment?'

'No. They prefer other people – non-technicians – to stay out. It all sounds very mysterious.'

'Is there anyone you know who knows about recordings? How it's done, and if it can be done in a hotel room?'

'I know an engineer at a studio I've recorded at, Wilson Studios. Frankie Jules. A nice guy. I've always found him very approachable. He used to work for the BBC, so he really does know about recording. He was part of the team that recorded Neville Chamberlain's declaration of war.'

'In that case I'd like you to take me to meet him.'

'All right, but only after I've had another of these fantastic cakes and another cup of tea. With the war on and rationing, it's been ages since I've had anything like this.' She took another bite and said through a mouthful of tart: 'I think I'm going to suggest we have more meetings like this.'

Chesney Warren looked up as the small, thin-faced man entered his office and stood looking at him with what appeared to be obvious disapproval. Warren was puzzled, he'd never seen this man before, but everything about him told Warren to be wary. The small man reminded Warren of Hitler, with his small tuft of a moustache and his hair combed to one side. He also had the same humourless look on his face as the German Führer.

A civil servant, thought Warren. But a very minor one. He had that air of sneering superiority. His clothes were worn, but clean and immaculate, as were his shirt and tie.

'Mr Chesney Warren?' he said, and his high-pitched voice sounded as if he was being strangled.

'Yes,' said Warren.

'I understand you are in charge here.'

'I am,' said Warren. 'Who are you and how may I help you?'

'My name is Hector Stanley and I am from the licencing

232

department of the local council.'

'The licencing department?' queried Warren. 'I believe all our vehicle licences are in order, as are those of our drivers.'

'Yes, I know. I checked before I came.' He pointed to the poster advertising Rosa's forthcoming concert, which had been pinned up on the wall. 'I am here because of that.'

'You wish to buy a ticket?' asked Warren. 'You're lucky, I do have some left. They're going like hot cakes. How many would you like?'

'None, because there isn't going to be any concert,' said Stanley.

'Of course there is,' said Warren. 'Miss Weeks has agreed, the church hall have given their permission, the posters and tickets have been printed. What's to stop it?'

'The fact that you have not applied for, nor received, a licence for this concert from the council.'

'We don't need one,' said Warren. 'It's not a commercial enterprise, it's to raise funds for St John Ambulance.'

'Nevertheless, you are charging the public money for the tickets.'

'Yes,' said Warren. 'That's how it works. People pay to come in and the money goes to St John Ambulance.'

'For any event where tickets are being sold at a set price a licence has to be issued.'

'All right, we'll apply for a licence.'

At this, the man smiled, a smug self-satisfied smirk. 'I'm afraid that won't be possible. The next meeting of the Licencing Committee won't be for three weeks, and I note this concert is planned for a week today. A licence cannot possibly be issued in that time. Therefore, you will have to cancel, or face prosecution.' He gave his hideous smirk again, then added: 'The law is there to be carried out, not ignored.'

With that, he left.

Chesney Warren stared after him, resisting the urge to rush after him and kick him in the seat of his trousers. The bloody bloated bureaucrat! Well, not bloated so much as shrunk. A weasel. A rat.

No, he thought grimly. You're not going to stop this. There must be a way round this. And I'm going to find it.

Wilson Studios were based in a small building in west London, not far from Ealing film studios. Frankie Jules was a man in his middle fifties and looked like a laboratory scientist with his long white coat. He was tall, thin, and with a luxuriant handlebar moustache, similar to those favoured by some RAF pilots. Coburg was relieved to notice that he seemed genial and approachable.

'Frankie, this is my husband, Detective Chief Inspector Edgar Coburg,' Rosa introduced Coburg.

Jules smiled and held out his hand.

'A pleasure to meet you, Chief Inspector.'

'Edgar will do fine.'

'Edgar wants to know about recording.'

'Oh? That's a pretty wide field. What, in particular?'

'Would it be possible to record a conversation that was happening in one room, in the room next to it?' asked Coburg.

'That's pretty particular,' grinned Jules. 'The answer's yes, if you had the right equipment.'

'What is the right equipment? For example, Rosa says

you recorded Neville Chamberlain's speech about the declaration of war.'

'I was part of the team. We used a Blattnerphone for that, recording on magnetic steel tape. Do you know much about recording?'

'Nothing at all,' admitted Coburg. 'How big was the equipment you used for that recording? Could it fit in a standard hotel room?'

Jules laughed.

'No way! The Blattner recorder is a massive piece of equipment. And since then it's given way to the Marconi–Stille, which is just as big, if not larger. We've got one here. Come and see.'

Coburg and Rosa followed Jules through a set of double doors into a room that resembled part of a small engineering factory, and then to a thick door with a sign on it: RECORDING MACHINE. NO ENTRY. There was a red lightbulb above the door, but it was unlit.

'When the machine's recording, that red light comes on,' explained Jules.

He opened the heavy door and they entered a room that was covered in carpet, not just on the floor but on the walls and the ceiling. A large piece of apparatus in metal stood in the centre of the floor. It was a metal box about five feet high, six feet wide and three feet deep, supported on a leg at each corner. The top section of the front of the machine was adorned with a variety of buttons and switches. Beneath these most of the front of the machine was taken up by what looked to Coburg like a pair of narrow wheels.

'It works with magnetic steel tape running from one reel to the other, going through a recording head, which you can see is set between them.'

He pointed to a door at one side of the room. 'That's the studio, where the artiste stands or sits at a microphone. Rosa has done that on many occasions.'

'But this is the first time I've been in here and seen the actual recording equipment,' said Rosa.

'The microphone is connected to the machine,' Jules continued.

'I see what you mean about it being a large piece of equipment,' said Coburg, disappointed. He'd been hoping for something that could be put in the hotel room. 'Could you record a telephone conversation?'

'What do you mean?' asked Jules, puzzled.

'Well, say someone somewhere made a phone call to your studio. Could you pick up whatever the caller was saying on your microphone in the other room and make a recording of what they said?'

'If it was amplified enough. It would also depend on the sound quality. What's it for?'

'Private use only.'

'In theory it's possible, but I wouldn't bank on it.'

'But you'd be able to hear the words? What was being said?'

'That would depend how close the people talking were to the microphone. Am I right that what you're thinking of doing is eavesdropping with a listening device on some people in a room, that conversation being picked up by listeners in an adjoining room? And those listeners in turn have got a telephone, which picks that up and relays it to a telephone here, in the studio, and we record that?'

'Yes, that about sums it up nicely,' said Coburg. 'Can it be done?'

'As I said, theoretically,' said Jules. 'But there's so many things that could go wrong with that. For one thing, the steel tapes are quite fragile, and the edge is sharp. They break. The tape travels at one point fifteen feet a second and when it breaks it's like having flying razor blades, which is why only the engineers are allowed in here when it's in use. The engineers wear protective equipment. But even with all that, there have been occasions when people have had the tips of their fingers sliced off.

'Once the tape breaks the recording has to be started all over again. That's all right if you're recording someone, you just get them to do it again. But it obviously wouldn't work on recording someone who doesn't know they're being recorded.'

'In short, you wouldn't advise it,' said Coburg with a sigh.

'No,' said Jules. 'Far too many things to go wrong. The quality of the sound. The equipment.' He sighed as he added. 'The Germans are ahead of the game. The Blattner recorder, which I mentioned as the forerunner of the Marconi–Stille, was invented by a German, and by all accounts they're doing some things with recordings using flexible magnetic tape. Better, more versatile equipment.' He gave them a rueful look. 'But we can hardly ask the Germans to help us with this.'

'No,' admitted Coburg.

'I'm guessing I wasn't much help,' said Jules ruefully.

'On the contrary,' said Coburg, 'you were invaluable. You've saved me from spending a great deal of time on something that is unlikely to get the results I want.'

As Edgar and Rosa returned to the car, Rosa said: 'So, it's no go?'

'I'm afraid so,' sighed Coburg. 'I'll just have to make do with the way we're doing it at the moment. Eavesdropping and writing down what's said. But it was good to meet Frankie. He's a nice bloke.'

'What's next?' asked Rosa.

'For me, back to Scotland Yard. What about you? Back to Paddington?'

She shook her head.

'No. It's a quiet day so I thought I'd take the opportunity to go browsing for sheet music, see what's new. I know what I'm doing tomorrow at Claridge's, but I thought I'd give a different programme for St John. People get bored hearing the same tunes all the time.'

'I don't,' said Coburg.

'Yes, but you're biased.'

'I certainly am,' said Coburg, and he hugged her to him and kissed her.

'Well really!' came a voice of disapproval.

They turned and saw a middle-aged, matronly woman regarding them with disapproval. Next to her stood a sad-looking man in his sixties.

'We are married, madam,' smiled Coburg.

'So are we, but we don't carry on in public,' sniffed the woman. 'Come, Stephen.'

With that, they walked off.

'Perhaps they should,' smiled Coburg, and he kissed Rosa again.

CHAPTER THIRTY-FOUR

Coburg dropped Rosa off in Charing Cross Road, the centre of London's music industry, then drove to Scotland Yard, where he was told by the sergeant at the reception desk that a Mrs Peters was waiting to see him. He looked around and saw a short, thin, grim-faced woman get up from the benches where people were waiting and make for him.

'DCI Coburg?' she asked.

'Indeed,' said Coburg. 'What can I do for you, Mrs Peters?'

'It was my husband, Patch Peters, who got shot. I've come to tell you who did it.'

'In that case, I suggest we go to my office,' said Coburg.

She followed him up the stairs to the first floor and his office. When they were inside, he offered her a seat, then said: 'You say you know who shot your husband.'

'I do. It was Hooky Morton.'

'You're sure of this?'

She nodded. 'And I'm prepared to go to court and say that on oath. I want him to hang. There was no call for him to do that to my Patch.'

'Do you know why he did it?'

'Patch had had enough of working for Hooky. He was a bully, and he didn't pay fair. Patch wanted more, so he started asking around to see if there was anything better for him. And this bloke approached him and offered him a deal.'

'Who was this bloke?'

'Someone called Fitt.'

'Roly Fitt?'

'I don't know his first name. Patch called him Mr Fitt, out of respect. He had a club in the West End. Somewhere posh.'

'What was the deal?'

'Patch never told me the details, just that this bloke was going to pay him good money for information.'

'About Hooky Morton?'

'I don't know. I suppose so. Patch said we had to keep it quiet. He didn't want Hooky or any of his mob finding out about it. But somehow Hooky must have, because Hooky and two of his men turned up at our house and they took Patch away in a car. Next thing I know, his dead body's been found in Mayfair.'

'Did Hooky and his men have guns on them when they picked up Patch?'

'I expect so. Hooky always carries a gun. It makes him feel big.'

'Mrs Peters, why have you come to me with this?' asked Coburg carefully.

'Because Patch always said to me that if anything happened to him, you was the person to go to. He didn't trust any of the others. He had respect for you. You nicked him a couple of times, but he said you was always fair. And honest. You weren't looking for a handout like a lot of the others. If I'd gone to some of the others, they might have sold me out to Hooky, and it would have been me gone next.'

'But you realise that by coming forward like this, you're putting yourself in danger. If you appear in court and testify—'

'I don't care,' she said angrily. 'So long as Hooky Morton swings for what he did.'

'Inspector Lomax wouldn't have sold you out,' said Coburg. 'He must have come to see you. He was in charge of the case.'

'I know that now,' she admitted. 'Especially after he got shot. And it must be Hooky who did it, because I heard that Lomax made him look small in front of everyone. Hooky can't abide that.'

'Why didn't you tell Inspector Lomax about this?'

'Because I didn't know him and I didn't like him. When he came to see me, he treated me like I was dirt, just 'cos my husband was a crook. Yes, Patch was a crook, but he always treated me right.'

After Mrs Peters had left, Coburg turned his attention to his desk. There was a large envelope addressed to him, and inside was a transcript of that morning's meeting between Braithwaite and what the constables had termed UYM (unidentified young man).

B: How can I help you?
UYM: A pal of mine told me you're arranging a commission for him. I'm hoping you can do the same for me.

241

B: And the name of your friend?

UYM: He asked me to not say, in case anyone else heard about it.

B: But if he's already a client of mine . . . ?

UYM: He still said he doesn't want his name mentioned. If that's a problem, then we'll forget it. I'm sure someone else will be able to help me.

B: I doubt it. There are very few people in the know about how things are done. But, the fact that he gave you my name and how to contact me is verification enough. What branch of the service are you interested in?

UYM: I thought the artillery. That's where most of the action is.

B: True. May I ask why you've elected to go through this route, rather than apply through official channels?

UYM: Yes, well, that's a bit awkward. Do you really need the details?

B: It would help.

UYM: Well, the fact is that last year, before war was declared, a chum of mine told me that an uncle of his had cheated him out of an inheritance, and he was set on getting what he was owed. He asked me if I'd help him liberate some art works from his uncle's flat, items that he said were his by rights. Well, of course, when a chum you've known and trusted tells you that, you believe him. He said his uncle would be away on a certain weekend, but unfortunately he wasn't.

B: You got caught.

UYM: Yes. Unfortunately for me, my chum legged it, so I was the one taken to court. I couldn't tell the whole story without dropping my chum in it.

B: So you were found guilty.

UYM: Yes. Will that be a problem?

B: I'm fairly sure it can be fixed. Most things can be fixed, for a price.

Coburg read through the rest of the transcript, with details of how much it would cost the unidentified young man, to which he agreed and promised to pay Braithwaite in a couple of days' time. 'Once I can get the old man to cough up. He'll be delighted.'

Excellent, smiled Coburg.

CHAPTER THIRTY-FIVE

Coburg knocked on the door of Braithwaite's suite at Claridge's.

'Sir Julian Braithwaite?' he asked when the door was opened by a well-dressed man in his sixties.

'Yes?' replied Braithwaite, curious.

'I'm Detective Chief Inspector Saxe-Coburg from Scotland Yard.'

'Yes? How can I help you?'

'It would be easier if we talked inside, if that's all right.'

'By all means.'

Braithwaite stood aside and let Coburg walk in, then shut the door and gestured to a chair. Coburg sat, as did Braithwaite.

'We're investigating two possible frauds,' he said.

'Frauds?' echoed Braithwaite. 'Nothing to do with me, I hope.'

'That's what we're trying to ascertain. We've had a complaint that you obtained money from a Mr Ronald Kemp allegedly to pay for your services in obtaining him a commission in the armed forces.'

Braithwaite got to his feet and stared at Coburg, his face

and stance a picture of indignant outrage.

'That is an outrageous lie!' he thundered.

'The issue compounded by the fact that, according to the allegation, when he realised the commission wasn't forthcoming and asked for the money back that he'd paid you, you told him that the money couldn't be recovered. Mr Kemp was so distraught that he killed himself.'

'An absolute lie!' said Braithwaite. 'And, if he killed himself, as you claim, who made the allegation?'

'A relative of his.'

'Then I shall sue that relative, whoever it is, for slander.'

'So, you've never offered to obtain a commission in the armed forces for anyone in return for money?' continued Coburg calmly.

'Absolutely not!'

Coburg took from his pocket the transcript that had been left for him at Scotland Yard that afternoon. 'So how you do explain this? It's a transcript of a conversation you had earlier today with a young man.'

Braithwaite stared at him, bewildered. 'What do you mean, a transcript?'

'Made through a listening device planted in this room.'

Braithwaite goggled at him, his mouth opening and closing like a fish gasping for breath.

'A listening device?' he said hoarsely.

'Installed following due legal process, following the allegation,' said Coburg. He proceeded to read from the sheet of paper, but stopped after a few sentences. 'I can read the whole of it, if you wish. The guarantees you offered the young man, the senior military people who would receive payment.'

Braithwaite sat down heavily on a chair.

'This is outrageous!' he blustered. 'It's illegal.'

'As I've just informed you, all due legal process was adhered to.'

'It's . . . it's a fit-up. Someone's trying to ruin my name!'

Coburg looked at him calmly, then took the transcript of the earlier conversation from his pocket.

'This transcript is of a conversation you had in this room with one Henry Kenneth Morton – Hooky to his friends and associates – in which you discuss the black market of delivering fuel to people you know, for which you take a payment. But, according to this, it seems you have been taking more than the figure agreed with Mr Morton, and he became rather upset with you. It refers to the sound of slaps being heard, and a punch. I trust you weren't hurt too badly.'

Braithwaite sagged in his chair, all pompous outrage gone, like a balloon that had suddenly been punctured and deflated.

'So that's the fraud over the military commissions, and the matter of selling stolen fuel on the black market.'

'I didn't know it was stolen!' said Braithwaite desperately.

Coburg smiled. 'You really believed Hooky Morton was a legitimate dealer in fuel?'

As Braithwaite sagged further, Coburg continued: 'We're talking about quite a lengthy prison sentence for each of these offences. And I do believe that some of the prisoners you'll meet in jail may be quite unforgiving about the selling of commissions to gullible young men. I've usually found that the common criminal is often quite patriotic.'

He fell silent and watched Braithwaite, now completely defeated. The man's lips quivered, and Coburg thought that he was about to burst into tears.

'Isn't there a way out of this?' he asked hoarsely.

Coburg looked at him with disapproval. 'I hope you're not suggesting a bribe or something, which would compound the situation?'

'No, no!' said Braithwaite desperately. 'I meant, might there be any information I might be able to help you with?'

'Your accomplices?' asked Coburg. 'I was under the impression that your so-called accomplices in the commission-selling scam were unaware that you were using their names. Of course, I can always check that.' He paused: 'However, with regard to Hooky Morton . . .'

'No, no,' said Braithwaite, and there was no mistaking his terror. 'I can't grass him up. He'd kill me!'

'You don't have to grass him up. All you have to do is invite him here to give him some of the money you owe him. And, while he's here, engage him in conversation.'

'He'll know!' said the terrified Braithwaite.

'How?' asked Coburg. 'We'll swear you had no idea your hotel room had a listening device installed. He just got caught up in something that was nothing to do with you. As far as listening in goes, that is.'

Braithwaite shook his head.

'No,' he said. 'You don't know what Morton's like.'

'I know exactly what he's like, and what he's capable of. Which is why I want him off the streets. Your choice is simple. You invite him here and get him talking; or you do a very long stretch of hard time.'

Braithwaite looked hopefully at Coburg.

'You'll drop all charges against me if I do that?'

'We'll see you get a reduced sentence on a lesser charge, and you'll serve your short time in a nice, easy prison, the other inmates mostly old lags long past their best.'

'You want me to get him talking about the fuel business?'

'Not particularly. I want you to get him talking about Inspector Lomax.'

'Who?'

'A policeman.'

'A bent one?'

'Possibly,' said Coburg, thinking it wisest not to frighten Braithwaite by telling him they suspected Morton had killed Lomax. 'He's the officer who first started investigating the murder of the man in the kitchen here at Claridge's, before it was given to me.'

'So you want me to ask him about that murder?'

'Yes, and no,' said Coburg. 'I'll leave it to you to pick your own words, but what I'd like you to do is tell him that Inspector Lomax visited you and that he asked you about Hooky Morton.'

'Why would he be asking me about Morton if he was looking into the murder in the kitchen?' asked Braithwaite suspiciously.

'You can tell him that somehow or other Lomax had heard about the fuel scam, and that you're involved. Tell him Lomax started leaning on you.'

'Leaning on me?'

'Threatening you. Tell Morton that Lomax seems to hate him and is determined to get him. Tell him he threatened you, trying to force you to grass Morton up.'

'He won't like it.'

'No, he won't. But he might like you for telling him, tipping him the wink.'

Braithwaite looked thoughtful. 'He might. But he also

might try and bump me off to make sure I stay quiet.'

'He won't,' Coburg assured him.

'How can you be so sure?'

'Because I know Hooky. He only gets upset if he finds that people are hiding things from him. Like you and the money you've been creaming off the fuel. In this case you're being open with him. Giving him valuable information.'

Braithwaite regarded Coburg warily. 'This money I'm supposed to pay him. It's coming from you?'

'From the police account. I'll drop it in to you shortly.'

'Say he tells me to bring it to him at his pub at King's Cross?'

'Tell him you're scared to go out carrying that much money with you in case you get robbed.'

Braithwaite lapsed into thought again, then asked: 'How do you know he'll come here in person? He might send one of his blokes.'

'Because Hooky Morton doesn't trust most of his blokes, not where hard cash is concerned. He'll come.'

CHAPTER THIRTY-SIX

Detective Constables Arkwright and Wemyss sat by the receiver, listening to distant noises in the suite next door: footsteps as Braithwaite moved about, a bottle being opened, drinks being poured.

'What time did the boss say Morton was expected?' asked Wemyss.

'He didn't say,' said Arkwright. 'Just that he expected him to be here some time this evening.'

The sound of a knock at the adjoining suite's door made them both sit up.

'Here we go,' said Wemyss. 'This is him.'

They heard the door being opened, and then, to their surprise, a woman's voice. 'Sir Julian Braithwaite?' she asked.

There was a moment's hesitancy, then Braithwaite said: 'Indeed, dear lady, but you must excuse me. I am expecting a visitor.'

'One of your victims?' she asked, her voice heavy with anger.

They heard the door shut, then Braithwaite said: 'I'm sorry, I don't have any idea what you're talking about. What victims?'

'My brother, Ronald Kemp, for one. You tricked him into

paying you six hundred pounds by telling him you could get him a commission in the armed forces. It was a fraud, and when Ronald discovered he'd been duped he shot himself.'

'I'm sorry, but I think you must be confusing me with someone else. Now I must ask you to leave. If you don't, I shall call the management.'

They heard the woman say: 'Put that telephone down.'

There was the sound of a telephone being replaced, then Braithwaite said: 'What are you doing with that vase?'

'I'm going to have you arrested, and if it means causing a disturbance here to achieve that, so be it. You should be in jail, you despicable cheat.'

The next thing Wemyss and Arkwright heard was the sound of something being smashed.

'She's thrown the vase at him!' exclaimed Arkwright. 'We've got to get her out of there before Morton arrives!'

Wemyss was already out of the door and running to the door of Braithwaite's suite. He tried the door handle, but it was locked. He stepped back and launched a kick against the lock, the kick being delivered with such force that the door jamb splintered and the door crashed inwards.

Wemyss ran in and stopped. The woman was standing, looking shocked at this interruption. Braithwaite was also looking shocked. A vase lay in shattered pieces on the floor beside him.

'This woman attacked me!' Braithwaite blurted out. 'Arrest her!'

'Who are you?' the woman demanded of Wemyss.

'I am a police officer, madam,' said Wemyss. 'Detective Constable Wemyss. I must ask you to accompany me.'

'Where to?'

251

Wemyss hesitated, then said: 'To the room next door. My colleague is already making contact with our chief inspector, who will be here shortly.'

Coburg and Rosa sat and listened to records, Rosa still weighing up what numbers to include at her performance the following evening. As they listened to Ella Fitzgerald's delivery of Rodgers and Hart's 'Manhattan', Rosa gave a sigh that was both delight at the sound, mixed with sadness.

'I can never equal what she does,' she said ruefully.

'No one expects you to,' said Coburg. 'You do your own version, your own interpretation. That's what people want to hear.'

They were interrupted by the phone ringing. Rosa answered it, then held out the receiver towards Coburg.

'It's for you. Detective Constable Arkwright phoning from Claridge's.'

Coburg took the receiver. 'DCI Coburg.'

'DC Arkwright here, sir. A woman has just invaded Sir Julian Braithwaite's room and thrown a vase at him.'

'What?'

'Her name is Mrs Linda Farnsworth. She arrived at his suite and said she was here to take revenge for a fraud he'd carried out on her brother, which led to him killing himself.'

Oh God, thought Coburg. I should never have given her Braithwaite's name.

'Is he badly injured?' he asked.

'No, sir. She missed him. The vase is broken.'

'Any sign of Hooky Morton yet?'

'No, sir. What shall we do?'

'Take the woman into your room and put her in the

252

bathroom. I'm on my way. I'll pick her up while you two carry on as planned. Oh, and clear away the broken vase. We don't want Morton to get suspicious when he arrives.'

'Are you sure he'll come, sir?'

'I hope so.'

Coburg replaced the receiver, then said: 'I have to go out.'

'To Claridge's?'

'Someone just launched an attack on a suspect we've been watching. A woman who felt he was responsible for the death of her brother.'

'And was he?'

'Indirectly. I'll be as quick as I can, once I've charged and processed her.'

'Did she injure him?'

'No, she threw a vase at him, but missed. The vase is broken.'

'It's a pity she has to be charged,' said Rosa. 'Can't she just be given a warning? I mean, if he was responsible for her brother's death . . .'

'I'll see you later,' he said, and picked up the car keys from the sideboard.

Coburg made a quick examination of the scene in Braithwaite's suite on his arrival. It had to be quick because there was the possibility that Hooky Morton could appear at any moment. The broken vase had been removed, but there was little that could be done about the splintered door jamb.

'Tell Morton that an angry person kicked your door in, but you managed to get away from him and had him arrested. That way, if Morton had anyone outside watching and they saw me draw up in my police car, there'd be an explanation that would satisfy him.'

He then went next door to where Arkwright and Wemyss sat by their radio receiver.

'Where is she?' he asked.

'In the bathroom, as you ordered.'

Coburg knocked at the bathroom door, then walked in. Linda Farnsworth was sitting on the edge of the bath. She looked completely crushed and downcast. He noticed that she'd been handcuffed.

'We didn't know what else she might do, sir,' said Arkwright defensively when he saw Coburg's quizzical observation of the handcuffs. 'She might have started smashing up the bathroom.'

'Yes, of course,' said Coburg.' He looked at the woman. 'Mrs Farnsworth, I'm going to drive you to Scotland Yard where you'll be processed. I'd prefer to do it with the handcuffs off. Do I have your word that you won't attempt to escape, or interfere with my driving?'

She looked at him, and he saw her face was streaked with tears, a picture of misery and despair. Slowly, she nodded.

'In that case you can take the handcuffs off her, Constable,' said Coburg.

Arkwright looked at him, his face showing his concern and doubt.

'Are you sure, sir?'

'I am. I'll take full responsibility.'

Arkwright undid the handcuffs. Coburg took Farnsworth by the arm and gently led her towards the door.

'Well done, the pair of you,' he said to the constables. 'And keep listening.'

They drove in silence, Coburg at the wheel, Farnsworth beside him in the passenger seat. Finally, she said in a mournful voice full of shame and embarrassment: 'I'm sorry.'

'You didn't think we were doing anything?' asked Coburg.

'I thought you were just watching him. I couldn't see how you were going to get the evidence you needed. You should have told me you were having his suite listened to.'

'No,' said Coburg. 'If I had you might have told someone else, and that information might have got back to Braithwaite. To be frank, I shouldn't have given you Braithwaite's name. As it is, you were lucky we were listening in and our man broke in when he did. Say the vase had hit him and he'd been badly injured? You'd be facing a charge of grievous bodily harm, or even attempted murder.'

'I didn't try to hit him. I just wanted to scare him and have the police brought in. I didn't know you were already there.' She let out a groan of unhappiness. 'What will happen to me? Will I go to prison?'

Coburg hesitated before replying, then he said: 'The only thing you can be charged with is criminal damage. To wit, breaking a vase. But I suspect Claridge's has had more than its share of breakages in the past. I'm sure if you offered to pay for the vase that would lay that to rest. There is the possibility of threatening behaviour in your attitude towards Braithwaite, but I don't believe he would want to press charges with the publicity that would result, exposing him for what he is. So, in short, the worst that can happen to you is a caution not to do this sort of thing again in the future, which I shall issue to you when we get to Scotland Yard.'

'And that will be it?'

'It will be.'

'And what about Braithwaite? I now realise you were gathering evidence against him by whatever listening devices you've been employing. But because of me, now he knows that you're listening to what goes on in his suite.'

'He already knew.'

She looked at him, bewildered. 'What?'

'We have an even bigger investigation going on, and we've used the fact that Braithwaite is aware that we have evidence of his guilt to put pressure on him to nail someone much more dangerous.'

'Who?'

'That doesn't concern you, Mrs Farnsworth. All you need to know is you will get justice for what Braithwaite did to your brother. I hope that what happened tonight showed that to you.'

'Yes, it did. And I'm so sorry. Will I have to have my fingerprints taken and other things like that when we get to Scotland Yard?'

'No. A simple caution, and then you're free to go. Providing I have your word that you will now leave this case to us and not interfere again.'

'I promise.'

'Good. Then we can call this episode finished.'

CHAPTER THIRTY-SEVEN

Sunday 20th October

Coburg was preparing a fried breakfast when Rosa walked into the kitchen. They'd been saving up their ration coupons and he'd been looking forward all week to a full breakfast of eggs, sausage, bacon, all on toast, to be eaten at Sunday leisure.

'You've got your ambulance uniform on,' he said.

'Ah, the ever-observant detective,' she smiled, and kissed him.

'Careful,' he said. 'Man at work in the kitchen. I don't want to spill anything on you. I didn't think you were going in today. I thought you'd be practising for this evening.'

'I'll do that this afternoon,' she said. 'Sunday is supposed to be a quiet day, but invariably there's a leftover from Saturday night.' She looked appreciatively at the food sizzling in the frying pan. 'But not before I've tucked into this glorious feast.'

Coburg served the food on to the two plates and took them to the table.

The telephone rang.

'Don't you dare,' she said warningly.

'It could be important,' he said.

'More important than breakfast?'

'You start while it's hot,' he said, and he picked up the phone.

'DCI Coburg, it's Scotland Yard reception,' said a voice. 'An envelope's been delivered for you, marked urgent. It's from DC Wemyss.'

'Keep it there. I'll be in shortly.'

As he sat down, Rosa asked: 'You'll be in where shortly?'

'The Yard. A transcript's arrived for me that I hope will nail Hooky Morton for the murder of Inspector Lomax.' He picked up his knife and fork. 'But first: food.'

Coburg dropped Rosa off at the ambulance station, and then made for Scotland Yard where the transcript was waiting for him. He took it to his office and read through it. Wemyss and Arkwright had done a good job. After an initial exchange, in which Braithwaite handed over some money, he was then heard to say: 'I had a visit from an Inspector Lomax.'

The rest of the conversation continued, with Morton identified as M and Braithwaite as B.

M: When?

B: A couple of days ago.

M: What did he want?

B: He's investigating the murder of a man in the kitchens here, and at the same time he asked about you.

M: About me?

B: He hates you. Somehow or other he picked up about the fuel business, and the fact that I might be involved. He started leaning on me.

M: Leaning on you?

B: Threatening me. He wants me to give evidence against you. I didn't. I won't. But I thought you ought to know.

M: You don't have to worry about Lomax. I've handled it.

B: What do you mean, handled it?

M: I've dealt with it.

B: In what way?

M: In a way that you don't want to know about. Is that clear?

B: What do I say if he comes back?

M: He won't be coming back.

B: You don't know that.

M: Believe me, I do.

After reading it through again, Coburg put a telephone call through to the detectives in the suite next to Braithwaite's. DC Wemyss answered.

'DCI Coburg here.'

'Yes, sir.'

'I've got the latest transcript. Good work.'

'Thank you, sir.'

'Of course, the one thing a transcript can't do is give me the tone of what was said.'

'The tone, sir?'

'Yes. When Morton said that he'd handled Lomax, how did he sound? Angry? Smug?'

'Yes, sir. Smug would be the word I'd use. He sounded very pleased with himself. I could almost picture him smirking as he said it.'

'Thank you, Constable.'

'Do you want us to carry on listening, sir?'

'One day more, just in case we pick up anything else. What you've done has been invaluable.'

Coburg then put through a call to Superintendent Moffatt.

'I'm sorry to trouble you at home on a Sunday, sir,' he said. 'But I've got a transcript of a conversation in which I believe Hooky Morton incriminates himself over the murder of Inspector Lomax.'

'You believe?' said Moffatt guardedly.

'If we could meet and I could show it to you, I think you'll agree it gives us what we need to at least bring Morton in and charge him.'

'Very well. I'll contact Sergeant Potteridge. Meet us at Mayfair station in half an hour.'

Superintendent Moffatt studied the transcript, then passed it to Sergeant Potteridge for him to read.

'It's not a confession, as such,' commented Moffatt doubtfully.

'It's close,' insisted Coburg. 'It's enough to bring him in and keep him on remand. Especially when I tell the prosecutor's office that we have a witness that places Morton at the scene of the shooting, and he was seen loading the inspector's body in his car.'

'But Mrs Randall went back on that,' pointed out Potteridge, concerned. 'She won't say that, and especially she won't say it in court.'

'At this stage she doesn't have to,' said Coburg. 'Nor do we have to reveal her name. At this stage it's a preliminary hearing at the magistrates' court where we ask for him to be remanded in custody pending his trial at Crown Court. And if we get that, while Morton's out of the way we can lean on the members of his gang. If they think they're also in the frame to be hanged for Lomax's murder as accomplices, one or two of them will talk soon enough.' He looked at Potteridge. 'What do you think, Sergeant?'

'I agree,' said Potteridge. 'It gives us something to bring him in. At least it'll put the frighteners on the bastard. So far, he's getting away with everything, like killing Patch Peters.'

'Very well,' said Moffatt. 'I'll leave it to you two to bring him in.'

'I thought it would be best to take him to Scotland Yard rather than here, sir,' said Coburg. 'It lets him know we mean business.'

'Agreed,' said Moffatt. 'His lawyer will try and spring him, of course.'

'We may be able to pre-empt that if we can arrange for him to appear at the magistrates' court tomorrow. It's a straightforward appearance, no major arguments in court, just enough evidence from us to prove that he's dangerous and needs to be held on remand until it comes to trial at the Crown Court.'

'Again, his lawyer will argue against that.'

'He will, but once we've brought Morton in, I'm going to get in touch with Jerry Sturgess at the prosecutor's office. He's a top man and I'm sure he'll be able to help us on this.'

'You were at school with Sturgess, as I recall,' commented Moffatt.

'Yes, sir,' Coburg admitted.

'Very well. But keep me informed.'

CHAPTER THIRTY-EIGHT

As Coburg and Potteridge drove to King's Cross, accompanied by uniformed officers, Potteridge muttered: 'The boss always resented that, you know.'

'Resented what?'

'You having been at Eton. He said it was all a conspiracy of the people at the top. And now, here we are hopefully able to put Morton behind bars because you were at school with a top prosecutor. Sounds like he was right.'

'Not completely,' said Coburg defensively. 'Yes, it's true that close friendships were formed there that have continued into adult life, but there were just as many enmities. Quite a few people I was at school with loathe me, and the feeling is mutual. But in this case, it's not just old boys tipping the wink to one another, it's evidence. The transcript, for one thing. Plus the fact that a car was spotted at the place where Inspector Lomax was last seen and two men were seen loading a body into it. That evidence should keep Morton in jail on remand, and Jerry Sturgess is the best there is at presenting it.'

When Coburg and Potteridge walked into the Dark Horse pub at King's Cross they found Hooky Morton genially holding court with Dobbin Edwards and a few more of Morton's gang.

'Well, well,' beamed Morton. 'The top man himself. DCI Coburg, welcome to my humble abode. Are you here on official business, or can I get you and your acquaintances a drink?' He smirked as he looked at Potteridge. 'And that includes even you, Sergeant Potteridge. I'm feeling in a good mood today.' He gave a leer as he added: 'I wonder why that might be?'

Coburg produced the warrant from his pocket and held it out towards Morton.

'Henry Kenneth Morton, I am arresting you on suspicion of the murder of Inspector Arnold Lomax.'

Morton laughed, a loud guffaw.

'Hear that, boys? They think they're going to pin Old Slowcoach Lomax's murder on me!' And he laughed again.

Coburg, for his part, continued with his warning that anything Morton said would be taken down and used in evidence against him.

Morton chuckled and shook his head.

'You're flogging a dead horse on this one, Chief Inspector. My mouthpiece will have me out on the street in no time.' He got up and turned to Dobbin. 'Dob, get on the blower to Mr Wisden. Tell him I'll be expecting him at Scotland Yard toute suite because the filth are trying to fit me up with the murder of Inspector Lomax.'

'Right-ho, Hooky,' said Dobbin, and he made for the telephone behind the bar.

Morton turned to Coburg and Potteridge with a mocking smile. 'Shall we go, gentlemen? Perhaps you'd like to phone ahead and tell them I'd like two sugars in my tea. If they've run out, I can always bring my own.'

And with a further chuckle, he pulled on his overcoat

and was heading for the door to the street, when Coburg stepped in front of him.

'Not so fast,' said Coburg. 'This is suspicion of murder. That merits handcuffs. Would you like to do the honours, Sergeant Potteridge?'

'With pleasure,' said Potteridge, and he stepped forward, producing a pair of handcuffs from his pocket.

At the sight of them, Morton recoiled, and for the first time a flush of anger came into his face.

'Oh, no you don't,' he snarled. 'No copper puts me in cuffs.'

'Resisting arrest?' asked Coburg calmly. 'I've got four constables outside in case such an event occurred. After all, this is the murder of a detective inspector we're talking about. If you like, I'll call them in, with their truncheons drawn.' He then looked at Dobbin and the members of Morton's gang. 'I've also got a police van outside in case we met any resistance from Henry Kenneth's associates. So it's up to you, gents.' He turned back to Morton. 'But especially you. We can have a battle royal where you and some of your blokes get a sound beating, and anyone who fights back does time for assaulting a police officer; or you can have the cuffs put on and we all leave quietly.'

Morton glared angrily at Coburg, and they could see the rage inside him he was battling against. Finally, he thrust his two hands out towards Potteridge.

'I won't forget this, Coburg!' he rasped. 'Trust me, I won't forget it.'

'I'll make sure you don't,' said Coburg.

With that, Sergeant Potteridge snapped the handcuffs on Morton's wrists and they led him out to the waiting police car. Just before the doors closed on him, Morton shouted: 'Make sure you tell Wisden about this, Dobbin! I'll have this lot sacked!'

Coburg had Morton put into the custody cells in the basement of Scotland Yard, then Sergeant Potteridge left for Mayfair to report on his arrest to Superintendent Moffatt, while Coburg went to his office to await the arrival of Walter Wisden, Morton's solicitor. While he waited, he put through a phone call to Jerry Sturgess at the prosecutor's office.

'Jerry,' he said. 'Edgar Coburg. I'm sorry to trouble you at home on a Sunday but something big has come up.'

'How big?' asked Sturgess, intrigued.

'We've arrested Hooky Morton for the murder of Inspector Arnold Lomax.'

'Lomax?' said Sturgess, startled.

'He was shot dead and we're fairly sure Morton did it. We've certainly got circumstantial evidence that gives us enough to bring him in. We've also got a potential witness.'

'Potential witness?' repeated Sturgess warily.

'We're talking to her at the moment. The thing is, as it's a police officer that's been killed, we'd like to move on this quickly. Could you arrange for Morton to be up before the magistrates tomorrow morning for a formal hearing? My hope is that he'll be remanded into custody until he comes up for trial at Crown Court.'

'That depends on you being able to prove to the court that leaving him free could be an endangerment to the public.'

'I think I can do that. I've got transcripts of conversations Morton had which point to his guilt.'

'Secret eavesdropping?'

'Legally authorised,' said Coburg. 'I'll have them copied and sent over to you by messenger.'

'It could all fail,' warned Sturgess. 'I'll have a word and get this in motion. I'll call you later to confirm tomorrow's court appearance as soon as I've got it authorised. Providing I can get it done that quickly, of course.'

'This is a senior police officer that's been murdered. Shot in cold blood on the streets of London.'

'And that's the ace in our hand I'll be playing. Have you questioned Morton?'

'No,' said Coburg. 'I'm expecting his mouthpiece, Walter Wisden, at any moment. I'm going to let Morton sweat. He'll hate that, not knowing what we're doing. The angrier he gets, the more chance there is of a meltdown from him in court on Monday, ensuring he gets remanded to stay in custody. And while he's there and off the streets, we work on his gang. Someone in that crowd will fold and give King's evidence in exchange for a deal. And once one gives up Morton, it only needs a few others to follow and we'll have him. Providing, of course, we can get permission for Morton to go before the magistrate tomorrow.'

'Leave that to me. I'll call you back. If you're not at the Yard, I'll phone you at home.'

'If I'm not there, Rosa will take a message.'

'Ah, the lovely Rosa! How is she? Is her arm healed?'

'So far, so good,' said Coburg.

'I've booked tickets for tonight's performance at Claridge's. As soon as I saw she was appearing I was on the phone. You're going, I trust?'

'Of course.'

'In that case, Deirdre and I will see you there tonight.'

CHAPTER THIRTY-NINE

At Paddington St John Ambulance HQ, it was a relatively quiet day. Rosa and Doris had had just one call, a pedestrian hit by a bus who'd suffered a broken leg and arm. When they returned to the station and found it was still quiet, Rosa sought out Chesney Warren and asked him if she could take time off to visit Elsa Peers.

'I'd like to offer my condolences about Derek.'

'I think that's a lovely idea. It would mean a lot to her. Derek told me she was very impressed when she heard you were working here. Have you got her address?'

'No.'

'It's not far. Derek and Elsa liked to keep everything local, within walking distance.' He wrote down the address on a piece of paper and handed it to her.

'Thanks,' said Rosa. 'You'll know where to find me if you need me urgently.'

'By the way,' said Warren, 'I'd better let you know in case anyone tells you that the concert is cancelled, it isn't.'

'Of course it isn't,' said Rosa, puzzled. 'Why would anyone say it is?'

'Because I had a visit from the Licencing Officer of the local

267

council, informing me that we could not go ahead with a concert where we are charging for tickets unless we have a licence.'

'Well, can't we get one?'

'Not according to this idiot. Any application has to go before the Licencing Committee, which won't be meeting for another three weeks.' As Rosa opened her mouth to express her dismay, he held up his hand and continued: 'However, there is a way round it. I spoke to a pal of mine who arranged a similar entertainment to raise funds for another good cause, and he came up against the same thing. But he discovered that if you don't charge for tickets but instead ask for donations on the day, you don't need a licence. So that's what we'll do. On the day of the concert, I will tell everyone about the problem, and offer everyone the chance to have their money back, or they can donate it. And anyone coming on the day will simply be told there's no ticket price, they can donate what they like.' He smiled. 'I reckon we'll make even more money that way than by selling tickets.'

When Walter Wisden arrived at Scotland Yard, Coburg took him to an interview room rather than his own office. Coburg didn't like Wisden. His claim to be representing the law didn't ring true – he made his living by protecting people like Hooky Morton. Coburg had to admit he employed talented people, like Wesley Stipes, an excellent barrister who – like Wisden – earned a very good living from keeping Morton and other rich gangsters out of jail, even though both men knew what Morton and people like him did to earn their riches. Criminality of all sorts, the black market, prostitution, blackmail, enforced by physical violence and often murder. As far as Coburg was concerned, Wisden and Stipes were accomplices and ought to be in jail, but neither had so far put a foot wrong as far as transgressions of the law were concerned.

'I'm here to see my client, Mr Morton,' Wisden told Coburg.

'I shall arrange that,' said Coburg.

'Why exactly has my client been brought here and held?' demanded Wisden.

'I'd have thought you'd have already been told the reason by Dobbin Edwards,' said Coburg. 'We heard Mr Morton issuing instructions to Dobbin to phone you.'

'I prefer to hear it from yourself.'

'Mr Morton has been arrested on a charge of murdering Detective Inspector Arnold Lomax.'

'That's nonsense.'

'We shall see if the magistrate agrees with you at the preliminary hearing tomorrow.'

Wisden looked at Coburg, stunned. 'You can't do that!' he protested.

'I can,' said Coburg.

'On what evidence?'

'Evidence that will be revealed in detail at his trial. But it includes at least one witness to the shooting, with more to come.'

'Who?' demanded Wisden.

'That will be revealed later.'

'You've got to share the evidence,' insisted Wisden.

'And we will, when it comes to trial. Until then, this is just a preliminary hearing. But, in view of the seriousness of the charge, we shall be asking for your client to be remanded in custody pending his trial at the Crown Court.'

'This is outrageous!' said Wisden. 'My client is a respectable businessman who has never been charged with any crime.'

'That's not strictly true,' said Coburg. 'Some years ago,

he spent time in prison for various offences.'

'The follies of youth and bad companions,' said Wisden.

'As I'm sure you'll argue tomorrow,' said Coburg. He stood up. 'I'll now have your client brought to you.'

'Wait,' said Wisden. 'Have you formally questioned him yet?'

'Dear me no,' said Coburg with a slight smile, 'as if I'd do such a thing without his solicitor being present.'

'Then, when you bring him to me, I presume you'll be questioning him then?' queried Wisden.

'No,' said Coburg. 'He and I have already had an informal discussion at his licensed premises. I intend to have a formal question and answer session later.'

'This is most irregular!' bristled Widen.

'But legal. However, if your client has a confession to make, I'm happy to hear that in your presence.'

'My client is innocent.'

'You know that, even though you haven't yet spoken to him?' queried Coburg.

'I know my client,' said Wisden.

'Yes, I'm sure you do,' said Coburg. 'I'll have your client brought to you, and I'll see you tomorrow morning at the magistrates' court.'

Rosa approached the small terraced house, the address she'd been given for Derek Peers. She would have preferred it if she could have telephoned Elsie first, to check that it would be all right for her to call on her, but Derek had not been on the phone. She'd deliberately left it for a few days since Derek died before making her visit to let Elsie grieve in some kind of peace. If she'd been allowed to, that is. Rosa expected that friends and neighbours would have been calling ever since it happened to offer their sympathies. She knew from Chesney Warren that Derek and Elsie had no children, and apparently no family. At least, none that lived locally. Mr Warren had told her that as far as he knew neither Derek nor Elsie had any living relatives. He'd also told Rosa that Elsie's real name was actually Elsa.

'She's German,' he'd told her. 'Derek met her during the First War, when he was injured in France. She was working at the hospital he was in. How a German woman came to be working in a French hospital, I don't know. But then, not all Germans supported their own side in that war, just as there are plenty who don't support Hitler in this one.' He then added ruefully. 'Just as there are plenty of Brits who seem to support Hitler. Lord Haw-Haw, for one.'

Lord Haw-Haw: William Joyce, the American-born Fascist from an Irish family, educated and raised in Britain, who put on a contrived plummy British accent and made anti-British, pro-German propaganda broadcasts on German radio, which were transmitted to Britain.

Rosa reached the door of number 14, the Peers' house, and knocked. To her surprise the door swung open.

'Mrs Peers!' she called.

There was no answer from inside the house.

Maybe she's popped out for a minute to call on a neighbour, she thought.

'Mrs Peers!' she called again. 'It's Rosa Coburg.' Then she added: 'Rosa Weeks, that is!'

Still there was no answer. She walked to the house next door and knocked on the door, but there was no answer from there either. Nor from the house on the other side. It was the next house along where a front door opened and a woman

271

wearing an apron and holding a tea towel peered out.

'I heard all the knocking,' said the woman.

'I'm looking for Mrs Elsie Peers,' explained Rosa. 'Her door's open but she isn't answering. I wondered if she might be with a neighbour.'

'She's not here, dear,' said the woman. She came towards Rosa, wiping her hands on the tea towel, which she then put in the pocket of her apron. 'Strange,' she said. She stopped at the open door and called out 'Elsie! It's Mary!'

Still no answer. The woman stepped into the house, a look of concern on her face.

'I hope nothing's happened to her. She was devastated over Derek. They were so close. I hope she hasn't done anything stupid.'

Rosa followed the woman into the small living room, which came straight off the street, and then into the back kitchen.

'Oh my God!' cried the woman, stopping and recoiling.

Rosa looked over her shoulder. A middle-aged woman lay on the floor, her eyes and mouth wide open, and Rosa knew at once she was dead.

'Look at her neck!' said the woman in horror.

Rosa looked. A ring of blood had seeped out from a narrow wound encircling her neck, and immediately she recalled what Coburg had told her about the victims whose murders he was looking into. 'Have you got a telephone?' she asked the woman.

'No, but Mrs Harris at number 20 has,' said the woman.

'I'll phone the police,' said Rosa.

'It's 999,' said the woman.

'I know,' Rosa assured her. 'My husband is a detective chief inspector at Scotland Yard, so I'll get a message to him at the same time.'

272

CHAPTER FORTY

Coburg was in his office, sorting out paperwork in case it might be needed at the magistrates' court the following day, when his phone rang.

'DCI Coburg.'

'Switchboard here, sir. We've just had a message from your wife. She's discovered the body of a woman at a house she was visiting. She says she's been murdered, strangled with wire.'

'Did she leave an address?'

'Yes, sir.' The operator gave him the address.

'Thank you. If she calls again, tell her I'm on my way.'

Morton looked up as Wisden walked into the interview room.

'About bloody time,' he scowled. 'Right, what's happening? How soon can I walk out of here?'

'It's not that simple, Hooky,' said Wisden awkwardly. 'You're charged with a capital offence, and because it involved the murder of a senior police officer, they've got the prosecutor's office jumping through hoops. You're down to appear in the magistrates' court tomorrow morning.'

'Tomorrow? You mean I've got to spend the night in this piss-hole? Why can't you get me out on bail? You've done it before.'

'As I say, this is a more serious charge than anything you've faced before. However, I have hopes that we'll get you out tomorrow. I've been on the phone to Wesley Stipes and he'll be at the magistrates' court representing you tomorrow. As you know, he's very good.'

'He ought to be, the money he charges!' said Morton angrily.

'It's worth it if he gets you out.'

'I shouldn't even be appearing in court! What evidence have they got against me?'

Wisden looked uncomfortable at this question. 'Coburg reckons he's got a witness.'

'Who?'

'He isn't saying.'

'He can't do that! He's got to share what he's got with my defence team.'

'That's when it comes to the Crown Court.'

'This is ridiculous! What do I bloody pay you for? You mean he's going to lay out the evidence he reckons he's got against me in open court tomorrow . . .'

'It's just a preliminary hearing.'

'But say he's got something? Some people he's persuaded to fit me up? Lies. Made-up stories.'

'If he has, we'll challenge them.'

'Say the magistrate is on his side?'

'There are no sides. The court is impartial.'

'Don't you believe it!' He looked urgently at Wisden. 'What's he got? Who is this witness?'

'He hasn't said. Did he question you when he arrested you?'

'No. He just said he was arresting me on a charge of murder of Inspector Arnold Lomax, and then came the usual about "anything you say will be taken down and may be used against you". You know the drill. This can't be legal! He's got to talk to me, surely? Ask me questions so I can prove my innocence.'

'I'm sure he will, once the session at the magistrates' court is over and you're free. Although I have a fear that your bail will be set quite high.'

'I don't care how much it is, I just want you to tell me that I'm going to get bail and walk out of there.'

Wisden hesitated, then said: 'Wesley will do the best job possible. The only problem is that we don't know what Coburg's got.'

'He's got nothing!' roared Morton in a rage. 'There's nothing to get!'

He forced himself to calm down. A witness, Wisden said. But where? Not when they'd dumped Lomax's body at the bomb site at King's Cross, that was for sure. Everyone in the area knew of Hooky Morton and what he'd do if someone crossed him. If anyone had seen anything at the bomb site they'd keep their mouths shut. So it had to be at the other end, the Lisson Grove end. But there'd been no one around on the street when Lomax had been shot. Maybe some nosey git had seen something from their window.

Morton reached out and grabbed Wisden's jacket, pulling him close to him.

'They're trying to fit me up,' he said. 'I bet they've persuaded someone to say they saw me. Lomax was shot near Lissom Grove, right?'

'That's what the police think. They reckon it must have happened after he got off the bus going home.'

'Right, I want you to get a message to Dobbin. I want him and a couple of the boys to work their way along from that bus stop, knocking on doors. Say they're private detectives investigating, asking everyone if anyone had seen anything. They'll soon spot if anyone seems nervous or jittery. Anyone acts like that, that'll be this so-called witness.'

'And if they find someone, you want me to have a word with them?' asked Wisden.

'You?' said Morton scornfully. 'No. Tell Dobbin to deal with them.' He chuckled. 'He can be very persuasive.'

A local constable was already at the house when Coburg pulled up. Rosa and the neighbour, Mary Perkins, hurried out of the house, along with the constable, when they heard the police car's alarm sounding.

'DCI Coburg from Scotland Yard,' Coburg informed the constable.

'Yes, sir,' nodded the constable. 'The body's in the kitchen. I'm waiting for the doctor, although there's no doubt she's dead.'

Coburg turned to Rosa and asked: 'Are you all right?'

'I am now you're here,' she said.

Hooky Morton looked around the cell with a deep emotion of anger and a burning desire for vengeance that ate at his stomach. That bastard Coburg. To take him out of his own pub, in handcuffs, for everyone to see. Well, he'd have his revenge on him. He had no doubt that he'd walk out of the magistrates' court tomorrow. He'd have preferred it if Wisden had assured him of that – that there was no real case against him. But the fact of Coburg refusing to tell Wisden the basis on which he was being charged ate at his stomach like acid. But there couldn't be anything, except this so-called witness. And Dobbin would deal with that when he found them. If there was one to be found.

The other alternative, though it didn't bear thinking about, was young Hopkins. Hooky had chosen him to be the driver, to make him feel he was really part of the gang. Could young Hopkins have grassed him and Dobbin up? He'd get Dobbin to have a serious word with Hopkins.

Or maybe this stuff about there being a witness was a bluff. Maybe that bastard Coburg was playing with him, that's what this was about. Trying to mess with his mind. But Wesley Stipes was good. The best. Tomorrow he'd walk out of that court, and once he was free, he'd deal with DCI bloody Coburg. He'd teach him to humiliate him in his own pub, on his own manor.

He thought of shooting him, then dismissed it. Too similar to what had been done to Lomax after he'd humiliated him in his pub. It would set tongues wagging. It would also be too easy. He wanted Coburg to suffer.

Coburg was married to that jazz singer woman, Rosa Weeks. Only now she was driving an ambulance. He'd remembered reading about it in the paper: 'Music star does her bit for the war effort'.

That would be his revenge. Kill her. That would make Coburg suffer. He wouldn't do it himself. After Lomax, that would be too risky. No, he'd get Dobbin to do it. Maybe not shoot her, maybe stab her. Slice her up. Maybe rape her as well, that would really crucify Coburg. A couple of his blokes holding her down while Dobbin did her.

Yes, he thought, smiling smugly to himself. That's what we'll do. I'll fix it up once I walk out of that court. I'm in jail on Sunday, in court on Monday, she's dead on Tuesday. Let's see how you like that, DCI bloody Coburg.

CHAPTER FORTY-ONE

The doctor who'd taken the call to examine the dead body of Elsa Peers, Dr Wirdle, was the same who'd examined the first victim, Janos Mila.

'This is identical to that victim,' he told Coburg. 'A thin wire garrotte. I understand the second victim, Mam'selle Corot, was killed the same way?'

'Yes,' confirmed Coburg.

'I'll have Mrs Peers taken to the Middlesex where I can do a fuller examination,' said Dr Wirdle. He gave orders to the ambulance crew waiting for instructions, and then left.

'It could have been me coming to pick her up,' commented Rosa as she watched the two ambulance crew lift the dead body and take it out to their waiting vehicle. She looked puzzled. 'But why?'

'Yes,' said Mrs Perkins. 'Why? That doctor said two other people had been killed the same way. What's going on? Is there a madman on the loose?'

Coburg took the photo of Yvette Corot from his pocket and showed it to Mr Perkins. 'Do you recognise this woman? Did she ever call on Mrs Peers?'

Mrs Perkins look at the picture, her brow creased in a

frown. Then suddenly her face lit up. 'Yes. She was here, visiting Elsie. I saw her coming out of the house. I noticed her because she didn't look like the usual sort we get round here. Her clothes were better, if you know what I mean.'

'Did you mention her to Elsa?'

'Elsie,' Mary Perkins corrected him. 'She said she preferred being called Elsie because it made her feel more English. Yes, I did. You know, just neighbourly curiosity. That's what we do, watch out for one another. Elsie said she was some sort of government official. She said that since the war started, she had to be checked because even though she was a British citizen through marrying Derek, she was still listed as an alien having been born in Germany. Munich, I think it was.' She shook her head. 'I thought it was a bit much, coming round harassing her that way. She was as good a Brit as anyone. She'd been here twenty years.'

'When was it this woman called?' asked Coburg.

Mrs Perkins thought. 'About a month ago.'

'Was Derek here when she called?'

'No, he was out with the ambulance.'

'Thank you, Mrs Perkins. You've been enormously helpful.'

'I hope you catch whoever did it. She was a really good person, was Elsie. Do anything for anyone.' She shot a glance at the clock, then said: 'I'd better get back home. Michael, that's my husband, comes home about now and he likes his tea on the table.'

After she'd left, Rosa turned to Coburg and asked: 'What does it mean? That one of the other victims came here?'

'It means she and Elsa knew one another.'

'Yes, but what does that mean?'

'I think it means they were both spies for Germany.'

'Elsa a spy?' said Rosa, shocked. 'Derek's wife!'

'I'll tell you more when I know more,' said Coburg. 'Right now, I'd like to check the house over.'

'What are you looking for?'

'Whatever I can find that'll help us.'

With Rosa watching, Coburg set about a systematic search of the house, starting at the top and working his way down, room after room, looking in every cupboard, every chest of drawers, lifting the edges of carpets, looking behind pictures and framed photographs. It was in a wooden box with the label 'food mixer' stuck on the lid, which had been pushed to the back beneath the shelves in the pantry, that Coburg found what he was looking for. He put the box on the kitchen table and tried to open the lid, but it was locked. He went out to the coal shed and returned with a hammer and chisel, with which he forced open the lock. Inside was what looked like a wireless set, but with headphones, a small microphone, and a tangle of wires.

'That doesn't look like any food mixer I've ever seen,' said Rosa.

'It's not. It's a radio receiver and transmitter. I'm guessing she hid it there because it's unlikely that Derek, with his one arm, would have got involved in anything too intricate in the kitchen.'

'What are you going to do with it?'

'I'm going to bring in someone who I hope will be able to tell us more about it. Inspector Hibbert from MI5.'

Rosa looked at her watch.

'Will it take long?' she asked. 'I really ought to be getting to Claridge's to start preparing for the performance.'

'Yes, you should,' said Coburg. He looked at the radio

transmitter. 'Tell you what, we'll take this to Scotland Yard and lock it up safely for tonight. Then tomorrow I'll bring Inspector Hibbert in. I doubt if he'd be free anyway, now. It's a Sunday, and I get the idea he likes to take his time off.'

The two men sitting in the car watched as Coburg and Rosa left the Peers' house and walked to the police car. After their mission had been accomplished, the two men had left the small microphone their technical people had provided them with next to the domestic wireless set on the sideboard, connected to the radio set's aerial. It had been left permanently on and tuned in to the frequency of the small radio set in their car, enabling them to hear any conversations in the house. As soon as they'd picked up the first shouts from Rosa when she called on Mrs Peers, they'd driven to the house and parked a few doors away to watch and see who arrived, and listen to what they talked about. The two men hadn't been able to do this at Yvette Corot's flat, because the technology hadn't been available at that time. This particular listening device had only recently been received by their people.

'Excellent technology,' murmured one in admiration. 'The Germans are very good with this sort of thing.'

The other didn't respond, just glowered in anger at this comment, before saying: 'This English policeman, Coburg, is good.'

'Yes,' agreed the other. 'Dangerously so. I think we need to stop him getting any closer. After all, that's what we do. Stop dangerous people.'

His companion looked at him, concerned. 'That would be crossing a boundary,' he cautioned.

'In war there are no boundaries,' said the other.

281

'What do you suggest?'

'We stop him, but we do it carefully.'

'But we send a message so that others know where to stop?'

'We do,' agreed the other.

'When shall we stop him?'

'Very, very soon.'

The middle-aged woman rummaged under the folded blankets stored in the chest of drawers, her fingers closing on the butt of a pistol her deeply loved late husband had kept hidden 'for emergencies'. To her, this was an emergency. An emergency of revenge. That scum of a gangster, Hooky Morton, had shot her husband dead. It hadn't been proved he'd pulled the trigger, that's what the police said, but she knew he'd done it.

He was going to stand trial, they'd told her. Well, she knew what that meant, she thought angrily. His clever barrister would cast doubt on the whole thing, insisting that there was no concrete proof that Morton had either pulled the trigger himself, or got someone else to do the shooting. Even if there was some evidence – circumstantial, they called it – that would show he was guilty, his gang members would threaten the members of the jury, warning them off. And Morton would walk free.

Well not so long as I've got breath in my body, she muttered to herself, vengefully. Morton is going to die, and I'm going to be the person who does it.

CHAPTER FORTY-TWO

The Hon. Jocelyn Walbrook-Staines poured himself another brandy and looked at the ticket on his dressing table for tonight's show by Rosa Weeks. He'd been really looking forward to that, but it had been tainted by Saxe-Coburg's visit, and his warning to Joss to stay out of sight on the night. How dare he!

Worse for Joss was the fact that ever since that bully Coburg had come and browbeaten him, here in his own hotel room, which was supposed to be his sanctuary, he hadn't dared to call and fix up for another companion for himself in case the police were watching and they burst into his room and arrested him and the girl.

Joss gulped down the brandy and then poured himself another. He knew he was getting drunk, but what the hell, he wasn't going to see Rosa Weeks tonight. He wasn't going to be seeing anyone tonight. Everyone else would be having fun, and he'd be stuck here, cowering in his hotel room.

He had to do something to get himself out of this dreadful state.

He opened the drawer of the beside cabinet and looked at the pistol lying inside. It was the one his father had carried during the First War. His father had given it to him as a hint for him to enlist and play his part in this war. Well, the old man was mistaken if he thought that Joss was going to put his life on the line like that. No, Joss was a survivor. He'd survived his public school with its sadistic bullying senior boys and the creepy groping staff. And he was going to survive the mental trauma that damned Saxe-bloody-Coburg had inflicted on him. The police detective had taken Joss to the edge of fear. Well, now it was time for payback. Time to balance the books.

Coburg was bound to come to Claridge's tonight to watch his wife perform. Joss would check with the reception desk, but he was fairly sure the couple would have booked a room for the night. Rosa Weeks would be in her dressing room, so the chances are that Coburg would be in their room. Even if he wasn't, some way or other tonight Joss would have his own back on the bullying chief inspector. He'd catch him on his own, preferably in his hotel room, but if not there, somewhere else away from everyone else, and he'd show him the gun and force him to get down on his knees and beg for Joss's forgiveness for the way he'd abused him. If Coburg tried to make an issue about it afterwards, Joss would tell whoever came calling it had just been a practical joke; the gun hadn't even been loaded. It had been a bit of fun. And to make sure Coburg didn't take it anywhere, Joss would show him the gun was empty of bullets once he'd been down on his knees and begged for forgiveness. Once Joss had shown him the gun was empty, there'd be no way Coburg would do anything about it, he'd be too ashamed and embarrassed.

Yes, he thought, and a smile spread across his face. That would break this cloud hanging over him. Seeing Coburg on his knees, begging for his life. That would take the power away from the bastard.

Dobbin Edwards and three others of the gang were knocking on doors, working their way from the bus stop in Lisson Grove just as Hooky Morton had ordered.

'Hooky thinks they might have a witness to when Lomax was shot,' Wisden had told him. 'Or it might be a bluff on the police's part. He wants you and a couple of others to work your way along the street, knocking at doors. Tell them you're private detectives who've been asked to look into a recent shooting. If anyone looks jumpy or edgy when you ask, make a note of who they are.'

Dobbin had been wary about taking part in this questioning himself. After all, he'd been with Hooky when it happened. All right, he'd been in the car with young Hopkins when Lomax had actually been shot, but he'd got out to help Hooky get the body in the car. He'd made sure his scarf was pulled up over most of his face and he'd worn a hat, but you could never tell with people and what they might have seen – or thought they'd seen.

So far, with the five doors he'd knocked on, no one had seen anything. Most of them said they hadn't even been at home and only knew there'd been a shooting because the law had come door-knocking, just like they were doing now. It was when the sixth door opened and the woman who looked out at him suddenly seemed nervous.

'I'm sorry,' she blurted out. 'I don't buy at the door.' And she started to push the door shut, but Dobbin stuck his foot in the gap and gave the woman what he hoped was a reassuring smile.

'We're not selling anything,' he assured her. 'We're private detectives. There was a shooting here a couple of days ago. I'm sure you must have heard about it.'

'No,' she said hastily. Too hastily. 'I wasn't here. And my husband will be home in a minute.'

With that, she shut the door firmly, Dobbin just pulling his foot back before it was squashed between the door and the jamb.

That's her, he thought. That's the one.

He moved on to the next house. The woman who opened the door to his knock looked fed up as he started to explain the reason for his visit.

'We've had the police round already,' she complained. 'Don't you people talk to one another?'

'I'm sorry to trouble you, but we're double-checking. Did you hear anything? Gunshots, anything like that?'

'When was it?' the woman asked.

'I thought you said the police had told you,' said Dobbin.

'Yeh, but I can't remember. What with everything that's going on, my Albert's arthritis playing him up, the gas stove not working properly, our Alice getting laid off work. Was it at night?'

'No, it was an afternoon. About five or six.'

'In that case I'd have been out. I've got a cleaning job every afternoon at an old people's home. I don't get home till seven.'

'Thank you,' said Dobbin. 'I'll try some of your neighbours.' He gestured towards the house he'd just called at where the woman had been nervous. 'Your neighbour there thought she might have seen something, but I forgot to ask her name, and I don't want to disturb her again.'

'Randall,' said the woman. 'Peggy Randall.'

'Peggy Randall,' repeated Dobbin. 'Thank you.' And he smiled and let the woman close the door.

So, he thought. We know who their witness is. That look of alarm in her eyes when she opened the door – was that because she recognised him? One thing was for sure, she was frightened. The question was, did he put the frighteners on her a bit more, warn her what would happen to her and her family if she said anything? Or might that just tip her over the edge and she'd go to the police and tell them?

An accident was possibly the best thing. A road accident. Tragic, but there were so many of them these days.

He gestured to the other three for them to return to the car. First, he'd find out if any of them had got anyone else in addition to Mrs Randall. He hoped not. One accident would be understandable. Two or more would definitely arouse suspicion.

Coburg had brought them to Claridge's early to allow Rosa plenty of time to sit quietly in her dressing room and go through the programme she'd planned. She liked to do that, envisaging the piano, the movements of her fingers on the keys, and singing snatches of some of the songs she'd be doing.

For his part, Coburg had gone to the room they'd booked. He took his evening suit from its case and hung it from the shower rail in the bathroom, then turned on the hot tap in the bath. The steam would take out any creases in the jacket, which had spent a long time unworn in the wardrobe of their flat.

We must do this more often, he thought. Even if Rosa

isn't appearing anywhere, we'll treat ourselves to a night at a top hotel. For one thing, rationing wasn't an issue for the best hotels, and they could enjoy a good meal without worrying about their ration books.

There was a knock at his door. Room service, he guessed, with some complimentary gift from the management. One of the side effects of having a famous jazz singer as a wife, he thought with a smile. He opened the door, and came face to face with Jocelyn Walbrook-Staines, and he was startled to see that he was holding a pistol. There was no mistaking the angry malevolent expression on Walbrook-Staines's face, nor the fumes of brandy coming from him as he opened his mouth and grated: 'Put your hands up and get inside.'

Coburg raised his hands and stepped back into the room. Walbrook-Staines followed him, kicking the door shut. His hand holding the pistol was steady, Coburg noted, despite the brandy. He'd seen that before. People whose hands shook when holding a gun sober suddenly found courage after a few glasses.

'You bastard,' snarled Walbrook-Staines. 'You came to my room and ruined my life. You . . . bully! Well, now it's my turn. You're going to get down on your knees and apologise to me for the way you treated me. And a proper apology. There'll be grovelling. You'll beg my forgiveness.' He smiled. 'So, let's do it. Get on your knees.'

Coburg just looked at him, unperturbed. To Walbrook-Staines's shock, Coburg actually lowered his hands and looked with disdain at him.

'On your knees!' barked Walbrook-Staines angrily, and he pushed the gun menacingly towards Coburg.

'I can tell you're not used to guns,' said Coburg calmly. 'You've left the safety catch on.'

Walbrook-Staines mouth dropped open and he looked down at the pistol in bewilderment. Which is what Coburg had been hoping for. Coburg smashed the edge of his hand down hard on Walbrook-Staines's wrist, and the man dropped the pistol with a yell of pain. Coburg followed it up with a punch to his stomach, doubling him over, and then chopping him on the back of the neck to send him tumbling face first to the carpeted floor.

Coburg kicked the pistol away, and as he turned towards the fallen Walbrook-Staines the young man threw up his hands protectively around his face.

'Don't hit me!' Walbrook-Staines begged plaintively.

'You were going to shoot me,' said Coburg coldly.

'No! The gun isn't even loaded! Take a look! All I wanted was for you to apologise.'

'Down on my knees,' snapped Coburg.

'You did it to me!' whined Walbrook-Staines defensively.

'I never touched you, or threatened you. Get up.'

'Why? What are you going to do? You'll hit me.'

'I wouldn't waste my energy on you. Now get up.'

Walbrook-Staines reluctantly pushed himself up off the floor. As he did, he winced in pain.

'You've broken my wrist.'

'Sit down in that chair,' said Coburg, pointing at one of the armchairs.

He walked to the door and locked it, putting the security bolt in place. Then he walked to the telephone and picked it up.

'What are you doing?' asked Walbrook-Staines.

'I'm telephoning for a couple of constables. They'll take you and remand you in custody. I'll come in tomorrow morning and have you formally charged.'

'With what? I didn't do anything. The gun isn't loaded!'

'Menaces with a weapon.'

'You can't!'

'I can. And I will.'

Coburg asked the operator to put him through to the detective constables in the room next to Sir Julian Braithwaite. DC Wemyss answered.

'DCI Coburg,' said Coburg. 'As of this moment you are both relieved from your current case. But I have a new job for you. I'm currently in Claridge's and I'd like you to come to my room and take a suspect I have here with me into custody. There's also a pistol to be taken as evidence.'

'Yes, sir,' said Wemyss. 'What do you want us to do with him?'

'Charge him and put him in a cell. I'll deal with him in the morning.'

'Yes, sir. Will it be all right if we pack up our things first, before we come and collect him?'

'It will. I'll leave you to arrange for transport. Use my name.'

Coburg hung up and looked at Walbrook-Staines. He cut a pitiful figure, hunched up in the armchair and near to tears. As he looked at the agonised Walbrook-Staines, he debated with himself whether the young man had had a lesson enough and perhaps he should just let him go with a warning. But then he remembered what he'd said to Ted Lampson when his sergeant had suggested letting George Wiggins go: the next time he does something like that, someone could be seriously injured, even killed. It was the same here. This young man was certainly capable of doing the same thing again, and the next time Walbrook-Staines got angry with someone and wanted revenge, his gun might not be empty. It was very different from Linda Farnsworth throwing a vase at Braithwaite.

'I hate you,' said Walbrook-Staines.

'Think about why you're here,' said Coburg. 'You're the one who's responsible for what's happening to you, not me.'

The room was packed for Rosa's performance, with people even standing at the back. Rosa ran through her repertoire, standards from Gershwin, Cole Porter, Rodgers and Hart and Hoagy Carmichael, along with less familiar ones. At the end there was a standing ovation with the applause going on and on and calls for 'Encore!' Rosa sat down for one final reprise of 'Summertime', and then bowed and said goodnight. But even then the audience wouldn't let her go. Coburg smiled as he watched her being congratulated and praised by some of the most eminent people in the country who were either guests at the hotel, or had come especially for this evening.

Afterwards, they made their way to their hotel room.

'I'm so glad you suggested staying here,' she said.

'So am I,' smiled Coburg. 'You were magnificent tonight. And that's not just my opinion, if that audience had their way you'd still be performing.'

He poured her a glass of whiskey. 'Irish,' he announced, as he handed her the glass.

'Thank you,' she said. 'You've made this a perfect night.'

'No, you did that, I just joined in.'

She settled back on the luxuriously cushioned settee with her drink and said: 'By the way, I overheard a couple of the guests talking about someone being arrested here tonight. There was talk of a gun.'

Yes, there would be, Coburg groaned inwardly to himself. It always amazed him that everything sooner or later got talked about by people who were nothing to do with it. A member of staff, he guessed, who'd seen the two detective constables escorting Jocelyn Walbrook-Staines through the corridors. Had they put handcuffs on him? It was possible, as they'd been told to collect the pistol he'd been armed with. Even though he'd told them it wasn't loaded – after he'd checked that fact for himself. He'd talk to the two tomorrow and get their version of events.

Aloud, he said: 'Yes.'

'You know about it?'

'I do,' he said.

She looked at him quizzically. 'You were involved in some way?'

'Yes,' he admitted awkwardly.

'And you weren't going to tell me about it?' she demanded, indignant.

'I didn't want to spoil the evening for you.'

'Are you kidding? Some kind of excitement happens here, which I'm all agog to find out about, how could that spoil the evening for me?'

'Because it involves the man who thought you were a prostitute.'

She stared at him, stunned. 'Him? That loathsome creep?'

'The very same.'

'How? What did he do? Did he try it on with some other woman? Only this time armed with a gun?' She shuddered at the thought. 'That could have been me!'

'The gun wasn't loaded,' said Coburg. 'He just used it to threaten.'

'But a woman wouldn't have known that if he pointed it at her and tried to . . .' She shuddered again.

'It wasn't a woman he threatened with it. It was me.'

'You?'

Coburg nodded. 'It seems he took umbrage at the way I called on him and got the information about the prostitution ring from him. He called me a bully.'

'Because you threatened to punch him on the nose?'

'I never threatened to punch him. I just sort of . . . leant on him a little. But with words, not physically threatening him.'

'He deserved it!' said Rosa, outraged.

'He did,' agreed Coburg.

'So why did he come after you with a gun? And an unloaded one at that?'

'He wanted me to apologise to him for pressurising him to give me the information I needed.'

'But that's your job. You're a policeman.'

'Yes, but he doesn't see it that way.'

'So what happened? He turned up and pointed a gun at you?'

'That's about the size of it.'

'And then what?'

'I disarmed him.'

'Did you know it wasn't loaded?'

'Not at that time, no. I found out after I took it off him.'

'Oh my God, you are a hero!'

'I wouldn't go that far,' said Coburg.

'Well, I would.' She put down her glass. 'Come and make love to me.'

'Because I took an unloaded gun off a man?'

'No, because I've wanted you all evening. Even when I was sitting at that piano, every time I looked at you I thought: I want that man tonight. I want to feel him close to me, feel his arms around me, feel him inside me . . .'

Coburg got up and went to her, lifted her out of the chair and carried her towards the bed.

'I was thinking the same all evening,' he said.

'Why didn't you do anything about it as soon as we got back to the room?' she demanded.

'I was biding my time,' he said.

'Well stop biding. Take my dress off me, very slowly, kissing every bit of me you expose.'

He reached round to her back and slowly began to unzip her dress, then lowered his head and kissed one bare shoulder, then the other.

'Keep going,' she said.

'We have to stay here more often,' he whispered as he kissed the tops of her breasts.

CHAPTER FORTY-THREE

Monday 21st October

The following morning Coburg arranged a taxi to take Rosa home while he headed for Somers Town to pick up Lampson.

'We've got a busy day today,' he told his sergeant as Lampson took over the wheel and drove off. 'First, we're going to Mayfair nick to pick up Sergeant Potteridge, because we're all taking Hooky Morton to court.'

The news so startled Lampson that he momentarily lost concentration and almost ran over a pedestrian who'd decided to take a chance and run across the road in front of them.

'Hooky Morton?' he queried.

'We arrested him yesterday. He's been in the cells overnight. I've arranged a hearing at the magistrates' court for this morning at ten o'clock.'

'Why didn't you come and collect me to do it with you?' demanded Lampson, obviously put out.

'It was your day off. And God knows you don't get many of those. One Sunday a week and every other Saturday afternoon.'

'Yes, but this was Hooky Morton!' said Lampson, still obviously upset.

'And you've had worries about Terry and these Purvis brothers you talked about. I felt it was more important you concentrated on him. How did the football go?'

'Very good,' said Lampson. 'A good number of kids turned up. What was more important was it showed up the Purvis brothers as a couple of cheats and dirty players. That did it for Terry. He wants nothing more to do with them.'

'Excellent!' said Coburg.

'How about the concert Rosa gave last night? How did that go?'

'It wasn't so much a concert, more of an intimate evening of songs and some great piano. It went really well. The only awkward spot in the evening was a young man who took exception to me because I quizzed him about the prostitute he'd booked at Claridge's, which gave us our lead into Jimmy Mussels and the whole racket. He'd obviously been getting worked up about it ever since, and he came looking for me with a gun.'

'To shoot you?' said Lampson, horrified.

'No, it was all a front. It wasn't even loaded. He just wanted to scare me. He'd had too much to drink, anyway.'

'So what did you do?'

'Took the gun off him and had him locked up. We'll deal with him after we've delivered Hooky Morton to court. Oh, and there was another murder yesterday. Garrotted, just like the others.'

'Where?'

'Paddington. The widow of a woman who Rosa crewed with on the St John Ambulance.'

'Why her?'

'It looks like she was an agent working for the Germans,

but we'll get more confirmation later today. We found a radio transmitter hidden in her house. I took it to Scotland Yard for safety, and I'll get Inspector Hibbert in to look at it once we've finished with Hooky Morton.'

'Bloody hell, guv! It all happens when I'm off!'

After collecting Sergeant Potteridge from Mayfair police station, they drove to Scotland Yard where they picked up Hooky Morton, once again handcuffed, along with a burly uniformed sergeant. Morton was put into the back of the car with Coburg and the uniformed sergeant on either side of him, with Sergeant Lampson in the driving seat and Sergeant Potteridge next to him. Coburg had arranged for himself and the uniformed sergeant to be armed with pistols, just in case there was any attempt by Morton's gang to intervene in the proceedings and try to spring Hooky.

'I'll have you,' growled Morton as they drove to the magistrates' court. 'All of you.'

No one answered him.

Coburg was counting on Morton being remanded in custody until his trial at Crown Court, but he knew there was always a chance that his lawyers would ask for – and get – his release on bail. If that happened it would be a disaster: Morton would swagger around town, claiming he'd beaten the coppers, and his menacing power in London's streets would increase. Coburg hoped that today their barrister would be at the top of his form to ensure Morton stayed behind bars.

Lampson pulled into the kerb in front of the magistrates' court, where two waiting policemen were on duty. A small crowd of onlookers had gathered, curious to see who was being brought to court that merited such a police presence. As Potteridge got out of the car he looked at the crowd and recognised some of the men there from the encounter in the Dark Horse pub. So Morton's gang had turned up. Were they here to watch the proceedings, or to try and spring him?

Coburg and the uniformed sergeant assisted Morton out of the back of the car, then walked with him towards the steps that led up to the court entrance. Sergeant Potteridge fell into step behind the three men, along with one of the constables, protecting against any attack from the back.

They were nearing the steps when a middle-aged woman stepped forward from the crowd and thrust her hand forward towards Morton. With a shock Coburg saw she was holding a pistol.

The first bullet took Morton in the chest at heart level, and as he fell to the pavement the second bullet ripped into his face, blowing his brains out at the back of his head along with parts of his skull.

One of the men standing watching gave a yell of rage and ran towards the woman, pulling a gun from his pocket as he did so. Coburg recognised him as Dobbin Edwards. Coburg beat Edwards to it, pulling out his pistol and firing, and Edwards crumpled to the pavement.

Sergeant Potteridge ran to the fallen Edwards and knelt beside him, checking for a pulse.

'He's dead, sir!' he called to Coburg.

The woman then stood stock-still and held out the gun, butt first, to the policemen and looked defiantly at them.

'That's justice for him killing my husband,' she said.

Coburg sat with Sergeant Potteridge across the table from the woman in the interview room at Mayfair police station. Sergeant Lampson sat apart from them. A woman police constable sat next to the woman, who looked calm, satisfied.

'Why, Muriel?' appealed Potteridge.

'Because he would have walked, and you know it,' said Muriel Lomax. 'The courts won't ever put people like Morton away. If they did, he'd be in prison already, instead of walking the streets.'

'I didn't know you knew how to use a gun,' said Potteridge.

'There's a lot about me you don't know, Joe Potteridge. I worked in a munitions factory in the First War. We made all sorts of weapons, including guns.' She smiled. 'I don't care what you do to me. My Arnold has been avenged, and that's all that matters.'

Coburg and Lampson left Muriel Lomax in the charge of Sergeant Potteridge and Inspector Moffatt, and drove back to Scotland Yard, where Coburg reported to Superintendent Allison on the morning's events.

'Arnold Lomax's widow shot Morton in front of you?' said Allison, stunned.

'I'm afraid so, sir. There was no time to stop her. And I was forced to shoot dead one of Morton's gang who was about to shoot Mrs Lomax.'

'My God, the press will have a field day with this!'

Leaving the superintendent to report the incident to the commissioner, Coburg made his way back to the office where Sergeant Lampson was waiting.

'The killing of Hooky is going to open a whole can of worms,' predicted Lampson unhappily. 'Rival gangs looking to move in on his territory.'

'True, but it'll take time. In the meantime, it's still one less murderous gangster off the streets,' said Coburg sagely.

He picked up the phone and put a call through to Inspector Hibbert at Wormwood Scrubs.

'Inspector, we've got an interesting situation,' he said. 'Another garrotting yesterday. And at the house where this one occurred, we found a radio transmitter.'

'Where is it?' asked Hibbert. 'Did you leave it there?'

'No, I brought it back. It's here at Scotland Yard. I'd be grateful if you'd come and take a look at it.'

'I'm on my way,' said Hibbert. 'I was intending to get in touch with you today, as it was. Something's come up about those photographs.'

'Oh? What?'

'I'll tell you when I see you,' said Hibbert.

Hibbert sat in Coburg's chair and examined the contraption on the DCI's desk while Coburg and Lampson watched him.

'Well?' asked Coburg.

Hibbert nodded and got up, vacating the chair so Coburg could sit. 'It's a German radio for receiving and transmitting. Where was it?'

'It was hidden in the larder at the home of a woman called Elsa Peers. She was German but she'd married an Englishman and had been living in Britain for twenty years. Everyone called her Elsie and said she was as good as any British person.'

'An ideal cover for a spy,' mused Hibbert. 'Do you think her husband knew?'

'I doubt it,' said Coburg.

'My guess is she was a sleeper, non-active and activated by the Germans once everyone knew war was going to be declared. You say she was connected to those two you showed me photos of?'

'Certainly to the French woman, Yvette Corot. I expect if we dug around, we'd find she also had a connection to Janos Mila, the kitchen hand at Claridge's.'

'Actually, we had some luck with the photos. Well, the one of the French woman. I circulated them around our double agents; enemy agents we turned who are now definitely loyal to us because they know the alternative is being shot. One of them reported recognising her. She was an assassin.'

'Who for?'

'The Germans. My man met her at a training camp in Bavaria a year ago, where they were taught all sorts of methods of killing.'

'Garrotting?'

'Among others.' Hibbert looked enquiringly at Coburg. 'Do you think she killed the kitchen hand? Mila?'

'No. Mila was killed by the same person who killed Yvette Corot and Elsa Peers. My guess is she was killed to stop her killing other people. Which suggests that Janos Mila and Elsa Peers were killed because they were also seen as dangerous.'

'So they were more than just a nest of spies.'

'Yes. I think Corot and Mila were assassins, sent to dispose of key figures. Elsa Peers was the contact, passing on to them who their targets were. Someone found out about it, and stopped them.'

'Well, it wasn't us,' said Hibbert.

'No, I never thought it was,' said Coburg. 'My guess is they were sent to kill key European figures in exile here in London. You said yourself, London has become the centre for resistance to the Nazis with so many European governments and monarchs and what-have-you all over here.'

'So who do you reckon killed the three of them?' asked Hibbert. 'And does it really matter? They were the enemy. They'd have been executed by us, anyway. We should count ourselves lucky someone bumped them off before they assassinated someone important. The last thing we want is a foreign king or prime minister being killed here in London.'

'I thought you preferred to turn enemy agents so they work for us?' said Coburg.

'Enemy agents, yes. Assassins, no.' He picked up the radio set. 'I'll take this to the Scrubs and get our boffins working on it, see if they can work out where the signals come from.'

After Inspector Hibbert had left, taking the radio set, Lampson said: 'He's got a point, guv. Yes, someone killed them, but they were the enemy.'

'That's still speculation,' said Coburg.

'But pretty solid when you look at the evidence. The French woman was trained as an assassin by the Germans. Mrs Peers had a secret radio to communicate with the Germans. Does it matter who killed them?'

'It does to me,' said Coburg grimly. He went to the coat stand and took down his coat. 'If anyone wants me, I'll be out for about an hour.'

'You know who did the killings?'

'Possibly,' said Coburg.

'It won't have any effect,' said Lampson.

'Maybe not, but I just want word to filter back to those responsible that I know what happened and they'd better be on their guard.'

CHAPTER FORTY-FOUR

Captain Dupont appeared neither surprised, not disturbed, when Coburg came calling. He invited him to his office, and when the two had sat down he looked enquiringly at the DCI.

'What can I do for you, Chief Inspector?'

'You know we are investigating the murder of Yvette Corot, who worked here.'

'Yes.'

'We are also investigating two other murders in which the same method was used to kill them, a garrotte made of thin wire. One was a kitchen hand at Claridge's Hotel, a Romanian named Janos Mila. The other was a woman called Elsa Peers. She was the widow of a volunteer with St John Ambulance, Derek Peers, who died recently while on an emergency call.'

'He was not murdered?'

'No, we're just looking at those three: Mam'selle Corot, Janos Mila and Mrs Peers. I've now received information from a very reliable source that Yvette Corot was actually an assassin, trained by the Germans. She arrived to work here in July, the same time she moved into the flat where she was killed. I believe she was sent here by the Germans in order to kill someone.'

Dupont stayed silent for a few moments, watching Coburg carefully, before asking: 'Who do you think she was sent to kill?'

'With the current high level of protection against unwanted people coming into Britain, getting her in must have taken a great deal of careful management. That indicates her target was someone of great importance, whose death was seen as vital to the Germans.

'In the middle of June, Brigadier-General de Gaulle arrived in England, and on the 18th of June he made a broadcast on the French-language service of the BBC, Radio Londres. Radio Londres is broadcast from the BBC studios, but is operated by the Free French. That broadcast made a major impact across France. It inspired the rise of the Resistance movement in France. The Brigadier-General made a further broadcast the following day, 19th June, and since then he has broadcast two or three times a month. His voice is the one the Germans fear. I believe Yvette Corot was sent to England in order to kill de Gaulle.'

'That is speculation,' said Dupont quietly.

'It is,' Coburg agreed. 'But when I investigated what sort of connection there could be between Yvette Corot, Janos Mila and Elsa Peers, one thing stood out. Janos Mila may have been just a lowly kitchen hand, but he was working at Claridge's, which has become the base for many of the leaders of European countries that have been invaded by the Germans, and whose leading politicians and monarchs have come to London.' As Superintendent Allison had done to him, Coburg listed them, ticking them off on his fingers: 'Queen Wilhelmina and Prince Bernhard of the Netherlands, King Peter and Queen Alexandra of Yugoslavia, King Haakon of Norway, King George of Greece. All staying at Claridge's, and all of them fiercely opposed to the Germans, and leading their people in exile.' Coburg then ticked off on his fingers another list he'd kept in his head: 'Governments in exile based in London: Poland, Norway, Belgium, Holland, Czechoslovakia, Yugoslavia, Greece, Luxembourg, and your own Free French.'

'You are suggesting they are all targets for an assassin?'

'For at least two assassins: Yvette Corot and Janos Mila. There are possibly others, but although we found the radio set secreted at the home of Elsa Peers with which she kept in touch with her German masters, any list of her contacts had gone. So we expect more people to suddenly die.'

Dupont was silent, then he said simply: 'It is war. People die. They are the enemy.'

'But by killing them so openly it brings it into the public eye. Why not just . . . disappear them?'

'I can only speculate that it is to send a message,' said Dupont. 'We know who you are and we will kill you.'

The same philosophy as Hooky Morton, thought Coburg: scare off the opposition.

'The problem is, by doing it so openly, it becomes a murder that the police have to investigate,' said Coburg.

'So what exactly is the purpose of your visit here today? Are you accusing us, the Free French, of organising the deaths of these people?'

'No,' said Coburg. 'But I thought it was politic for me to share our thinking on the reasons for these murders with you.'

Dupont was silent for a moment, studying Coburg's

face, before he said: 'It seems to me you have just said that you have no actual evidence as to who committed these murders. Just speculation.'

'That is true,' agreed Coburg. 'But now we have some firm evidence, the witness linking Yvette Corot with Mrs Elsa Peers, we will be concentrating our investigation on the possibility that the murders were carried out to protect prominent figures who advocate strong resistance to the Germans.'

Dupont nodded, then rose to his feet. 'In that case, we will be interested to see where your investigations take you, Detective Chief Inspector.'

As he left the Free French building at Carlton Gardens, Coburg wondered: what happens now? Had the French killed them, or were they involved in some way, possibly in conspiracy with other foreign Intelligence services based in London? By telling Dupont their suspicions, he'd thrown down a challenge. The question was: how would Dupont and his conspirators react? His answer came when he arrived back at Scotland Yard and Lampson told him there'd been a telephone call for him, asking him to telephone Inspector Hibbert at Wormwood Scrubs.

He telephoned straight away, and noted the tetchy tone in Hibbert's voice as he said: 'There's someone who wants to talk to you.'

'Who?'

'Let's say, someone very important in this organisation.'

Warning bells rang for Coburg. Someone at the top of MI5. Dupont had obviously set things in motion to protect his organisation.

'What does he want to see me about?'

'He'll tell you that when you get here.'

'That suggests he wants to see me now.'

'He does.'

'In that case, I'm on my way.'

When Coburg arrived at Wormwood Scrubs there was none of the usual waiting, Inspector Hibbert was in reception watching out for him. He looked unhappy.

'Don't worry, Inspector,' said Coburg. 'I don't believe any of this is your doing.'

Hibbert didn't respond, just gestured for Coburg to follow him. They walked through a maze of corridors before arriving at a door on its own, with no name on it or any form of identification.

Hibbert knocked at the door, and at the command 'Enter!' pushed it open.

'DCI Coburg is here, sir.'

'Thank you, Hibbert. Come in, Coburg.'

Hibbert retreated, closing the door behind him. The man sitting to attention behind the large desk gestured to Coburg to take the chair opposite him. Coburg guessed he was in his sixties, his white hair neat, cut to an almost military length. His dark, three-piece suit indicated a bespoke tailor, and his tie was a legacy of a Guards regiment. There was no introduction. No handshake, just a silent stare.

'These murders you're investigating. The French woman, the kitchen hand at Claridge's, and this German woman. We think it's time to pull the plug on it.'

'We, sir?'

'Let's just say, Top Brass.'

'Do I assume the French have spoken to you, sir?'

The man bristled. 'No, you may not assume that.'

'Then can I ask why the investigation is to end?'

'For God's sake, man, you know why! Don't play the idiot!'

'The different Intelligence services gathered in London working together,' said Coburg.

'It has been decided this is a matter of national security. You will close the files and mark them as murder by person or persons unknown.'

'And those are your orders, sir?'

'They are not just my orders, they are the orders from the very top. The very top. Is that understood?'

'It is, sir.'

'You may go.'

'Thank you, sir.'

Coburg got to his feet and left the room. Hibbert was outside.

'You waited?' asked Coburg.

'I had the impression it was only going to be a short encounter,' said Hibbert as he led the way to the exit.

'I've been warned off,' said Coburg.

'What else did you expect?' asked Hibbert. 'There's a war on. As I said before, the dead people were our enemies. Whoever killed them is our ally. End of story.'

The two men shook hands at the exit, and Coburg made for his car. He'd guessed it would end this way once they made the connection between Elsa Peers and Yvette Corot. Still, on the other murders, Patch Peters and Inspector Lomax had been avenged. But not by the justice system. What would happen to Muriel Lomax? Would she hang? There'd be plenty of people who'd say she should be given a medal for ridding London of an evil murderous gangster like Hooky Morton. There'd be a clamour in the popular press for leniency for her. Doctors would be brought in to say she was suffering from traumatic stress as the result of her husband's murder. And Arnold Lomax would finally receive the fame he'd hungered after, depicted as a hero, shot down in the course of his duty. There would even be a memorial to him: a plaque raised by subscriptions from his fellow coppers. And Coburg, of course, would be a generous contributor.

CHAPTER FORTY-FIVE

Lampson looked at Coburg's doleful expression as he entered the office and said: 'So, I suppose it's over?'

'It is as far as us investigating these murders is concerned. National and international security has priority.'

'In a way it's understandable. They were all enemy agents.'

'True, but they were still murdered.'

'Executed,' said Lampson. 'That's the price of treason, and they were all here in England trying to undermine our war effort.'

'Yes, I suppose that's one way of looking at it.'

'It's the only way to look at it, guv. The Germans would do the same to any of our agents they discovered.'

'Yes, that's true.'

'So the French did it?' When Coburg looked at him quizzically, he said: 'You said you were going to filter information back. The only exiled Europeans we've spoken to about it are the French.'

'It was the French I went to see,' said Coburg, 'but I'm not sure if they actually did it. They were involved, I've no doubt about that. But I get the feeling it might have been a team effort. The different intelligence services pooling their resources: French, Dutch, Polish, Norwegian, Belgian, Yugoslav, Greek, Czech, Luxembourg. They work together to take action, then tell the British about it afterwards.'

'Why not before?'

'They don't trust us.'

'Why not?'

'The business of the RAF sinking the French naval fleet didn't help. It also possibly goes back to the scramble for colonies in Africa when we were fighting one another. Or earlier wars between us.' He gave a rueful sigh. 'But, at the moment, as long as we're working on the same side for the same end, I can live with that.'

Rosa recognised he was in a thoughtful mood when he arrived home.

'Something bad happen today?' she asked.

He gave a sigh. 'Something bad seems to happen every day. Which is why last night was so special.'

'So what went wrong today?'

He told her about being warned off by MI5 about investigating the murders any further. 'It's pretty obvious the foreign security services were working together to bump them off to stop them killing important European leaders here in London. If they'd alerted our own security people at the very outset, we wouldn't have spent a huge amount of time poking around. We could have got on with proper police work.'

'Why didn't they? Tell British security what they were doing early on, I mean?'

'They don't trust us, even though we're allies.' And

he told her what he'd told Lampson, about the rivalries between supposedly friendly nations, and the effect the raid on the French navy had had.

'We're not going to find it easy to win this war if those on our side don't trust us,' said Rosa.

'It's not just them. British Intelligence doesn't trust any other nations. In fact, MI5 and MI6 don't trust one another, and neither of those trust the police.'

He was interrupted by the telephone ringing.

'Edgar Coburg,' he said.

The voice, in French, informed him that Captain Dupont was calling him and added: 'There is someone who wishes to speak to you. Someone very important.'

'There's no need, Captain,' said Coburg. 'I've already been warned off. There will be no further investigation.'

'That is good to know. But this person would still like to see you. Could you come to Carlton Gardens tomorrow morning at seven o'clock?'

'Seven?'

'The person who wishes to speak to you is an early riser.'

'I'll be there.'

As he hung up, Rosa said, 'I wasn't aware you spoke French so fluently.'

'My Latin's pretty good as well,' he smiled wryly, 'but there aren't as many Latin speakers to practise with.'

CHAPTER FORTY-SIX

Tuesday 22nd October

When Coburg arrived at Carlton Gardens at 7 a.m. he found it to be a hive of activity. Captain Dupont was waiting for him by the entrance.

'I hadn't realised your staff began work this early,' said Coburg.

'There is no clock when fighting the war against the Nazis,' said Dupont. He added, with a wry smile: 'Of course, when a certain person is here, so is everyone else.'

A certain person? mused Daniel. Could it be . . . ?

It could. Dupont led him to a room where none other than Brigadier General Charles de Gaulle stood studying some papers on a shelf. He was an imposing and immediately recognisable figure. Six foot six, he towered over Coburg, his back ramrod straight. He looks down on everyone because of his height, thought Coburg. The nose, too, which he'd seen lampooned in cartoon versions of the man in the newspapers, was indeed large. It was a nose with which to look down on people.

There was certainly a superior air to De Gaulle, but his look at Coburg was also inquisitive.

'Detective Chief Inspector,' he said. Or, rather,

'*Inspecteur-Detective en Chef*'. So we're going to be talking in French.

'*Brigadier Général,*' returned Coburg.

De Gaulle gestured for Coburg to sit, then sat down behind his desk.

'Captain Dupont says you are to be commended for your intelligence.'

'That is very gracious of the captain. I would like to return the compliment to him.'

De Gaulle studied Coburg for a moment, then said: 'Captain Dupont believes that you merit an explanation.'

'That is very kind of the captain, and greatly appreciated.'

'It has been said that we are all allies against the Germans – we French, the British, the Dutch, Norwegians and many others. But there is one major difference. Those of us who have established governments in exile here in London, our countries have been invaded and appear lost to us. You British, thanks to *La Manche*, have not felt the Nazi jackboot on your precious soil.'

La Manche, Coburg noted, not the English Channel.

'And we will resist that happening as long as we have breath,' he said.

'Ah yes; we shall fight them on the beaches, we shall fight them on the landing grounds. The words of your Prime Minister Churchill.' He gave a look of disapproval. 'It is a pity he does not speak French as well as you.'

'I thought he made a pretty good job of it in his broadcast yesterday,' said Coburg amiably.

The day before, Churchill had made a radio broadcast direct to the people of France, speaking in French, in which he appealed to them not to hinder Britain in the war against Germany: 'We are persevering steadfastly, and in good heart in the cause of European freedom and fair dealing for the common people of all countries for which, with you, we draw the sword. Remember, we shall never stop, never weary, and never give in, and that our whole people and Empire have bowed to the task of cleansing Europe from the Nazi pestilence and saving the world from the new Dark Ages.'

Some felt Churchill had made the speech because he was determined not to let De Gaulle get the upper hand in the propaganda war to keep the French onside. The two men were notoriously jealous of one another when it came to courting popularity with the public. Churchill already had the approval and backing of most of the British, but De Gaulle had the lead over him when it came to the French. At least, those French who did not support the Nazi-backed Vichy regime.

Coburg suspected Churchill had made the speech because some of the British government's actions had not gone down well with the French, especially the sinking of the French fleet. Churchill was desperate to stop the enmity between the French and the British escalating into an all-out war; hence his radio broadcast to the French people.

'He made an attempt,' scowled de Gaulle grudgingly.

Coburg was tempted to say: I'm sure Churchill's French is as good as your English, but decided against it. De Gaulle was notoriously a prickly character, yet he had invited Coburg here as a kind of peace offering. It would be churlish, and also politically foolish, to disturb that goodwill.

'I requested you come here because, after talking to

Captain Dupont, I wished you to know that although we have some reservations about certain of your politicians, we do not feel any enmity towards you personally, Chief Inspector. Captain Dupont feels we can work together. To that end, if a situation arises in which you feel we may have a mutual interest, you have my permission to contact Captain Dupont.'

A personal endorsement from De Gaulle himself, thought Coburg. Unlimited access to the Free French forces in London. It was more than Churchill and his War Cabinet had. But was he being played as a pawn in someone's political game? Who else had been involved in the negotiations to achieve this? Inspector Hibbert? But Hibbert was too low down the ladder. Someone at the top. But who? And why?

De Gaulle rose from his chair. Coburg took the hint and also stood.

'Thank you for seeing me, *Brigadier General*,' he said. 'I look forward to co-operating with Captain Dupont in the future.'

There was no offer of a handshake, just a slightly formal bow of the head from De Gaulle, which Coburg returned.

When he left the room, Captain Dupont was waiting to escort him out.

'Thank you for arranging that meeting,' said Coburg. 'He is a great man.'

'He will be the saviour of France,' said Dupont proudly.

'I know the case is closed, but – off the record – I'd be interested in how you found out that Mam'selle Corot was actually a Nazi assassin. Did you suspect her early on?'

'You said yourself, Chief Inspector, there were questions

as to how she made it to England.'

'Did you ask her?'

'I did. She said the Resistance had arranged it, but she would not give details. To protect them, she said.'

'You didn't believe her?'

'No. If her arrival in England had been arranged by the Resistance, we would have known about it.'

'So you set a team to watch her?'

'I did. They saw her go to the house of a woman called Elsa Peers.'

'Who was a sleeper agent. We found the radio set hidden in her house. She must have received messages from her controllers in Germany and passed them on to Yvette Corot and other assassins. How many other assassins were there? We know of just Yvette Corot and Janos Mila. How did you get on to Mila?'

'We had Mrs Peers watched by friends in another agency. One day she paid a call to Janos Mila at his house. We discovered that Mila worked at Claridge's in the kitchen. The deduction was made that he was there to . . . assassinate one of the guests. There are many prominent people in residence there, many of them as vital to the war effort against the Nazis as the brigadier is for we French.'

They had reached the front door. Dupont opened it, then held out his hand to Coburg.

'Au 'voir, Chief Inspector.'

'Au 'voir, Captain.'

They shook hands, then Dupont jerked to attention and made a smart salute. 'To victory,' he said.

'To victory,' echoed Coburg.

As he walked to his car he reflected on the last

week. Janos Mila, Yvette Corot and Elsa Peers, dead – assassinated. Inspector Lomax dead. Along with Hooky Morton, Dobbin Edwards and Patch Peters. Seven dead in just over a week. Meanwhile, the death toll in London because of the war numbered in the thousands.

He thought of the famous line by the poet John Donne: 'No man is an island . . . any man's death diminishes me.'

If Donne had been alive now, he'd be so diminished he'd be the size of a flea.

JIM ELDRIDGE was born in central London in November 1944, on the same day as one of the deadliest V2 attacks on the city. He left school at sixteen and worked at a variety of jobs, including stoker at a blast furnace, before becoming a teacher. From 1975 to 1985 he taught in mostly disadvantaged areas of Luton. At the same time, he was writing comedy scripts for radio, and then television. As a scriptwriter he has had countless broadcast on television in the UK and internationally, as well as on the radio. Jim has also written over 100 children's books, before concentrating on historical crime fiction for adults.

Jimeldridge.com